Surviving Magic
School of Magic Survival 1

CHLOE GARNER

CONTENTS

The Natural

Valerie looked over her shoulder as the boys continued to follow her down the sidewalk. She was about four blocks from home, and she could run flat out from here if she had to, but she didn't like giving them the satisfaction. If she ran from them now, they'd just find her another day and make her run again. Her mom had had her in self-defense classes at eight, because of the neighborhood, and Valerie was comfortable in her own body. If someone tried to touch it without permission, she knew she could hurt them, hard and fast, and get away.

That was the kind of thing that stupid boys wouldn't come back for.

"Valerie," someone called, crossing the street, and Valerie looked over to see Hanson, long-suffering friend and one-time test dummy for the various moves Valerie had learned in her classes.

She slowed to let him catch up and walk alongside her. He looked back once, making eye contact with the guys who had been following her, then pretended like it hadn't happened at all, shouldering her playfully.

"Want to go get something to eat?" he asked.

"Do you ever think about anything but your stomach?" Valerie answered, grinning.

"Sometimes I play basketball," he answered. "Come on, my treat. I'm celebrating."

Valerie adjusted her backpack and raised an eyebrow at him.

"Did Nikki finally agree to go out with you?" she asked, and he waved her off.

"No, we both know that's never going to happen. Coach put out the list for varsity."

Her eyes flew open.

"You made it?"

He grinned.

1

"Power forward," he said.

"You say that like it should mean something to me," Valerie said, still grinning. "Well, if you're celebrating, then it ought to be my treat."

He shook his head and was about to say something when a car rolled up to the curb and a man got out.

"Valerie Blake?" the man asked. Hanson took a half step in front of her and Valerie walked around him.

"Who are you?" she asked.

"Valerie, your mother asked me to come get you," he said. Valerie checked her phone, but it didn't have anything from her mom.

She glanced at Hanson.

"No," she said after a moment. "Just no."

She took a step back and started down the sidewalk again.

"I have this," the man said, taking out an envelope and showing it to her. "I don't know what it says. She signed the envelope after she sealed it."

"Hold up," Hanson said. "We're, like, four blocks away from her apartment. Why would Mrs. Blake send a man in a *car*?"

Valerie looked at her phone again, then shook her head and texted her mom.

There's a guy here who says you sent him to get me. Bogus?

She lifted her eyebrows and looked at the man once more. He flipped the envelope over and she frowned. It was actually her mom's signature.

She stepped forward and took the envelope, going back to stand next to Hanson again as she ripped open the end of it and took out a folded sheet of legal paper.

She knew that pad of paper. Lived on the counter in the kitchen.

Val,

I've got a lot of explaining to do, and it needs to happen fast. This is Roger. I don't know if you can trust him or not, in general, but he'll bring you back to the apartment. Please come with him quickly.

Mom

"What's your name?" Valerie asked.

"I'm Roger Haem," he said. Valerie glanced at Hanson.

"He comes, too," she said. "I'm not getting in your car by myself."

Roger looked at Hanson for a moment, then shrugged.

"We need to move quickly. They'll be watching."

He went to get in the car as Valerie lingered. Hanson looked like he'd rather go get pizza.

Valerie looked at her phone again.

I wrote the letter. He isn't lying to you. Stop using your phone.

She showed the text to Hanson.

"I don't know," he said as she put her phone away again. "You don't know this guy?"

She shook her head.

"Mom said to go with him."

"And how do you know someone didn't steal or hack your mom's phone?" he asked.

"Look," she said, bending over to look into the car again. "We'll just walk. Okay? Meet you back there."

"You are exposed, completely out in the open," the man said. "You aren't safe. She said I had to get you first, but you're putting all of us in danger."

"What are you talking about?" Valerie asked. "Danger?"

"She hasn't told you *anything*, has she?" Roger asked. Hanson again was edging around to stand in front of Valerie.

"You need to just roll on," Hanson said. "Creepy."

"It's a busy street in the middle of the afternoon," Valerie said. "I'm certainly in more danger getting into a car with some strange dude than I am walking down the sidewalk."

She straightened and turned to continue on the way they'd been going originally.

The sidewalk buckled in front of her.

She stopped short, staring down at the trench of shattered concrete in front of her, jerking her head around as she tried to figure out what had just happened.

She heard Roger curse quietly as he got out of the car again.

"They don't have to be able to see you to take aim at you," the man said quietly. "You need to get in the car right now. Even if they do miss again, they might kill someone else."

"What?" Hanson asked, staring down at the sidewalk. It was like someone had smashed it with a pipe the size of a beach ball. It wasn't possible.

That thing.

It couldn't have just happened.

"How do you know my mom?" Valerie asked, taking an involuntary step back away from the damage.

"I only know *of* her," Roger answered. "The people who know her are the ones who sent me."

That helped her *none*.

"What's she wearing today?" Valerie asked, scrambling.

What was *happening*?

"Purple sweater and khaki slacks," Roger said. "And it's ninety out here. Will you please get in the car?"

"If you're lying to me and kidnapping me or hurt my mom or *anything*, I'm going to be *so* angry," Valerie said, sliding past Roger into the car. Hanson stood on the sidewalk for just a moment longer, then when it became evident that Roger had no intention of waiting for him, Hanson shouldered him out of the way and went to sit next to Valerie.

"What kind of villain rides around the city in a limousine?" Hanson whispered. Valerie shook her head.

"Shut up," she said. "I don't understand what's going on, but he isn't a Bond villain."

Hanson snapped.

"That," he said. "That's exactly what I was thinking about."

She looked over at him, and he dropped his head, chastened, as Roger closed the door. The sunlight from outside cut off abruptly and the car started rolling as Valerie scrambled to put on her seatbelt.

Roger was on his phone the moment the car started moving.

"We're on our way," he said. "Someone needs to clean up here."

He hung up and looked at Valerie, but he didn't say anything.

She dropped her head a fraction.

"Tell me what's going on," she said. "Why did mom send you?"

He shook his head.

"You don't know anything," he said. "I'm not getting in the middle of *that*. I only just *met* Susan, and I know better."

Valerie looked at Hanson.

It did *sound* like her mom.

It was actually comforting.

She leaned her shoulder against Hanson's arm for the entirety of four blocks, where Roger opened his door and made an urgent motion at them to get out. Valerie glanced over her shoulder at the driver, feeling quite absurd to have ridden in a car for four whole blocks, but the way Roger moved, he just didn't quite move right. Prey. He moved like prey. Either the man was nuts, or something *big* was going on.

She tried not to think too hard about the sidewalk.

Not yet.

They took the elevator up to the sixth floor, where Susan Blake was standing in the hallway waiting for them.

"Hanson," she said. "You need to go home."

"Mrs. Blake," Hanson answered. "Is everything okay?"

"Yes," Susan answered. "Roger is a bit dramatic, but everything is fine. Tell your mom we'd love her to come over for dinner one night next week, okay? I'll make stir-fry and she can bring that Thai salad she made last time."

Every word of it rang true.

Valerie looked at Roger, but the man still wasn't moving right. Susan waved again as Hanson stalled at going back to the elevator, then the woman took Valerie's elbow and casually steered her into the apartment. Roger closed the door and Susan shook her head at him.

"You're a disgrace," she said. "I asked you to do one simple thing, and you put up a magic signal I caught from here, *and* you freaked out my daughter and her civilian friend."

"Civilian?" Valerie asked. Susan sighed, at Roger rather than at Valerie.

"I don't know what you expected," Roger answered. "You

haven't prepared her at all, and they *know* you're out here unprotected. If they're going to get you before you come back in, now is their last chance, so I have to move fast."

Susan looked at Valerie and shook her head.

"I didn't want it to go this way," Valerie's mom told her. "I didn't want you to find out at all, but here we are, and there's no time."

"Mom," Valerie warned. "What's going on?"

Susan sat down on the couch, pulling Valerie down to sit next to her.

"We won the war," she said, as much directed at Roger as at Valerie. "And I retired. All I wanted was for you to have a normal life and not have to worry about…" She waved a hand at Roger. "Everything."

"We won, but we didn't chase them *all* to ground," Roger said, and Susan's dismissive wave turned into a very sharp point.

"I'm not going to discuss it with you," she said. "You weren't *there*."

"Mom," Valerie warned again.

"I know," Susan said. "I'm sorry. Here's the fast version. Magic is real. I'm good at it. Your dad was the best, before he went quiet. There was a war and he and I helped win it. When he didn't come back, I lost my stomach for it, and I came here and you have been a normal girl ever since then."

"Such a waste," Roger commented, getting another very sharp point. It almost sounded like he wished he could suck the words back up again.

Went quiet.

Her mom's words for her dad's death.

She'd been using them, just like that, Valerie's whole life.

And somehow she'd never heard them *just like that.*

"Mom, what happened to Dad?" Valerie asked. Susan shook her head.

"On the list of important things I never told you, that doesn't get to the short list of things I have to tell you *right now.*"

Valerie widened her eyes and started to argue, drawing that sharp finger around to her own face.

"Young lady," Susan said, then paused, recollecting her place in whatever she was trying to tell Valerie. "The war is back. *Whatever* reasons there might be for it not being completely over, it apparently isn't, and I am tactically valuable, which means that you are in danger."

"Mom," Valerie said, and Susan dropped her hand, looking over at Roger.

"She needs to go to one of the schools," Susan said, and Roger shook his head.

"She's nowhere near qualified," he said. "They're all too competitive."

Susan shrugged.

"Either you do it, or I run and you will never find either one of us again. You know I can do that."

"Magic is *real?*" Valerie asked, but neither of them so much as glanced at her. Susan stood.

"Which school would you even want her to go to?" Roger asked.

"Show me the latest faculty lists," Susan said. Roger flicked his hand off to the side, like opening a napkin, and a piece of paper unrolled where his hand had clearly been empty a moment before.

Susan took the list and looked down it, muttering to herself as Valerie stared at it.

That.

Just.

Happened.

After a moment, Susan smile dryly.

"Jamison," she said. "Survival."

Roger's nostrils flared and he shook his head.

"That's one of the top schools," he said. Susan flicked a glance over at Valerie without actually looking at her.

"You think there is a set of skills she needs *more* than survival, right now?" she asked.

"Mom," Valerie demanded.

"Let me see the enrollment," Susan said.

"It isn't *public* yet," Roger answered with an outraged tone.

"I can read a calendar," Susan said. "It's finalized. They're just

7

making sure that there isn't enough money sitting on the sidelines to change their minds."

Roger tightened his mouth, then flicked his wrist once more and handed Susan another roll of paper. Valerie pulled her feet up onto the couch with her and in the same motion found herself sitting up on the back of it, staring at the two adults.

"Mills," Susan said. "That would be Ivory Mills' daughter. Put them in a room together."

"I can't," Roger sputtered. "It's all already settled. And she's completely unqualified."

Susan looked over at Valerie and gave her a half a smile.

"I'm not worried about her at all," she said. "She's going to be a natural."

So many things to explain.

No freaking kidding.

And she hadn't explained *any* of them.

No.

Oh, no.

Instead, Susan Blake had gone back into Valerie's room and packed up her gym bag.

"I'm sorry, baby," she'd said. "If I thought I could, I'd just keep running forever, but you don't want that life, and… they need me."

She'd pushed Valerie toward the door and Roger had given her one more uncertain look.

"You're sure she's a natural?" he asked.

"I've been testing her for years," Susan had answered, looking over her shoulder. It had sounded like something was back in a back room, like a dog trapped in the spare bedroom with the door closed.

Roger had pulled Valerie by her elbow to the elevator and Valerie had just stared at the apartment door, willing her mom to come out, to laugh and throw her arms around Valerie's shoulders and tell her that it was all just a mistake, that she'd figured it out and that nothing *really* had to change.

But no.

Oh, no.

Roger had put her back into the limousine and they'd driven for forty-five minutes out of the city, through early-fall forests and rolling countryside, to a long drive way. A long, long driveway.

Roger was on his phone the entire way, fighting with the entire world, but when they'd finally gotten to the end of the driveway, there were three people standing out front of a huge red-brick building.

He'd made a shooing motion at Valerie, continuing to fight with his phone, and she'd dragged her bag out of the car, looking at the two women and one man who stood on the front steps.

"Valerie Blake," the woman in the center said. "It is not just an honor, it is a lovely surprise to have you with us this year."

Valerie looked around, trying to adapt to the size of the building. The woman put her arm back, indicating.

"This is the School of Magic Survival, and I am Lady Harrington, the headmistress. This is Mrs. Gold, the girls' dormitory supervisor, and this is Mr. Benson, the head of academics."

Lady Harrington wore a plaid, fitted skirt that went to her knees, a white blouse, and a matching plaid beret of some sort, and she might have been fifty or she might have been eighty. Valerie was bad at that game. Mrs. Gold looked like she was in the act of sucking on a lemon, and Mr. Benson was already on his way back up the stairs for something important. He gave Valerie a half a wave over his shoulder and said something, but Valerie didn't catch it. Lady Harrington watched after him for a moment, then shook her head.

"You'll have to forgive Mr. Benson. We are very, very close to the start of our school calendar, and there are a lot of things left to sort out. Mrs. Gold will see you to your room."

The limousine pulled away and Valerie turned to watch after it.

It took an act of will not to *chase* after it, and it was everything she could do to not cry.

She turned to face Lady Harrington once more, and the woman gave her a pressed-lip smile.

"Oh, dear," the woman said. "I know that you have not come

to us under traditional circumstances. We need to get you signed up for your classes and test your aptitudes, all of that, but it can wait until you're settled into your room. Mrs. Gold?"

The other woman gave Valerie an appraising look and sighed.

"This way," she said, motioning. "Dorms are to the right."

Valerie picked up her bag and went up the stairs, pulling open one of the huge doors and going in.

The floor was traditional school-quality tile, but the walls... There was nothing normal about the walls. They were covered with designs... artwork, perhaps? or, well, that there was a symbol of some kind...

"Warding on the building is more than a century old," Mrs. Gold said. "Never been broken. You stay on the property and you'll be safe from any outside magic."

"Magic," Valerie whispered.

Mrs. Gold glanced over at her.

"If you're expecting me to answer you, you've got to speak up so I can hear."

"Sorry," Valerie said.

They walked past offices and trophy cases, classrooms and lockers, turning several more times, first away from the front of the building and then outward again, into a carpeted wing with periodic doors.

"These are the dorms," Mrs. Gold said. "That's my room, there. You tell me if there's something I need to deal with, but think carefully about the meaning of the word emergency before you knock on my door at three in the morning, you hear?"

"Okay," Valerie said slowly. "So... I *live* here now?"

"Unless you've got enough pull to get yourself into one of the cottages as a freshman," Mrs. Gold said.

"I'm supposed to be starting my *junior* year," Valerie said and Mrs. Gold shook her head, getting out a ring of keys and unlocking a door.

"This one will be yours," the woman said. "No one else will be here until at least tonight, might not get your roommate until tomorrow or the next day. Some of the kids won't come for the first week, only turn up at the weekend, but the freshmen are required to be here for the first Wednesday."

Valerie's school had started two weeks before.

She looked at the dark room and then Mrs. Gold, and decided the room was better than the moody tour guide.

She went in.

"I have a key for you," the woman said, holding onto the doorknob. "I'll give it to you at dinner. Don't lock yourself out before that."

Valerie started to ask when and *where* dinner was, but Mrs. Gold had already closed the door.

Valerie shivered, rubbing her arms and going to sit on a naked mattress.

She didn't have sheets.

She didn't have a *pillow*.

She didn't have *anything*.

She went to press her back against the wall, wrapping her arms around her knees and staring out at the dark room.

Alone.

She'd never felt so alone.

Her mother had abandoned her.

Her friends at school - would they ever even know what happened to her?

Hanson.

There was no telling what he would do, if Valerie turned up missing. It had felt as though Valerie's mom would also be leaving soon after Valerie had... Hanson would call the police.

No one was ever going to know what happened.

She squeezed her knees tighter, tears breaking loose and rolling down her cheeks.

There was a quiet knock on the door and Valerie blinked quickly, looking around for tissues, but the room was absolutely bare.

She wiped her eyes on her sleeves and went to answer the door.

An attractive man her mom's age stood there. Kind eyes. He had an authenticity to his expression that Valerie would have trusted, anywhere else. Unconditionally.

"Miss Blake?" he asked.

11

She almost, *almost* asked him who else he might have expected her to be.

"Yes," she said.

"I'm Alan Jamison," he said. "Your mom called me. Told me you were coming here and asked me to help you figure out what's going on. Can we talk?"

Valerie put both hands over her mouth, the seeping tears from her room only a forerunner to the blinding ones she found now. She sobbed and he put his arms out, letting her step in to put her head on his shoulder and cry.

"It's okay," he said when she was able to hear him again. "It's really not as bad as it feels. There are a lot of kids, almost all of them who are going to be turning up over the next couple of days, who have been working their entire lives toward getting here. It's not a *bad* place to end up. It's just a shock. Come on. Come get something to eat, and let's talk, you and me. It's okay."

She nodded, not trusting her voice, and he indicated, leading the way back down the carpeted hallway.

"This is the girls' wing," he said. "The boys' rooms are upstairs, and they lock the stairwell at both ends at ten. You met Mrs. Gold…"

"She was *wonderful*," Valerie said, regretting it immediately, though he seemed unbothered.

"She's been watching over the girls dormitories since your mom and I were in school. She's seen too many shenanigans to give people the benefit of the doubt, but she's fair when push comes to shove. If someone does something to hurt you, she'll come down on them like a she-bear, make no mistake."

"You went to school with Mom?" Valerie asked.

"No," he said, shaking his head. "She was in the Light school, and I didn't even have the scores to get in *here*. No, she and your dad are most of the reason I've had enough credibility to land a job here. We just all graduated at the same time and went off… You know. The wars."

Valerie shook her head.

"I have no idea what you're talking about. You knew my dad?"

He frowned.

"You don't know about the wars? She told me you didn't know anything, but I didn't imagine… Well. I guess we have to start a bit further back, yet, then. When we were teenagers, well, basically as long as anyone can remember, the magical community has had divisions. The styles of magic align a certain way, the opinions about our relationships with the civilian community, the demonic community…"

"*Demonic*," Valerie said, stopping. He turned back to look at her, his eyes still earnest, but now with something akin to pity.

"Demons are real. Angels are real. Magic is real. Is that where we need to start?"

Valerie nodded slowly. He motioned.

"I'm hungry," he said. "Picking up where I was, we'll come back to the demon thing, we've always been divided, and we've always had *passionate* opinions, but somewhere along the way we stopped being even *friends*. There were men who thought that we were superior to the civilians and ought to rule them by natural selection, and there were those on our side who thought that it was our job to proactively prevent magic users from attacking or manipulating humans… Fringe groups, for a long time, but as time went along, they started getting into more and more fights, and then they were killing each other, and little by little and then all at once, the rest of the community picked sides and we were killing each other… just on sight.

"It was brutal and awful, but it wasn't anything compared to what happened when they got organized. They started orchestrating mass attacks on humans and on us, and that… Well, that was our senior year, when that started."

He stopped, opening a door for her and indicating.

"Cafeteria," he said. It looked exactly the way a cafeteria ought to.

"War," Valerie answered, and he nodded, leading the way to a stack of trays and going to a buffet table where Valerie served herself a portion of pasta and another of steamed vegetables. There were rolls and pats of butter… It wasn't as miserable as her school's cafeteria, but… It was mass-produced food, certainly.

"Right," he said, sitting down. "You have to understand that the magical community wasn't ever really *organized* before it all happened. We were flat-footed, and the first few years, they killed a lot of us, and a whole lot more humans. They enslaved hundreds or thousands of humans and... If it hadn't been for some luck on our side and some hubris on their side, they should have won the war before it even started. It wasn't until about maybe five years in, Susan, Grant, and I had been fighting since we graduated, and really just picking at it around the edges, learning who we were and what we were capable of, but around that time our side really realized that if we didn't get ourselves organized, we were going to lose control of the situation and, yeah, we were all probably going to die. They formed the Council, they affiliated the schools... They did a lot of things that are still really controversial today, but they did it to try to turn the war around, and it worked.

"By that point, the three of us were really out in the middle of it, and... Well, the details of that..." He shook his head, looking away. "Probably a story for another time. We won. Your dad..."

He looked at her, and Valerie shook her head.

"What about my dad?" she asked.

"What did your mom tell you?" he asked her, and she looked at her tray.

"That he died," she said, looking up again. He frowned, then he sat his fork down.

"I have no idea what she was going through," he said, meeting her eye. "And I really don't want to be in the middle of *that*. So. Let's agree to leave it?"

"What happened to him?" Valerie demanded, and he shook his head.

"She quit," he said. "We won the war, and Susan was just *done* with all of it. I don't think that she *hated* all of us, and I don't... I *can't* believe that she hated magic. I think she just felt like *magic* wasn't worth it. Not after everything. So she walked away and she took you with her, and..." He paused, smiling. "When Susan Blake decided something, you really didn't have a chance to tell her otherwise."

"That sounds like mom," Valerie muttered.

He nodded.

"She disappeared, and no one ever knew where she went. The idea that you've just been right there in the city all that time…" He gave her a half a smile. "She had the right to go. Before the Council, no one would have even thought twice about it. The Council didn't like her leaving, and that might be part of the reason she hid so well. I looked for her once or twice, just… Wanted to make sure she was okay, maybe sit and talk about old times once more… I couldn't find her with as hard as I was willing to look, but I expect they spent serious resources, tracking her down."

"Why?" Valerie asked. "Why would they come looking for her? Is she in trouble?"

"We need her," Mr. Jamison said. "The Superiors… When the war was over, we didn't know the half of who had been involved on the other side, by the end, or to what extent. Certainly not everyone helping *us* was happy about it, and there was a lot of argument about what to do with everyone who fought against us. We knew at the time that some of the hard-liners would slip through our fingers if we just let everyone go, and a lot of good men argued for stricter measures, but…" He licked his lips and leaned forward. "We're getting into the zone of politics, here. People are going to have impassioned opinions, so you have to be careful who you talk to and *how*, if you decide you want to have these kinds of conversations with other students. A lot of us remember the days before the magic community had *alignments*, back when we all just had *opinions*, and that was the vote that carried the day. Maybe we were wrong. Looking back…" He tapped his fork on his plate and shook his head. "No point questioning it, now. What's done is done. We let everyone go that we hadn't witnessed *actually* killing someone. The ones who had killed civilians or our side, we executed, but the rest went back to their normal lives. There was a lot of mistrust in the early days, but I thought we'd made a lot of progress, mending bridges, and now…"

"Jamison," a man said, coming into the cafeteria. "Jamison, I need your mind."

Mr. Jamison turned his head, looking as an older man in a gray jacket and slacks walked quickly over.

"I'm working on a cast, and it's not centering the way I want it to. It needs a verbal cast to supplement it, but I've tried three different languages and none of them are working."

Mr. Jamison raised his eyebrows slightly, sitting back in his chair and crossing his arms.

"I need more detail than that," he said.

"It's a type of ward," the man in the gray jacket said, glancing once at Valerie. "Should hit concrete walls and stick there like a flypaper, and the azara root I'm using is adhering to the hard surfaces quite well, but it smokes off after I cast it because I can't get it to balance long enough to set."

"Have you tried Cornish? Or one of the old Gaelic dialects?" Mr. Jamison asked.

"No, obviously not," the man said.

"Do you have *words* you like?" Mr. Jamison asked with a sort of bemusement.

"Yes I've *written* the cast," the man said, annoyed, glancing at Valerie once more. "Who is she?"

"Mr. Tannis, I'd like to introduce you to Valerie Blake."

The man paused, shifting on the table to look more squarely at Valerie. Valerie looked back, not sure what she was supposed to say or do.

"Nice to meet you?" she tried.

"I don't know you," he said. "You don't intend to start classes, I hope."

"She will be starting with the rest of the freshman class," Mr. Jamison said.

"I didn't test her," Mr. Tannis said, standing. "I test all of the incoming students."

"She was last-minute," Mr. Jamison said. "Lady Harrington signed off on it."

"Then she will hear from me," Mr. Tannis said. "What's the point of me testing all of the students before we select them if she can just choose them at random? Were you tested at all?"

"No," Valerie said, hoping that the truth was the right answer.

"And what aptitudes have you identified for yourself without any external evaluation?" Mr. Tannis asked.

"Um," Valerie said, and he shook his head.

"I work hard to uphold the standards of this institution," he said. "I take it very seriously. We didn't *used* to compete with the School of Light Magic with any real seriousness, but we now have some of the best students graduating *here*. They want to come because they *know* it's competitive to get in. This only damages the school's reputation."

"You need to take it up with Lady Harrington," Mr. Jamison said, unruffled. "She can't answer you for any of that."

"Blake," the older man said. "Blake, Blake, Blake. I know that name."

"You *ought* to," Mr. Jamison answered.

The gray-suited man frowned, turning his attention more intensely on Valerie.

"Blake," he said. "Susan Blake."

She nodded.

He shook his head.

"Nothing but trouble, that woman. Best in the business, but she *would* think that she was entitled to bypass the entrance process."

"Again, she can't answer that," Mr. Jamison said. "Don't blow up the school with the wrong dialect. Give me your cast and I'll give you a few options on translation. Better yet, give me the entire cast and the text, and I'll see what I can come up with."

The man looked at Valerie once more, then shook his head, pointing a finger at Mr. Jamison.

"It will be on your desk in twenty minutes. I need it today."

Mr. Jamison nodded, then watched the man go and turned his attention back to the table.

Valerie's food was getting cold, but she had no appetite.

"He's going to hate me, isn't he?" Valerie asked, and Mr. Jamison shook his head.

"Impress him and he'll be impressed. Fail to impress him and he'll forget all about you."

She frowned, then closed her eyes and sighed.

"Mom is going to go fight again, isn't she? The people you let go at the end of the last war, they didn't *change*, any of them, and they're going to try to kill her all over again."

He rubbed his thumb and forefinger down the sides of his

mouth.

"Wow, you sound so much like her. Yes. You're exactly right. That's what is happening, and we lost so many key players, winning the war... I don't think we could win another without Susan Blake at the front of it."

"Why am I here?" Valerie asked, knowing the answer. Thinking of the smashed concrete of the sidewalk and how close it had come to being her or Hanson who had gotten smashed.

"Because the schools are the safest places we have," Mr. Jamison said. "Well, the safest places that are going to take in someone like you. Your mom... Both of your parents were... *polarizing*. Your mom still has friends in the community, but after all of those years, there's no way for her to have known who still feels about her the way they did the day before she left. She was smart, insisting that you come here. The faculty here... We care about the students first and the politics after. There are people here who blame an awful lot of death on your mom and the things that she said..." He held up a hand when Valerie's eyes flew open, as though she'd been about to speak. "When you're up against impossible decisions, looking at life and death everywhere around you, you see people's true colors come out, and you leave marks on each other that don't ever come off. She did what she thought she needed to, and she still has my whole-hearted support for everything she did, given what we knew at the time."

"Tell me about my dad," Valerie said after a moment, lifting her eyes once more to look at him. He shook his head.

"I told you, I don't want to get in the middle of that," he answered, and she clenched her hands under the table.

"Not how he died. Not, like, the stuff that my mom ought to have told me by now, but... You *knew* him. I don't even remember him. There are pictures of him holding me as a baby, but I never *knew* him."

Mr. Jamison drew a breath and nodded slowly.

"He was... quieter than your mom. He played pranks, sometimes... back then, we did that. You shouldn't do that, now. I'm a teacher. You understand. Pranks are bad. But he played these brilliant, cerebral pranks, back in the day..." The man smiled, thinking about it, then shook his head. "I always felt like your mom was the smart one, but then he'd go and do something like that, and you just realized how evenly-matched they actually were. He was funny, and anything he said, every *word* out of his mouth was worth hearing. He was... He was tough, and he knew his own mind. They said he changed a lot, coming out of school, but I only ever knew him from the war, and he was... He might have been the most *determined* person I ever met."

Again, that sounded very much like Valerie's mom.

Valerie shook her head.

"She should have told me. She should have *said* something to me..."

Mr. Jamison folded his hands.

"Is this about the war or your dad or magic in general?" he asked.

"All of it," Valerie said. "How could she keep a secret from me like that?"

"You've always known," he said. "Haven't you?"

She hesitated, and the corner of his mouth came up.

"You have. You... If all of this had come as a *complete* surprise to you, you'd be sitting on the bed in your room rocking back and forth, not talking to me."

"You don't know what I was doing before you knocked," Valerie said. "Besides, there aren't any bedsheets."

He frowned.

"I wouldn't have thought of that, either, if I'd only had a few minutes to pack. Let me see what I can do. I expect we can come up with the basics, at least. What *do* you have?"

"Some clothes?" Valerie said tentatively. "I wasn't watching very closely."

He nodded, then motioned at her dinner.

"You should at least eat something, then I'll walk you back to your room. I called Ivory Mills and she's bringing Sasha tonight, so at least you won't be alone. You've got a lot of catching up to do, the next few weeks."

Valerie nodded down at her dinner, still thinking hard, trying to make it all make sense.

"Is my mom in danger?" she asked after a moment as she cut the lasagna into bites and pushed them around with her fork.

Mr. Jamison sighed, resting his chin on his folded hands and frowning.

"I can't tell you that she isn't," he finally said. "Most of your childhood, you were probably very safe, but here recently, she's probably better off *with* us, rather than out on her own. They've been looking for her, I have no doubt, hoping to find her without anyone at her back to help her. Easiest time they'd ever have, killing her, and they…" He nodded. "They all know. We do, too. It's not fair. All she wanted was to be left alone and apparently for you to have a *normal* life, but today wasn't the moment everything changed for her."

Valerie shuddered.

"They tried to kill me," she said. "It was…"

He blinked.

"She didn't tell me that."

"I didn't… I didn't think to tell her," Valerie said. "It all happened so fast."

"You're safe here," Mr. Jamison said. "As safe as you can be anywhere. And, honestly… Man, your mom makes good decisions in a pinch. She sent you to the School of Magic Survival. You're about to go through the most aggressive self-defense training we know how to give you."

"I want to learn how to fight," Valerie said, and Mr. Jamison nodded.

"Of course Susan Blake's daughter wants to learn how to fight. But first we have to teach you how to survive."

Sasha

Sasha was thirsty.

This meant something, she was certain of it.

It was a tickle at the back of her mind as she worked, that she needed to pay attention to that, but she was focused.

Focused.

Magic took focus.

Focus.

Thirsty.

If she looked up now, the house of cards of ingredients and incantations she'd been weaving all afternoon stood every chance of falling down, and she'd have to start again.

And Proctor Tannis was watching her, taking notes.

Once more, the pen scratched on the paper, over there, and Sasha's mind twitched away from her work.

The smoke from the burning tell-weed curled, and she almost missed putting it right again. You had to whisper the air still or else… Well, she didn't want to think about how completely the spellwork would fail if the line of smoke broke.

Thirsty.

She blinked.

Looked over at Proctor Tannis.

There on his desk was what she had initially mistaken as a bird's nest, but it was actually a cast of drain.

He had been sipping at a coffee idly the entire time she'd been in the room, holding it off, but she'd been paying too much attention to her entrance exam to notice it.

He held her eye, seeing her figure it out, and she shook her head.

Tricky.

Her mom had warned her that it would be tricky.

Did she know how to break drain without interrupting her own cast?

Or…

She could weave it into the cast, add to the test parameters - had there been anything in the instructions against adding features to the cast? - and put a protection spell in on top of it to keep the impact of the drain cast off of her?

She'd been in too deep on the exam cast, and the break in her focus bewildered her.

Proctor Tannis' pen scratched on his paper again and he took a sip of his coffee.

Protection spell on a gullet base, designed for targeting death magic...

Her parents hadn't allowed death magic in the house, so she'd not done an awful lot of practicing around it, and the gullet... It was finicky. The tell-weed was keeping it in line, but tell-weed itself was one of the most ephemeral magics Sasha had yet mastered. Her mother was a master with it, though, and Sasha knew that the school would expect her to come in well-versed. It was only fitting she should use it as part of her entrance exam.

She was getting thirstier.

If she didn't work it out soon, the drain was going to hit the end of her water reserves and start sapping her energy. Water was a known defense against a wide variety of magics, but Sasha had been too nervous to eat her breakfast this morning.

She didn't want to complicate the spell any more than it already required all by itself, but at the same time, it needed to set, and she couldn't sustain it if the drain hit her solidly.

What did she have available?

She lifted her attention once more to look around the room.

She was in the upper-grades potions room, with boxes on the wall of everything she'd ever heard of and many, many things she hadn't.

Proctor Tannis' interest in keeping her from making a mistake only went as far as his own self-interest and her life's safety. Sasha had heard rumors that kids had died, mistaking one ingredient for another and having a proctor who failed to notice in time, but she thought that these were stories that they told the kids coming up into the Schools to keep them sharp at their lessons and then again here.

Mason powder.

She liked mason powder. It had a nice, smooth feel to it, when it was prepared correctly, and it was dormant in the context of most spells, but, if she remembered her lessons right - oh, how she wished she could refer to her notebooks for this part - it also remembered the ocean floors it came off of, the streambeds, and it associated with water.

Was it enough?

She added a layer of stabilizing influence to her cast, trying not to crush the spell underneath it, just keep it still and calm for long enough to get to the crate and get out a pewter hinge-lidded box full of mason powder.

She ran it between her fingers, marveling at how fine they'd ground it here, then she sprinkled it carefully down directly over the burning flame of the tellweed, watching the thin flame gutter. The smoke didn't come from the flame, it came from the burning weed itself, and she spoke cautious words, keeping her breath off of it, and the smoke maintained.

The cast continued to set.

She was still thirsty.

It wasn't like the mason stone was going to replenish what she'd lost.

She just had to wait to see if it would be enough to keep the drain cast on Proctor Tannis' desk from disabling her before the spell wholly set.

She just had to wait.

Valerie had eaten without tasting any of it, and then Mr. Jamison had walked her back to her room, where a woman in a pretty red dress had been standing in the doorway.

She was a dead-ringer for Snow White.

She took a step back when she heard their footsteps, quiet on the carpet, and she gave Mr. Jamison a tight smile, then looked at Valerie.

"Wow," the woman said. "Wow, can I see it."

"I know," Mr. Jamison said. "And I didn't even know her, back then."

Valerie looked from one to the other of them, then a girl's voice called out from the room.

"Is she here?"

"Come on out, Sasha," the woman said. "This is Sasha, my daughter. I'm Ivory Mills."

Valerie blinked and shook her head.

"I was a friend of your mother's from school," the woman said. "She's the one who first started calling me Ivory."

"You didn't tell me that," Sasha said, and Ivory nodded.

"Yes. Susan was the most gifted Light magic user I've ever known."

"Not that I'm not glad you're here, but why didn't you try for Light School?" Mr. Jamison asked. "I know your scores would have been good enough to at least test for it."

Sasha looked at her feet for a moment and nodded.

"I know how hard it was for everyone, during the war," the girl said. She had huge red hair that was held back - barely - in a ponytail. "I want to be able to keep people safe. I'm not…" She looked up at Mr. Jamison. "I don't want to go to war. I want to be a healer."

"Light magic is involved in a lot of healing," Mr. Jamison said. "Again, not to argue with you."

Ivory smiled, putting an arm around her daughter's shoulders.

"She has a plan, Mr. Jamison. Just you let her sit you down after a couple of weeks, when all of the new has worn off and when she's started talking everybody's ears off like she does at home, and you ask her about her plan. She's going to blow you away."

Mr. Jamison smiled, then glanced at his watch.

The man actually wore a watch.

"I need to go get back to my lesson plans," he said. "I'm sorry. Valerie, you come find me, if you need to talk or if you have more questions I can answer, but I… Start of school is always crazy. Good to see you, Ivory. Sasha."

Valerie looked at the two women, then dipped her head and edged around Sasha into the room.

"Your bed isn't made," Ivory said. "Do you need help with it?"

"I don't have any sheets," Valerie said. "Or a pillow."

Ivory put her hands on her hips, frowning.

"That won't do," the woman said. "What else are you missing?"

Valerie spread her fingers and Ivory looked at Sasha.

"Get out your list," she said. "We'll work off of that."

Sasha nodded quickly, going to a large backpack and digging through it for a moment to find a binder. She opened it on a desk and took the loose sheet of paper out of the front, offering it to Valerie.

"I don't even know what I *do* have," Valerie said, going to get her duffel bag and opening it.

"You were working quickly," Ivory said. "Sasha has two older brothers we've already done this with, and we've already made all of the mistakes. Sasha, you read them out and we'll go through and figure out what's missing."

The woman pulled a drawer open and put her hand out for the jeans Valerie had pulled out of her bag. Valerie hesitated, and Ivory motioned with her hand again.

"She'd do it for Sasha, if she was here and I wasn't," Ivory said. "We'll unpack, we'll do your list, and child, I'm going to buy you sheets. Best if you just move on and embrace it."

Sasha nodded as she threw herself onto her bed, running her finger down the list and looking at Valerie again.

"You don't argue with mom," she said.

"My mom, either," Valerie muttered, then nodded and started unpacking.

It was nearly midnight before Ivory Mills finally left.

Valerie had sheets, she had towels, she had bookends for her desk, she had a pillow, and she had a set of nail clippers.

Ivory had been oddly specific about the nail clippers.

Sasha went to close the door and turned to face the room. All night, families had been wandering past, talking and laughing and unloading things into rooms, and Valerie recognized that it was going to continue on all day tomorrow, too.

She didn't *want* to feel sullen about all of it.

Taking a step away from the circumstances under which her mom had sent her here, this was kind of a marvelous adventure: magic was *real*.

Mr. Jamison had been right - she'd believed in it her entire life, well past the point when normal kids embraced the fact that it was just make-believe. She'd always checked out of the corner of her eye, hoping to catch reality slipping up and being fantastic.

But she felt forced, cornered, and as friendly as Mr. Jamison and Ivory and Sasha Mills had been, Valerie wasn't ready to just go along, yet.

"So, that's done," Sasha said, coming to sit on her bed. She crossed her legs and wound her fingers around her ankles. "Sorry about her. Once she gets a plan in her mind, it's hard to convince her to do anything else."

Valerie nodded, looking over at the wall for a moment, and then rolling onto her stomach and balling her pillow up under her chin.

"I don't know anything about magic," she said and Sasha tipped her head to the side.

"What? How is that possible?"

Valerie shrugged.

"My mom didn't tell me anything. I didn't know it existed until... well, until today. A guy showed up at our apartment and told Mom she had to go fight, and she said she'd only do it if they sent me here, to room with you, actually, and... And now I'm here."

Sasha whistled, leaning over to lay on her own pillow.

"Wow," she said. "Mom didn't tell me. Did she know?"

Valerie shrugged.

"I don't know. I'm... I don't know what's going to happen *tomorrow*. I was going to school, just... normal, and... I don't know."

Sasha frowned.

"You shouldn't tell people you don't know anything about magic," she said.

"What, you don't think they're going to notice?" Valerie asked, and Sasha twisted her mouth to the side.

"It's *hard* to get in here. Not every magic-talented kid will get into *any* school, much less one of the top-tier ones. You being here..." Sasha shifted, looking uncomfortable. "You're taking a slot that a kid really wanted."

Valerie nodded, the pillow crushing under her chin.

"I didn't ask to come," she said.

Sasha's eyes went wide and she nodded quickly.

"No, I know, and... The way they whisper about the war when they think we aren't around to hear... Everyone I know was in the war. I think there were families that didn't participate, but everyone I've ever *known* was either in the war or too young when it happened. It was *bad*, and if it's coming back... I don't even want to think about it. They told Bradley some things, a few months ago... he's my big brother, graduated from Light School at the top of his class... and he told Newton and me pieces of it..." She shook her head again, squeezing her eyes closed. "I love magic, and I hate the idea of people using it to hurt other people. I wouldn't just... you know, walk away and say it isn't my problem... But I think my mom *killed* people."

"I think my mom was *good* at it," Valerie whispered, the realization coming to her as she spoke it.

Sasha nodded.

"I just want to take care of people. You know, build a place where they can't get in, where the kids can all come and hide."

"I think that's something someone *has* to do, right?" Valerie asked, and Sasha nodded again.

"After I graduate Magic Survival, I want to go to Light School, and then, if the war isn't happening, at that point, I want to go to the School of Natural Development."

Valerie shook her head.

"I don't know what any of those are."

Sasha nodded, rolling onto her back.

"Light School is the top school. Bradley and Newton both went there. Newton's a junior. My parents were surprised when I wanted to come here, but right now everyone at Light School is just *all about* fighting, and... I think you need a foundation of being able to take care of yourself and others before you should even think about learning to fight. Because if you don't respect how hard it is to keep yourself and everyone around you *alive*, you aren't going to truly value the life you're taking when you fight."

Valerie tipped her head to the side.

"I like you," she said, and Sasha smiled at the ceiling.

"Most people tell me that you don't have to be a survivalist to appreciate a hike, or to be a hunter, or whatever."

"Killing *should* be hard," Valerie said. "And I don't care how exciting it would be to go fight off the bad guys, we need people who can defend *home* and take care of the people who can't fight. I think it's awesome."

Sasha looked up and back at Valerie.

"Do you even know if you can *do* magic?" she asked. Valerie shook her head.

"Mom said that I was supposed to be a natural. Said she'd been testing me, but I don't know what that means."

"Probably the testing she's talking about is something you do by drinking a test fluid of some kind. You can measure the response to it, if you know what you're doing."

"I've never…" Valerie started, then frowned. "My mom is a good cook."

"Okay," Sasha said slowly.

"But she makes the *worst* soups on the *planet*."

Sasha smiled slowly and settled back onto her bed where she wasn't looking at Valerie anymore.

"I bet that's when she did it."

Valerie pulled the blanket and sheets back, shifting to get into the bed, and looked at Sasha again.

"I have a lot of questions," Valerie said, and Sasha nodded, yawning.

"I bet."

"You have to tell me if I get annoying," Valerie told her, and Sasha giggled.

"You have to tell me if I talk too much," she answered. "I love to talk about school stuff."

"But not tonight," Valerie said, reaching up to turn off her lamp."

"Yup," Sasha said, rolling onto her side to get her own lamp. "Not tonight."

Valerie couldn't remember where she was, when she woke up.

Her pillow was on the wrong end of the bed, or the wall was wrong, or something. It smelled wrong and she couldn't remember where the door was.

And then she heard Sasha get up and she remembered.

Valerie rolled over in bed, not sure if she was going to sit up and scream or pull the blankets over her head and cry, or if something else entirely was going to happen.

"Light School, the dorm rooms each have their own bathrooms, but we have a shared bathroom down the hallway. That's why the flip-flops. I'll wait, if you want to go with me," Sasha said.

Valerie swallowed and sat up slowly.

She wasn't screaming yet.

And she wasn't crying yet.

So far, so good.

She nodded, sticking her toes under the bed to find her flip flops and then digging in the top drawer of her dresser for toiletries. Lined up by size, just the way Ivory had left them.

"Your mom is…" Valerie started, then put her fingers to her eyes, trying to hold the tears there.

"You okay?" Sasha asked, and Valerie shook her head. There was a pause, then Sasha put her arm around Valerie's ribs and pressed her head against Valerie's shoulder.

"I miss home, too," Sasha said. "And I've been working toward this my entire life. I can't… I can't imagine."

Valerie nodded, steeling herself and putting the things she needed into the shower basket, then following Sasha down the hallway to a bathroom with six toilet stalls and six showers. There were a couple of girls there, already, and no one talked as Sasha and Valerie went to brush their teeth.

"They called me a Freshman," Valerie said quietly after she washed out her toothbrush and put it away, taking out the hair brush to put her hair up.

"I am, too," Sasha said, nodding.

"I'm *sixteen*," Valerie said. "I'm a junior."

"Oh," Sasha said, glancing over her shoulder and shaking her head quickly. "No. I'll turn seventeen this year, too. I finished my sophomore year at a civilian high school, last year. The magic schools are four year schools that graduate you at twenty."

"*Twenty*," Valerie said. "What about college?"

"You can go to another magic school after that and just do the upper class material, and as many as you want and you can get into, really."

"They all live in the dorms all that time?" Valerie asked, and Sasha shook her head.

"No, that's what the cottages are for. You can move out of the dorms after your sophomore year, if you choose to, and you aren't allowed *in* them, after you graduate your first school."

"How many kids are there, in all of the schools?" Valerie asked.

"I don't know," Sasha answered. "Hundreds. Maybe a couple thousand. There will be fifty girls and fifty boys in the underclasses at the Survival School.

Valerie's school back home had a class of more than four-hundred.

"Fifty," she whispered. "That's just two classes."

"Classes," Sasha said. "You haven't picked any. We should ask Mr. Benson for the list so that you can go through it."

Valerie looked at Sasha in the mirror, feeling helpless.

"I have no idea what I'd pick."

"Most of it's foundational," Sasha said. "A little bit remedial, if you've been working hard on your own. So… It'll be fine. Okay? We'll get the list, we'll just… you know, pick, and… I'll help you, okay? It's going to be okay."

Valerie looked at her own reflection, wondering just how much panic was showing.

"I need to tell Hanson I'm okay," she said. "He probably called me last night…"

Her phone.

Her mom had left Valerie's phone on the desk in her room, and it hadn't gotten into any of Valerie's bags.

"I need to call Hanson," Valerie said again. "Can I borrow your phone?"

"Is he your boyfriend?" Sasha asked, and Valerie shook her head.

"My best friend. And he was there when they came and got me. He's going to think that I've been *abducted*."

"I don't have a phone yet," Sasha said. "I'm not strong enough to manage it."

Valerie looked at her and frowned, holding out one finger.

"It's like… that heavy…"

"No," Sasha said. "It's that you have to ward it really hard to keep people from being able to track it or listen in on it. It's really, really advanced magic."

"So I can't call him?" Valerie asked.

"No, you can call, it just has to be from the office, and Lady Harrington has to be there," Sasha said lightly. "So... Well, I guess it would need to be really important."

Valerie nodded slowly, looking over at the showers.

"Why don't we get our own bathroom again?" she asked, and Sasha smiled, twisting her mouth to the side.

"They pay someone to clean this one," she answered. "If we had our own we'd have to clean it ourselves."

Valerie frowned with a slow nod.

"I can see how this could be better, then."

She picked up her things and followed Sasha back to the room, changing and going for breakfast.

"We only have a couple of easy days," Sasha said over their meals, turning her head as more new students showed up. "After this, classes start at seven-thirty and run through five, four days a week."

"Four?" Valerie asked. Sasha shrugged.

"Wednesdays are for special activities, studying and homework, and practicing. I'll show you where the labs are, once I find them, and that's where I'll be spending *all* of my Wednesdays."

Valerie nodded slowly.

"What do you do in the labs?" she asked.

"Try things," Sasha answered happily.

"Right," Valerie said.

She actually ate her breakfast with some appetite, then went to the main office with Sasha.

"This is Mrs. Young," Sasha said, indicating the woman at the desk. "She's the one with all of the *real* power."

"Miss Mills," Mrs. Young said. "You oversell me."

"You are," Sasha said. "She can get you into classes and move your schedule around, she can get you permission to be off campus, and she knows all of the teachers' favorite things. At the School of Light Magic, her name is Mrs. Pepper. Both of my brothers told me that I needed to meet Survival School's Mrs. Pepper first thing and make sure she liked me."

"And what favor is it you're hoping for today?" Mrs. Young asked, and Sasha held out a hand.

"This is Valerie Blake," she said. "She doesn't have a schedule yet."

Mrs. Young stood.

"I... Yes, I knew that you were here, but I hadn't had a chance to look over what was available. I was going to send for you, but I'm glad you're here. Mr. Benson said that he wanted to sit down with you and go over your final plans, given your... special situation, but I can give you the list of what has openings and when, and Miss Mills can at least help you work it down to your best idea. Mr. Benson is in faculty meetings all morning and won't be available until after lunch."

"I needed to make a phone call," Valerie said, and Mrs. Young shook her head.

"No, I'm afraid that isn't possible. Lady Harrington told me herself when we found out your circumstances that you will not be allowed to make contact outside of the school for at least a few weeks."

"I have a friend who is going to send the police looking for me, if I don't let him know I'm okay," Valerie said.

Mrs. Young pressed her lips and nodded.

"I do know it was rushed," the woman admitted. "If you wrote him a note and Lady Harrington approved of it, I could see that it made its way to him."

"I guess I can just e-mail him," Valerie said. "Do you have a wi-fi password?"

Sasha glanced at her, and Mrs. Young shook her head.

"Internet is not available on campus," the woman told her. "I'm sorry, but it's too much risk. You'll need to hand-write a note for your friend and have Lady Harrington sign off on it."

Valerie stared at her, and the woman spread her hands.

"I'm sorry," she said. "Those are the rules."

She pulled a stack of papers off of a printer and put them down on the counter.

"Is there anything else you need?" she asked, and Sasha swept the printout up and waved, heading for the door.

"No. Thank you."

Valerie looked at the woman for one more moment, and Mrs. Young gave her a very dry look, then turned her attention back to her computer.

No internet.

No phones.

No outside contact.

Surely Valerie's mother hadn't *meant* to send her to a convent, right?

Valerie followed Sasha out into the hallway and threw her hands into the air.

"What kind of people are these?" she asked. Sasha's arms flew out from her sides as she tried to motion for Valerie to be quiet without actually grabbing her.

"It's... Those are the *rules*," Sasha said. "And they're important. If we weren't careful with our phones..."

"What?" Valerie asked. "What would happen? Someone out *there* in the big bad world would know what color we're planning on painting our fingernails tonight? It's not like any of us actually *have* any important secrets."

"We do now," Sasha said, taking a step back. "That you're *here*."

Valerie let her shoulders drop, but then she was angry again.

"They didn't say that it's just a rule for *me*. This is the entire *school*. No computer, no phone. You *knew* those were the rules. Why? It's just a power grab. Do we have to wear *uniforms*, too?"

Sasha flapped again, looking around quickly.

"The magics we're learning," she hissed. "They're *secret*. You have to... You have to apply and get in and they have to *know* you, in order for you to be able to *be* here."

"What *is* this stuff, if it's all some big secret?" Valerie demanded. "I mean, is it all some big cult ritual that I'm going to go be in, now?"

Sasha backed into the wall, squeezing the stack of papers against her chest.

"It's because we have to protect it," she said. "From people who would steal it and use it against us."

"Who?" Valerie demanded. "Sure, there's a war on, whatever. Day in, day out, year after year, *who* is going to tap my cell phone to see if I *might* mention something about something I learned in class today? Nobody."

Sasha shook her head.

"You don't understand," she said.

Valerie closed her eyes, willing her temper back into its corner.

"I'm sorry," she said. "It's not your fault that they have *stupid* rules."

"They aren't stupid," Sasha said, and Valerie kept her eyes closed, wondering why Sasha wouldn't *take* an apology and just let it be.

She looked at the redheaded girl and pressed her lips between her teeth.

"Okay," she said. "Okay. I'm sorry. Can we go back to the room and look at a schedule?"

Sasha nodded quickly, walking along ahead of Valerie all the way back to the room.

Valerie didn't think she'd yet felt this alone, like she'd burnt the one bridge she had left.

She didn't know if she could do this.

But she knew she had to.

Basics of Magic Improvisation
Potions 101
New Old Languages
Tactical Herbtending
Diction
Stance
Traditional Magic
Group Spellcasting

"How can there be this many classes, when there are only like five students?" Valerie asked, and Sasha looked up from the class list.

"Because the classes are small and you might not get to all of them at once, so even the upper classes will still have a few people taking the last of their foundations courses," Sasha said without guile.

Valerie twisted her mouth to the side and lay on her back again on her bed.

"Do you think you're more interested in Color in Magic or Geometry of Magic?" Sasha asked. "You still have that gap at three."

"They both sound miserable in opposite directions," Valerie answered.

"You still have to do it," Sasha answered. "Geometry of Magic is really, *really* important, but if you don't understand the way that color plays into magic, you leave yourself really short on the things that you can do. I mean, the way that it ties into Improvisational Magic?"

Valerie sighed.

"I don't even know if I can *do* magic," she said, and Sasha sat up.

"Well, *that's* easy enough to test," she said, stacking the papers and tossing them out of the way under a desk chair. She motioned to the floor in front of her and Valerie sighed, sliding out of bed and going to sit in front of her roommate.

This had stopped being fun an hour ago.

When she found out that she was going to be expected to memorize a dozen or more *languages* in order to be able to *do* magic.

Apparently Mr. Jamison was the upper-level language teacher.

"Wow," Sasha said, putting her hands palm-up on her knees and shifting back and forth as though settling herself. "I haven't thought about this in a long time."

"Am I supposed to do that?" Valerie asked.

"You need to remember that right now I'm your only friend," Sasha said, her eyes closed. "Stop being so sarcastic."

Valerie frowned, looking at the girl's face.

She might not have been friends with her, at her regular school with Hanson and the kids she'd been in classes with her entire life.

She was kind of weird and *totally* a geek.

But.

35

She'd been really kind and really sweet to Valerie, and Valerie knew that she had been… unreasonably sour back at her, especially since she'd found out that she couldn't talk to Hanson.

"Okay," Valerie said. "Right. Magic. Let's do magic."

Sasha smiled.

"Just… kind of settle. Sit in a way that makes you feel calm and centered and strong."

Valerie thought about that for a minute, then shifted to sit on her ankles, drawing a deep breath and crossing her arms.

"Okay?" Sasha asked without opening her eyes.

"I'm here," Valerie answered. "But I don't get it."

"Your mom says you have power," Sasha said. "But words and ingredients are only as powerful as the person using them. And the precision with which you use them, but that's a different thing."

"Diction," Valerie said, and Sasha laughed.

"Yeah, I'm not *really* looking forward to that one, either. But it's mandatory for freshmen."

"Okay," Valerie said. "What do I do?"

"There are lots of families of magic, but they basically come down to three *types*. Things you mix, things you say, and things you *do*. The stronger and more specific a magic is, the more it tends to mix those three types together. Bradley told me that one of the first things you want to do when you get moved in is ward your room. Lock it down so that people can't cast on you."

"Who would do that?" Valerie asked.

"Well, normally it's just pranks and stuff, but it's kind of a lot more important now with the war and you and stuff. So the first thing we're going to do is just lock the door so that the only people who can open it are you and me. And the teachers and Mrs. Gold, but that's mostly because I don't think I'm strong enough yet to lock it against them. But the other underclassmen? We ought to be able to keep them out."

"Okay," Valerie said. "I'm good with that."

"The only way I know how to do it is for us to work together," Sasha said. "If I did it on my own, I'd probably lock you out, too. So this is a good test."

"Okay," Valerie said.

"You have magic," Sasha said. "Your mom said you do."

"So either she's right or she's crazy," Valerie said, and Sasha opened her eyes.

"Valerie," she said sternly, and Valerie twisted her mouth.

"Sorry. Just… It's a lot to just jump in with both feet."

"Okay," Sasha said, standing. "You stay. I'm getting my basic spell kit. You don't know any of the languages, so I'll do all of the incantation. We're going to mix noon oil with tell weed and burn it and… There it is."

She came and sat down across from Valerie again with a shower caddy full of bottles and bags and she started taking things out of it and laying them on the floor in front of Valerie's knees.

"Can I look at them?" Valerie asked, and Sasha nodded.

"Most of my basic stuff is pretty benign," she said. "You have to work it pretty well in order to get it to do anything, and I don't think there's even anything poisonous in there."

Valerie started going through the bottles first, holding them up to the light and spinning them to watch the fluids inside move. Some of them were just like water, and some of them moved more like oils. Others had things suspended in them, bits of leafy flotsam, mostly, and a couple she wasn't able to see through.

"What are all of these?" Valerie asked. Sasha sighed.

"You need to be able to name all of them, like, as soon as you can. I'll make a list or something to help, but if you can't name just *this* stuff? You're going to be so far behind…"

She'd taken out a black piece of slate and put it between them and then made a tiny pile of some kind of dry grass, which she set fire to with a flint-and-steel. Valerie knew *what* it was, watching Sasha work it, but she'd never seen one before.

"Are we allowed to burn things in here?" Valerie asked, siting straighter.

"Of course," Sasha said without looking up, as though it had been a dumb question. The redheaded girl was tipping a bottle of thick fluid slowly over the burning grass, murmuring words that Valerie couldn't make out. The oil hit the grass and for a moment it appeared it might put the whole thing out, but then it caught and burnt an ethereal green.

Valerie watched it burn for a moment, entranced, then put her hand out gently.

"Can I have it?" she asked, and Sasha handed her the bottle, still whispering in a language Valerie had no experience with.

Valerie took the oil and poured it out onto her hand, rubbing it between her fingers and just feeling the way it sat on her skin.

When she blew across it, it went cold.

More than just evaporation.

Cold, cold.

There was a reflex of instinct, and Valerie lifted her chin, looking at the slow curl of smoke coming off of the green flame and burning grass.

Just.

Do it.

Do it.

She pulled a piece of the grass out of Sasha's basket, rolling it in between her fingers hard enough to crush it to dust, and then rubbed one hand against the other in a quick slicking motion. The dust dissolved and disappeared, and both of her hands were coated in oil.

She blew across her palms, feeling the bone-deep chill come out of it, then put both hands down to the fire, letting it catch.

That was stupid.

Wasn't it?

It didn't feel stupid.

The green flame leapt to her palms and Sasha jerked away, looking at Valerie with alarm, but not interrupting whatever she'd been saying in her odd language.

Valerie stood and walked quickly to the door, putting both hands flat against it with a hiss.

There had only been an instant, there at the end, when her skin had felt hot, and the hiss startled her, and it felt as though something were *boiling* against her palms, but it wasn't *heat*.

She wasn't *burning*.

She let her hands drop to the side and she tipped her head, looking at the two black handprints she'd left on the wood.

Sasha was beside her in another moment, using her fingertips to paint the doorframe with the same oil. She put some on Valerie's fingers and indicated that she should do the other side, and the two girls met in the middle over the top of the door, then Sasha went to get a piece of green-burning amber grass and set fire to the damp oil at the bottom of each side of the door. The oil lit in a roll of green flame, burning out after just a few moments, then Sasha went and blew out the burning grass on the piece of slate.

"How did you know to do that?" she asked Valerie when she stood again.

"Don't know," Valerie said. "Just did. Is it wrong?"

"No," Sasha said. "It's awesome. Though I think I'm going to have a hard time getting into the room without focusing."

"Sorry," Valerie said, and Sasha shook her head, bending forward to look at the marks.

"They're perfect," Sasha said. "Usually you drip oil or miss something... Let me see your hands."

Valerie put her hands out and Sasha pored over them for several moments.

"Not a scorch in sight," the girl mused. "You did that better than I ever could have. And the *timing*. I wouldn't even try."

"I don't know better," Valerie said. She looked at the handprints again. "Am I going to get in trouble?"

"Oh, most certainly," Sasha said with an amused tone. "But not for that."

"What do you mean?" Valerie asked, and Sasha grinned.

"I mean that you are *definitely* a natural."

They spent a day going through the supplies that Sasha considered to be standard, quizzing on the ingredients and their properties. Valerie couldn't tell the difference between tell weed and angel hair, not for anything, no matter how often Sasha insisted that they were completely different.

Sasha told her about the various ways to group magic - the way it was cast, the nature of the things you used to cast it, the purpose of the cast - and the battling philosophies trying to encompass all of how magic worked.

"You seriously mean to tell me that you guys don't have this figured out?" Valerie asked, and Sasha grinned at the ceiling.

"Of course not," she said. "What else would the old people have to sit around and argue about, if not magic?"

Valerie picked the things up off of the floor and put them back into the caddy one by one, looking at each of them.

Magic.

Her handprints were on the door. There was no arguing about *that*. And it had a sense of connection to it, that she'd put a piece of *herself* into it, not in a dangerous soul-eating way, but the way she might have felt about a painting if she'd had a gift of art. Familiar and personal were those handprints.

She still had moments of complete and utter denial, but she *believed* that magic was real. It had been there on her hands, a part of her mind and her body forged together.

But the idea that this bit of dried grass clippings or that bottle of clear oil could *be* magic… It was completely disillusioning. She wanted it to be thunderbolts coming out of her hands and purple smoke. Everything in Sasha's box was clear or somewhere on the tan-yellow-gold axis. Like the bits of flotsam a child would pick up on a walk.

"Have you thought about what you're going to tell your friend?" Sasha asked, rolling onto her side. Valerie shook her head, the sullenness swelling in her chest without warning.

"I don't like them reading my mail," she said. "Maybe it would serve them right for the police to come looking for me, here."

"They wouldn't ever find it," Sasha said. "There's warding all the way up the drive. You basically have to know it's here to be able to find it."

"I left my cell phone in the apartment," Valerie said. "He's going to be frantic. There's no way to find me here… It almost feels like I really *have* been kidnapped. I mean, what am I *supposed* to tell him?"

"The closer to the truth, the better," Sasha said. Valerie straightened.

"Are there *rules*?" she asked. Sasha shook her head, draping her forearm across the bridge of her nose.

"No," she said. "But there are *reasons.*"

"That sounds like your mom," Valerie said, and Sasha laughed.

"It is. You don't tell civilians about magic because *knowing* about magic is enough to take away some of their protections, and there are worse things in the world than us."

"Than genocidal maniacs?" Valerie asked. "Prove it."

"The Superiors aren't mostly genocidal," Sasha said. "I mean, not the way my mom talks about them. Not most *of* them. Just the ones that we're always fighting with. Most of them just thought that we ought to be in charge, because we're more *powerful.* That just voluntarily being powerless around them out of some sense of consideration... I mean... You kind of see their point, don't you?"

"No," Valerie said, and Sasha laughed.

"Yes, you do," she said. "Why shouldn't we be allowed to use magic just because they don't know it exists or know how to use it? We keep it a secret voluntarily. Every one of us. And I can *see* why some people would just decide they didn't feel like doing it that way anymore."

"Okay," Valerie said slowly. "What's that got to do with Hanson?"

Sasha nodded, rolling onto her side to look at Valerie.

"Evil exists," she said quietly after a moment. "Mostly it doesn't care about us, but if it wanted to come mess with us, it could. Some of the Superiors, some of their magic... Magic goes on a spectrum from light to dark. The things that you use for it, the way that it *works.* The School of Light Magic *only* uses... you know, light magic. Survival School is a lot more pragmatic about using what *works.* I mean, we aren't using ravens' guts and stuff, but almost everything I brought from home is kind of there in the middle."

Valerie looked at the box and then over at the handprints on the door.

"Dark magic," she said quietly and Sasha sat up, pointing.

"That's not dark magic," she said. "So... don't think that it is. I used amber oil for it, and amber oil is one of the lightest oils I have. I actually picked it *because* it's going... Because you'll be safer if the Superiors come for you and try to open the door with dark

41

magic. It goes directly against it."

Valerie turned slowly to look at her roommate, frowning hard.

"You were thinking about that when you did the spell?" she asked. Sasha paused, awkward, then lay down again.

"I had six oils to pick from," she finally said. "Tell weed is okay with any of them - I use tell weed in almost everything I do… kind of a *thing* - so I was thinking about the reasons to use one over another and… Well, yeah."

Valerie's throat closed and she paused, waiting to be able to swallow again.

"Thank you," she finally said.

"You're welcome," Sasha said simply.

"Does my mom use dark magic?" Valerie asked, and Sasha shrugged.

"She went to Light School. Possible she *only* uses light magic. I don't know. My mom won't touch anything darker than that."

She motioned to her ingredients, and Valerie nodded.

"She doesn't feel like it's *corrupted* somehow?" she asked. "Using something that isn't *pure* light magic?"

Sasha shook her head.

"No. It's like… you want to be careful as you go over the middle, but… Anyway, it's not like you really get to *pick*. Some magic works for you and some magic doesn't. They'll probably do a whole bunch of aptitude testing to see where you are on the spectrum, so that they can tailor your classes to the kinds of magic that you're good at."

"Like, I'm going to be lighter or darker than you?" Valerie asked, alarmed.

"It isn't about your *character*," Sasha said. "No one knows what makes people able to do some things and not others. It's just… what it is. You'll figure out what your strengths are and you kind of play to them."

"Can I get *better*, if I'm not good at light magic?" Valerie asked, and Sasha twisted her mouth to the side.

"I don't know. Some yes, some no? You can practice and be more precise with how you do things, and that will make them work better, even if you're not very good at them, but you're never going to really be *better* at them. You'll just *do* them better. Does that make sense?"

Valerie went to sit on her bed, checking the clock - the *clock* - to see how long it was until dinner.

"How long have you been doing this?" she finally asked.

"Since I can remember," Sasha answered.

"And how good were your test scores, coming in?" Valerie asked. Sasha shook her head.

"They were good," she said.

"How good?" Valerie asked.

"Um," Sasha said. "Proctor Tannis told me that I had the highest marks of the incoming class."

Valerie nodded.

"I'm not going to survive here, am I?"

"You are," Sasha said. "I'm going to help you."

"No," Valerie said. "You've been studying your *entire* life. You know all of this *stuff*. And I don't know any of it. It's like... Oh, my gosh, I was going to say it was like trying to learn another language, but they actually *expect* me to learn another language."

"I was studying French at my old high school," Sasha offered, and Valerie shook her head.

"I was taking Spanish, but it's like, yeah, I can fill out some blanks on a vocabulary form and say some words that kind of sound like Spanish, but that won't *work*, will it?"

Sasha paused, then shook her head.

"No. You have to have perfect pronunciation and diction in the context language. And Spanish... I don't think they use Spanish much."

Valerie closed her eyes.

"Why didn't Mom tell me?" she asked.

"If you see them, they can see you," Sasha said, her tone ominous. Valerie sat back up again and looked at her.

"What does that mean?" she asked. Sasha burrowed the corner of her mouth into her cheek, then looked up at the ceiling.

"It's why you can't tell your friend *everything*. If he knows about magic, the demons can use him."

"Hold the phone," Valerie said. "*Demons?*"

Sasha nodded, still looking up at the ceiling.

"They can't *hurt* civilians. People who don't know *anything*. Like, there are... I don't know. My parents don't talk about them much. But they were involved in the last war, and they'll probably be involved in this one."

"Demons are real," Valerie said flatly, and Sasha nodded.

"They can teleport. Spontaneously manifest. If the school wasn't warded, they could just pop into the school if they wanted to, because we know about magic and we know about them."

"And do what?" Valerie asked.

"They're pure evil with a twisted sense of humor and a desire to ruin things," Sasha said. "They do whatever they want."

"Like, run through the hallways killing people?" Valerie asked. Sasha shrugged.

"I don't know. My parents never told me what they did in the war."

"So... me coming here, and you telling me all of this *stuff*... means that demons can come kill me now," Valerie said.

"Hopefully they don't ever show up again," Sasha said. "I mean, most magic users never have anything to do with them, in a lifetime. But... I guess so."

Valerie lay back down on her bed, weaving her fingers behind her head.

"Wow," she said. "I mean... I guess I can see why my mom would want to walk away from that."

There was a knock on the door.

"Dinner in ten minutes," Mrs. Gold said, her footsteps not pausing as she went to the next door down the hallway and knocked on it as well.

"Everyone ought to be here by now," Sasha said. "If you want to get to the cafeteria before the line is out the door, we can go early."

"What am I going to tell Hanson?" Valerie asked, still staring at the ceiling.

"The closer to the truth, the better," Sasha said. "Lies get complicated really fast. But you can't tell him everything. It wouldn't be safe."

Valerie closed her eyes and sighed.

"I have no idea what I'm doing," she said.

And, no, being *a natural* wasn't helping anything, just now.

Class

Seven-thirty in the morning.

Valerie sat bleary-eyed at a desk in a room that smelled funny. The kids around her whispered and shuffled, getting things out of their backpacks or writing in notebooks, but Mr. Benson had put Valerie into Botanicals and Herbs first thing in the morning, and Sasha was... Well, Valerie didn't remember, but her redheaded ally was somewhere else.

Valerie was on her own in a classroom that was about to discover that she had no business being here.

"Good morning," the woman at the front of the class said. "I am Mrs. Reynolds, and you are going to be on time to my class, or we are going to have trouble. I want all of you to know that I will not hesitate..." She paused as another girl came in, sitting down behind Valerie, then Mrs. Reynolds pressed her lips in silent commentary and went on. "I want you to know that I will not hesitate to send you to Mr. Benson or Lady Harrington if you are tardy more than once, and I will fail you if you are late more than twice in a semester. All magic requires promptness and attention to detail, and it doesn't matter if you know your herbs dead to rights, if you can't use them *on time*. You are warned."

She stood from her desk and looked up and down the rows. There were eight students in the room, in total, and Valerie was feeling a distinct lack of cover, compared to her real school.

There, if you sat in the back and didn't make eye contact, no one would even remember if you were *there*.

"Freshmen," Mrs. Reynolds said, shaking her head. "So full of themselves to have made it this far, and so far to go before they are anything *resembling* true magic users. Don't get ahead of yourself, in my class. Plants have distinctive traits that will keep you safe, so long as you know *all* of them. If you mistake wolfbane for sallow root in a potion that you imbibe, it will kill you before I can go through your potion closely enough to find your mistake. All right. Yes? Let's have some fun."

Valerie blinked as the woman transformed, figuratively. She tossed her hands out to either side at shoulder-level and went back to her desk, where she picked up a cafeteria tray with eight round plates on it.

"This is a selection of twelve different kinds of light-gray greenery ingredients. Rating sixty-five to seventy-five. I would like to see how many of them you can correctly identify by their spellcasting name, bonus points for being able to identify scientific or civilian-use name, where to find it, and which of these three you combine to form the most potent healing poultice."

She passed out the plates like it really was a treat, then she went back to lean against her desk, watching them.

"They aren't labeled, so you need to identify them by key characteristic in order to get any of the credit."

Valerie began picking through the so-called ingredients, smelling them, putting them down on the desk, piling them this way and that in ways that she hoped looked insightful, then she got a piece of paper out of her backpack and set it down in front of her with a pen, looking at the plants.

Lettuce.

Lettuce.

Tree branch.

Grass.

Celery.

Lettuce.

Leaf.

Leaf.

Leaf.

Vine.

They meant nothing to her. Just more stuff that a kid would take home from the park.

She remembered the way Sasha's oil and powder-stuff had felt on her hands, and she picked up each of the items more carefully, running her fingers over them, hoping that something would speak to her the way the oil had.

47

Celery.

Her fingers itched when she held the celery, and she broke the end of it, looking at the fibers inside of it. One by one, she started pulling them out, listening to the zippery way they peeled loose, feeling how cool they were to the touch as the water inside of the stalk - whatever it had been - hit the air.

It was satisfying.

She made little coils of the fibers on her desk, just for something to do with them, then put her pincered fingers under her nose again. It had a clean, earthy smell to it.

The red leaves, there, the way the green veins cut through the dark maroon surface of the leaf, that was interesting.

She had no idea what it meant, if it even *meant* anything, but it was pretty to look at. She split the leaf in half along the spine, enjoying how it split. It didn't tear; it broke.

She put the two halves into separate spots on the desk, one in the middle of the fiber coils and the other off by itself.

Turning her attention to one of the lettuces, she found the underside furry in an awkward, almost toxic way. She wanted to keep her fingers *off* of it. She broke the stem of that one, down at the base of the lettuce-y bit of leaf, and put it to her nose without touching it, then turned her head away at how acrid the fresh fluids inside of it were.

She put it down on top of the solo half of the red leaf, then changed her mind and put the red leaf top-side down on top of the fuzzy surface of the lettuce.

She browsed her fingertip through rest of the ingredients, coming up with the bit of tendril-y vine.

As long as she was doing it, she may as well make it look good.

She found the end of the vine hard, woody, but it split neatly with some force from her fingernails and the split ran down the length of it quite nicely. Inside, there was a pulpy fluid that she scooped out with another fingernail, just to feel the texture of it, then she wiped it off on the red leaf there with the fibers, and turned her attention once more to the other ingredients.

"Come with me," Mrs. Reynolds said, suddenly close. "Everyone else, turn in what you have. On my desk, face down, and put the plant subjects into the burn box. I'll be back in just a minute."

Valerie's heart beat hard against her chest as she stood to follow the woman to the door. Mrs. Reynolds paused to watch as everyone turned in their papers, then she opened the door and went out into the hallway, turning around to face Valerie as she pushed the door closed again.

"Are you mocking me?" the woman asked. Valerie swallowed the apology that was halfway out of her mouth. This wasn't what she'd expected.

"No," she said. "No. Um. I don't…"

"Who are you?" Mrs. Reynolds asked.

"Valerie Blake," Valerie answered, and Mrs. Reynolds straightened.

"Susan and Grant Blake's daughter?" she asked, and Valerie straightened.

"Yes," she said, prepared to be defensive at whatever the woman might say next.

"Well, I can't say I'm surprised they sent you in prepared, but mixing a poison in my classroom on the first day is hardly the way to win allies," Mrs. Reynolds said.

"Poison?" Valerie asked, and Mrs. Reynolds frowned, taking Valerie in down the length of her nose.

"Don't be smart with me," she said. "I don't take kindly to that sort of thing. How did you learn that preparation of gavon root?"

"Which root?" Valerie asked, confident that none of those things had been roots.

"Did your parents call it something else?" Mrs. Reynolds asked.

"The viney thing?" Valerie asked.

"Viney…" Mrs. Reynolds said. "What are you playing at?"

Valerie sighed.

"I have no idea," she finally admitted. "I… I didn't know magic was real until two days ago. Some guy showed up at our apartment and told Mom that she needed to come fight, and she sent me here for safe-keeping, apparently, but…"

She shrugged helplessly, and Mrs. Reynolds frowned deeply, considering her.

"Then *where* did you learn that preparation of gavon root?" she asked.

"I'm still back at poison," Valerie said. "I wasn't mixing anything."

"Child, you were extracting the essence of the olla leaf onto the rust weed. All it was going to take was adding in the green welk and you had a *classic* neurotoxin. I'm not going to let you make that kind of thing in my classroom, I don't care what you were doing at home."

Valerie shook her head.

"I was just stacking things in hope you wouldn't notice that I've got no idea what I'm doing," she said.

"But you *made* the gavon elixir," Mrs. Reynolds said, exasperated. "And I've only seen that preparation of gavon root a few times. Mr. Jamison does it that way."

"He knew my parents," Valerie said reflexively and Mrs. Reynolds snorted.

"I'll say he did," she answered. "You can't be trying to convince me that you don't know what you're doing. That was a very precise preparation. Non-traditional, I'll grant you, but that is probably the strongest gavon elixir I've ever seen a student make."

Valerie realized that if she tried to move, her knees were going to buckle and she was going to fall, but at the same time her body was entirely tensed, preparing to take off running the moment the woman realized that she was telling the truth. She didn't know where her body intended to *go*, when it took off, but the small of her back was beginning to hurt, it was so tight.

"Come with me," Mrs. Reynolds finally said, turning to walk away. Valerie worked each leg carefully to make sure it was going to hold her up before she followed, going back to the office and the woman who had liked Sasha so well and… Well, she gave Valerie a dark look as she followed Mrs. Reynolds in through the door.

"Didn't take you long to cause trouble," Mrs. Young said, turning her attention from Valerie to Mrs. Reynolds. "What can I do for you?"

"Is Mr. Benson in his office?" Mrs. Reynolds asked.

"He is," Mrs. Young answered slowly. "It's the first day of

school, though. You know he's very busy."

"She was in the process of making a welk-based neurotoxin during my evaluation quiz," Mrs. Reynolds said. Valerie wondered if maybe giving teenagers the ingredients necessary to *make* a neurotoxin might be a bad idea, but she kept it to herself.

"Let me go get him," Mrs. Young said, standing. "You can go sit in the counseling room."

Mrs. Reynolds led the way once more, opening a solid wood door and turning on the light in a small room with a smaller round table in it. The space was really only big enough to stand around the table, but they'd crammed four chairs in, anyway, and Mrs. Reynolds shifted her way around the table to sit, indicating another chair for Valerie.

"I'm sorry," Valerie said. "I didn't mean to. I swear I didn't. I… Please don't kick me out. I don't even know if my mom is at home anymore."

"Kick you…" Mrs. Reynolds said, then shook her head. "No. No, of course not. I just need to understand what I'm dealing with. If you're acting out, we will *deal* with it, but if you are genuinely without the first foundations of magic training…?"

She paused and was about to go on when the door opened again and Mr. Benson came in. He sat down in one of the chairs, shifting to try to get as much room as he could between the table and his chest, then he rested his elbows on the table and looked at Mrs. Reynolds.

"Mrs. Young said that you had a complaint about Ms. Blake's classroom behavior."

"No," Mrs. Reynolds said. "That's not it at all. I am *concerned* that she came into my room and promptly began mixing a neurotoxin, but I'm beginning to believe that that might have been your fault."

Valerie's shoulders dropped and she stared at the woman.

Mrs. Reynolds didn't turn her attention at all from Mr. Benson.

"Mixing…" Mr. Benson said. "Why was that even an option?"

"I like to know the capabilities and the proclivities of my students upfront," Mrs. Reynolds said. "You can tell a lot about a student's personal interests by which herbs he or she can quickly and easily identify."

Valerie found that a very interesting point, and she also found herself liking Mrs. Reynolds more and more as the woman spoke.

"There's a long way between identifying herbs and mixing neurotoxins," Mr. Benson said, and Mrs. Reynolds nodded.

"I'll agree that her tactics on identifying the ingredients were highly unusual in my estimation, something I've not seen in many years at this school, but it doesn't make them invalid methods. She says that she is new to magic."

"That's true," Mr. Benson said. "She came to us at the last minute because Roger Haem drafted Susan to go back to the war."

"Drafted?" Valerie asked, but neither of the adults looked at her.

"And her parents hadn't trained her at home *at all*?" Mrs. Reynolds asked.

"Grant Blake went quiet during the war," Mr. Benson said softly, and now Mrs. Reynolds did look over at Valerie.

"I hadn't heard," she said. "I'm sorry."

Valerie looked from one to the other of them and nodded.

"I don't really remember," she said. "It's... you know."

"She really wasn't trained?" Mrs. Reynolds asked Mr. Benson. He looked at her.

"I was given to understand that you were being raised as a normal, civilian teenager," he said.

"You guys aren't an army," Valerie observed. "I'm not sure I get this *civilian* thing."

Mrs. Reynolds nodded.

"I see," she said. "You know *no* magic?"

Valerie shook her head, considering mentioning the handprints on the back of her dorm room door, but not thinking that that qualified as *knowing* magic, since she wasn't sure at all if she could do it again.

Mrs. Reynolds looked at Mr. Benson.

"I am without a doubt that she was one step away from a welk-based neurotoxin, and she made one of the most elegant preparations of gavon elixir I've ever seen. If she can do that without a single *day* of magic training, I'm afraid I cannot teach her without better understanding her capabilities."

They both glanced at her, and Valerie twisted her mouth to the side, feeling like she was supposed to apologize at this point.

Mr. Benson looked once more at Mrs. Reynolds.

"What are you suggesting?" he asked.

Mrs. Reynolds smiled.

And so Valerie found herself in the upperclass potions room.

That's what they said it was, at least.

To Valerie, it looked like someone had let a storage closet get out of hand and take over a very large classroom.

There were only sixteen desks in the classroom, and every wall was lined with boxes and shelves and baskets. Everything was labeled, and none of it made the first bit of sense to her.

And there were nine adults standing at the back of the room watching her silently.

Mrs. Reynolds, Mr. Benson, and Lady Harrington were joined by Mr. Jamison and five others - one of whom had to be the potions teacher himself, though Valerie hadn't caught which one of them that was. The frowny-faced man from her first day at the school was scowling at her with crossed arms.

She sat down on a desk facing them and frowned.

"I don't understand what you expect me to do," she said, looking around.

"The same thing you did in my classroom," Mrs. Reynolds said. "Whatever that was."

Valerie spread her fingers.

"I was just playing around," she said. "I didn't think there was a chance you'd give us anything *dangerous* on the first day of school."

"Magic is fundamentally dangerous," Mr. Benson said. "Once you become familiar with it, some very dark, violent portions of the world have permission to involve themselves with you."

"Then why do you do it?" Valerie asked, still feeling very awkward with the adults all just... standing there. She wished Sasha was there. Or Hanson.

Anyone.

Just someone familiar.

"Because we can't let them go unopposed," Mrs. Reynolds said. "Those who embrace the darkness. And because there's a power to magic that you know, deep within yourself. You're safer, staying away, but if you did have the opportunity to choose, would you?"

"But I don't get a choice, do I?" Valerie asked. "I'm stuck here, and you won't even let me contact my friends to tell them that I'm not dead."

"Who told you that?" Mr. Benson asked and Valerie shook her head.

"I can write him a *letter*, and you'll read it and then give him the pieces you're willing to let him have," Valerie said. "He thinks I'm dead right now. My best friend."

"We'll discuss that after this," Mr. Benson said, shaking his head and stepping forward to sit down at the back-most desk. He wove his fingers and put them under his chin.

"This school is full of remarkable students," he said calmly, looking at her. "And we have a truly remarkable faculty here, trying to give them the opportunity to realize their full potential. Most of them have come to us through normal, predictable channels. You, though, are remarkable in a very different way, and we need to understand that, if we are going to help you."

Valerie thought suddenly of her mother's note, that she didn't know if Valerie could trust Roger or not.

There was a war.

Bad people.

Dark magic.

Some of these people might not be trustworthy.

Should she be considering keeping secrets?

She looked at Mr. Jamison, and he nodded.

"Whatever it is you did to impress Mrs. Reynolds so much, we would all like to see it," her mother's friend said, and Valerie drew a breath, looking once more at Mr. Benson, and then looking around the room.

"I really don't know what it is you're expecting," she said after a moment, but she got up and started walking along one wall, just letting her fingers brush across the fronts of boxes and mesh bags, dipping into containers to pick things up and setting them back down again.

Neurotoxin.

It was a fancy movie word, or something in the news. She didn't really know what it meant, other than the obvious translation that it was a brain poison.

She'd almost *made* one.

On accident.

With a pile of leaves.

What business did she have in here, looking at all of this *stuff*? What kind of awful potential was here, just behind the cardboard under her fingers?

Someone started to say something, and Mrs. Reynolds hushed them.

"Just wait," the woman said quietly.

And then Valerie stopped walking.

Her hand didn't leave the box she was touching, and she went back to look into it.

Vials.

Tall skinny ones with black screw-on tops. She took one out and looked at it, then read the label on the box, which told her nothing of any value at all.

All the same, her fingers closed around the cold glass and she went on, pulling things out of baskets, out of boxes, off of hooks. She came to a section full of wooden bowls and stone platters, glass trays and pewter plates. She took a stone bowl, going back to a desk and setting it down there, just looking at it.

What had that bowl seen?

She ran her fingers along the inside of it, feeling the angles there where the rough cut of the stone had been worn smooth through workman's tricks and long use.

And then she poured the vial in.

There was a reaction, but she didn't pause to measure it. Either she'd done something spectacularly *bad* or highly unexpected or... Well, she didn't know what they expected. They'd put her in a room full of boxes and asked her to do *stuff*. Of course whatever she ended up doing was unexpected.

She poked a small pewter box with her index finger, then opened it, taking out a soft green powder, like what you might get if you really mushed up green tea *really* well. She sprinkled it over the shiny red fluid in the bottom of the bowl, then tipped her head to the side, watching it.

There was a bit of rope, maybe a foot long and made of something that felt an awful lot more like reptile than cotton. She picked that up and let it dredge back and forth across the bottom of the bowl, just watching the swirl patterns of blackening green powder in red liquid.

She picked up a pair of stones, rolling them over each other between her fingers while she continued to drag the rope back and forth, then she held one of them over the bowl.

"Stop," one of the men said. "Just… stop there."

"I don't know that cast," Lady Harrington said. Mr. Jamison had his fingers over his mouth and Valerie watched him, trying to figure out if it was shock or horror or something else.

"That's just how Susan did it," her mom's friend said after a moment. "I've *seen* her do *exactly* that."

"It's a bomb," the man Valerie didn't know said. He was the one who'd stopped her. "Give me the pig's ears?"

Valerie looked around. She hadn't found anything that matched that description.

"The rocks, Valerie," Mr. Jamison said.

Valerie turned her hand over and let the man take them, and then Mrs. Reynolds came and took the bowl, rope trailing out of it. The two of them - the herbs teacher and the potions teacher - consulted, and Mr. Benson stood, looking at the rest of the things Valerie had picked up.

There were still a good dozen things that had caught her interest before she'd ran out of space in her hands and her bowl.

"I've never seen this variant," the frowny man with Mrs. Reynolds said after a moment. "But I know this model. I'm confident enough that it *would* work that I won't let her complete it."

"What else were you going to make?" Mr. Benson asked.

Valerie shook her head, looking at the handful of grass. She picked it up and started dropping it on the desk one piece at a time, forming a circle and Mrs. Reynolds gasped.

"The leather line," she said to the potions teacher. "How would it interact with tell weed?"

Tell weed. Is that what that stuff was? Valerie frowned at it. She probably ought to have recognized it, after how much Sasha had gone on about it.

"It's going to stabilize it, if you did it right," the other teacher said. "Could be a fuse. Could be a shield. It all depends."

They looked at her, and Valerie let her hands drop.

"Do you guys want me to keep going or… I don't understand."

Mr. Benson stood and looked back at the teachers once more.

"I think we need to have a discussion before we figure out what we're going to do about all of this," he said. "Mrs. Reynolds, can you take Miss Blake back to your classroom and ensure that she doesn't have direct contact with any additional magical ingredients, please? We will hold a meeting at lunch with her teachers to discuss the issue."

"I would like to be there, if I may," Mr. Jamison said, glancing at Valerie. "Her mother was a dear friend, and I owe it to her to watch over Valerie if I can."

"Can you spare the time?" Mr. Benson asked, and Mr. Jamison stretched his mouth to one side and nodded quickly.

"I'll make the time," he said. "I'll figure it out."

Mr. Benson nodded and motioned to the door.

"In the meantime, you all have classes waiting for you."

Including the potions class out in the hallway, just now.

The potions teacher came to look at the pile of things Valerie had and he nodded.

"I would have very much liked to have seen what you would do with those," he said. "I am Mr. Tannis, and I'd like to review your schedule to have you moved into my class next semester. You are dangerous, right now, and you need to learn… everything here. Most students wouldn't have *touched* any of these things without a written spell, but you worked with them more confidently than magic users who have been doing it for decades longer than you. You need to be taught, but without curtailing that ability. Do you understand?"

Valerie shook her head.

"Not really."

"Good," he said. "Ignorance isn't something to be praised, but truth is. We will see what the rest of the faculty agree to, but expect to be in my class this year."

Mr. Jamison was standing in the doorway, waiting for her, and Valerie went to go through to the hallway, watching as the older students filed back into the class.

Mr. Jamison was watching her carefully.

"She didn't teach you *anything*?" he asked.

She shook her head.

"No."

He drew a slow breath and sighed.

"With any luck, your penchant for creating weapons is something we can curb toward defense a bit more consistently," he said. "This is the School of Magic Survival, after all." He chewed the inside of his cheek for a moment, then nodded, looking over at where Mrs. Reynolds was waiting for her.

"We both have classes waiting for us, Mr. Jamison," Mrs. Reynolds said. "We'll discuss it privately and come up with a plan."

Mr. Jamison nodded again and Valerie slowly followed Mrs. Reynolds down the hallway and down the stairs toward the herbs and botanicals room again.

"Did I do something wrong?" Valerie finally asked.

"No," Mrs. Reynolds answered. "You're just going to be very challenging to teach. You have immense skill and no knowledge. It's the kind of combination that kills someone if you don't get it right."

Valerie's mouth went dry. Somehow, the woman putting it *just like that* had made it feel very real.

She could kill people.

On accident or *on purpose*.

She shuddered and shook her head.

"I don't want to kill anyone," she said.

"No," Mrs. Reynolds said. "That's why you're going to work so much *harder* than the rest of the students to make sure that you have the knowledge to choose what you want to make. If you can't get on top of it, we may never be able to let you use magic ingredients, and if you are just as skilled with the other magics… I can't imagine what we'll do."

"I didn't ask for this," Valerie said as Mrs. Reynolds put her hand on the door knob.

"No," the woman said, firmly but kindly. "No, you didn't choose any of this, but this is where you are and it's what you are, and now you have to do the best you can."

"I just want to go home," Valerie said quietly and Mrs. Reynolds drew a breath that made her chest rise.

"That is behind. You need to focus on ahead. Is that clear?"

If someone else had said it, it might have sounded cruel, but the way she spoke, it was bracing.

Encouraging.

Valerie nodded.

"Yes," she said, and Mrs. Reynolds gave her a tight smile.

"Let's go have some fun," she said.

Sasha sat with her at lunch.

The rest of the kids kept their distance, staring and whispering.

Valerie was a bit preoccupied with what the teachers were talking about just then, and not really invested enough to take it personally, but Sasha seemed uncomfortable.

"If you want to sit somewhere else, you can," Valerie said as Sasha hunched over her tray.

"They're saying that they cleared out the upper class potions room for you," Sasha said, the first she'd spoken to Valerie. "But no one knows what happened."

Valerie frowned.

"So?" she asked.

"You're Susan and Grant Blake's daughter," Sasha said, her voice still low. "They think that you're a master magic user, that you're just here for show, or that they're going to move you up to the upper classes because you're that advanced."

Valerie pursed her lips.

"Did you really split a gavon root?" Sasha asked after another moment.

"I don't know," Valerie said. "I don't remember which one that was."

"Sort of a green… tube, like a tulip stem?"

"Oh," Valerie said. "The viney thing. Well, yeah. Isn't it just asking for it?"

"You use it to wrap *around* things, and it keeps them thermally stable," Sasha said.

"Oh," Valerie said. "Okay."

"What *did* happen, when you went in the potions room?" Sasha asked. Valerie shook her head.

"I don't know," she said. "Stuff."

"You made me stand in the hallway," someone said, a tray clapping down on the table next to her and a guy a couple years older than Valerie sitting down next to her with an easy smile. "The least you can do is tell me why."

"Um," she said, glancing at Sasha. The girl had gone wooden.

"I'm Elvis Trent," the guy said. "And you are?"

"Valerie Blake," Valerie said. "Thought that had already gone around, though."

"Blake," he said. "Everyone's guessing, but it's not *that* uncommon a last name."

"Yes, my mom and dad are kind of famous," Valerie said.

"Your mom is Susan Blake?" he asked, and she nodded. "Then what are you doing, slumming it down here at Survival School? Shouldn't you be at Light School?"

Valerie shrugged.

"This is where my mom wanted me to go."

He grinned again, shifting to cross his legs and picking up his fork.

"You didn't get a say?" he asked, and Valerie snorted.

"Not really, just then," she said. He frowned, about to ask something, but a pair of guys came over and clapped him on the back.

"Hey man," he said, greeting them. They started talking about where they were all living this year, and Valerie turned her attention back to Sasha.

Elvis? she mouthed.

Trent, Sasha mouthed back. Valerie gave Sasha an exaggerated shrug and Sasha shook her head quickly. Don't do that.

Valerie looked at Elvis once more. He had a nice build to him, maybe a bit slighter than her taste ran. Hanson would have plowed through him at just about any sport that allowed that sort of thing.

She smiled at the thought of Hanson, then turned forward to look at her tray again, blinking sudden tears.

Elvis put his hand on her back and she slid sideways, grabbing his wrist. His eyebrows went up and Valerie very briefly considered whether she owed him an apology.

Not likely.

"Don't like to be touched unexpectedly by strangers," she said. "Mom put me in classes starting when I was little."

He held his fingers up. Surrender.

"Sorry," he said, taking his wrist back and waving off his friends. "So what's your story? No one *knows* you."

"Mom and I kind of kept to ourselves," Valerie answered, feeling more defensive of her secret, here. Here where everyone whispered.

"Still," he said. "You know Sasha. And we know Sasha. How do you two know each other?"

They knew Sasha? How? Was there like, pre-school or something? Sasha had talked about her normal school, her friends there.

"Our moms were friends, back during the war," Sasha said. "So when Valerie was going to come here, her mom said we should room together."

"Why did they clear out the potions room?" Elvis asked. Valerie shook her head.

"Because they didn't want you to be there," she said. "They didn't ask me."

"You in trouble?" he asked, and Valerie shook her head.

"Don't know. I guess I'll find out later."

He grinned.

"Big trouble for the first day of school, have Lady Harrington and Mr. Benson both turn up for it."

She shrugged, and he shook his head.

"No. We're all betting that you showed up and they didn't know how to deal with how good you were. That they're looking at skipping you up to upperclass. You thought about it at all yet?"

Valerie shook her head.

"Just trying to get through my first day at a new school," she said, looking around the room.

"Well," he said. "If they do and you're looking for what cottage you want to move out into, I've got some friends who have space for another roommate."

"I'm not moving out," Valerie said. "Thanks."

He raised his hand to clap her on the back once more, then thought better of it.

He stood and walked back over to a group of guys at another table, and Valerie looked at Sasha, who shook her head and returned to her meal.

No one else spoke to them during lunch, but after lunch, Valerie got a significantly cooler reaction from her classmates. She made it to the end of the day without breaking, and Mr. Benson was waiting outside of her classroom. The students ahead of her skittered away and those behind stayed in the room as Mr. Benson stood from where he'd been leaning against the wall and motioned to Valerie.

"I need you to come with me, Miss Blake," he said. She dipped her head and adjusted her backpack, following him down the hallway and into the main office once more.

They got a larger conference room this time, where Valerie found all of her teachers, plus Mr. Jamison and Lady Harrington waiting for her.

Mr. Benson sat down at one end of the table and indicated at the other end, for her.

Valerie sat, looking around with acute discomfort. She couldn't even recite all of their names, at this point.

"Miss Blake," Lady Harrington began. "None of us were quite prepared for your arrival, given it came in such proximity to the start of school, but Mr. Benson and I agreed that it was necessary that we take you on, regardless of your merit as a student, because of the service that your parents had done for the magical community, and how your mother was going to be pressed back into service again, putting you at risk."

She shifted, folding her hands in front of her and looking down at the table for a moment, then looking up at Valerie again.

"We find ourselves in a difficult position, because you are not only the least-qualified student the School of Magic Survival has ever accepted, but you may be the most talented. You are going to remain here for as long as you need to, in order to ensure your safety, but Miss Blake, if you want to *learn* from us, I cannot begin to express how hard you are going to have to work, not only to catch up, but to contain your latent talent until you are actually able to control it. Do you understand?"

Valerie swallowed.

"I don't know," she said.

"You have a decision to make," Mr. Benson said. "We have discussed it at length, and the teachers represented here are willing to start you at the very bottom and work their way up, because we are all eager to see what you are capable of, properly trained, but you are going to have two, three, perhaps four times as much work as any other Freshman, and that workload is likely to persist through to your Senior year, in order to get you ready to graduate. Most of our students have been studying magic since they could speak. A few of the parents don't introduce magical instruction until the pre-teen years, ten or eleven years of age, because they don't want their children playing with magic. But if you don't *start* instructing magic until the properly teenage years, thirteen, fourteen years old? You aren't going to be able to be ready for one of the Schools by the year of the seventeenth birthday. The freshmen in class with you have *all* been studying for at least four or five years.

"You are going to start from absolutely nothing, not even observational knowledge, and that's going to take time to overcome. If you choose to do it. If you decide that it isn't for you, we will find a way to get you access to correspondence lessons through a regular school, and you may yet be able to graduate from a civilian high school as you remain here on campus for your own safety. But you have to choose one or the other, and you need to choose quickly. Mr. Tannis has offered to be your faculty advisor - two years early, I'll point out - because he was most impressed with your performance today. I need an answer from you by the end of the day, what you would like to do."

She looked up and down the table at the curious expressions of the adults there, then Valerie looked at her hands, considering.

"I want to talk to Sasha," she said, and Mr. Benson nodded.

"You should take your time making your decision," he said. "But it must be today."

"You are safe and welcome here," Lady Harrington said. "We just don't know how to help you best."

Valerie looked at the woman and nodded, making eye contact with Mr. Jamison after a moment.

"I wish I could talk to my mom about it," she said, and he gave her a glum but understanding look.

"It is my understanding that she is already out of communication," Lady Harrington said. "The Council met with her the day that you came to us, and she was sent out with orders. They don't expect to hear back from her until they're completed."

Valerie's attention snapped to the woman, and Lady Harrington nodded.

"I keep up with what's going on in the lives of my students," the woman said. "I know that it's important to you, and I wish there was more I could tell you."

Valerie stood, unsteady, looking at Mrs. Reynolds. She was so stern sometimes, but her expression was so encouraging.

"You think I should do it?" Valerie asked her, and Mrs. Reynolds smiled.

"I think I would be delighted to see how far we can launch you, my dear," she said. Valerie nodded, then looked around the table again.

"I'll... Okay," she said. "I'll decide soon."

Mr. Benson stood and walked her to the door, opening it for her and closing it behind her to the beginnings of conversations among the teachers in the room.

Valerie looked at the closed door for a moment, then bolted

out of the office, going straight back to her dorm room.

Where she found Sasha sitting outside.

"I couldn't get in," Sasha explained cheerfully. "The lock was too strong. Can you let me in?"

"Oh, my gosh," Valerie said, horrified. "I'm so sorry."

Sasha shrugged, standing as Valerie went to try the doorknob. Whatever she'd been expecting, the door opened easily and Sasha breezed past as though she'd known it would be that simple.

"They were saying that Mr. Benson pulled you aside after Diction," Sasha said. "What happened?"

Valerie closed the door, considering the charred handprints there for a moment before going to sit on her bed. She dropped her backpack on the floor, then scooted across the bed to sit with her back to the wall.

"They said that they're going to keep me here," Valerie said. "That I'm not safe anywhere else. And that they're *willing* to teach me, but that it would be really hard. Like, I would have to work harder than anyone else, just to catch up, and I don't know if they'd let me *do* any magic for a long time."

"Why?" Sasha asked. "What *happened* today?"

Valerie shook her head, looking away.

"Well, first I made a poison and then I made a bomb, apparently."

There was a long silence, and Valerie turned her head to see Sasha creeping closer.

"How?" she asked. Valerie shook her head.

"I don't know. I didn't even know I was *doing* anything. I mean, Mrs. Reynolds said that I made the antidote, too, so I've at least got that going for me, but Mr. Tannis said that it was a bomb, and..." Valerie couldn't help but smile, just for a moment. "Well, he seemed like he was really impressed, actually, but still, they put me in a room with a bunch of ingredients and I just start putting them together. I don't even know what I'm doing."

"Like sleepwalking?" Sasha asked, and Valerie shook her head.

"No, more like doodling. Only I look down and I've drawn the Mona Lisa upside down or something. I'm *doing* nothing, but then they all freak out because I built a bomb by accident."

Sasha blinked.

"That's *awesome*," she said.

"No it isn't," Valerie said, unable to contain the grin at Sasha's glee. "I just want to go back to *school*, who thought I would ever say that?, and hang out with Hanson and see my mom. I don't want to learn the wild world of magic and have everybody constantly on edge that I'm going to kill them by mistake."

"Okay," Sasha said. "But that's not an option, is it? I mean, is it?"

Valerie shook her head.

"No. Someone tried to kill me, and… No. I just hope that they don't go after Hanson after all of that…" She paused. How had she not thought of that before? In the middle of everything, it had never occurred to her that *Hanson* might be in danger. "I need to talk to him."

"Okay," Sasha said. "So… Okay. Can you do anything to help him?"

"No, but they could bring him here to keep him safe," Valerie said.

Sasha twisted her mouth to the side.

"I hate to say it but the fact that he doesn't have any way to get in touch with you and that everyone knows it, because everyone knows the rules at the schools for freshmen… Maybe that keeps him safe."

"They tried to *kill* me," Valerie said. "And they could have killed him just as easily by mistake. He was standing right next to me. They aren't going to *not* hurt him, just because it isn't guaranteed that I'll know about it and do something about it. They'll do it in case I find out."

Sasha frowned.

"You have to tell Lady Harrington," she said.

Valerie put the back of her hand to her mouth.

"They're going to expect an answer," she said. "I'm supposed to tell them what I want to do."

"What do you want to do?" Sasha asked. Valerie looked over at the basket of ingredients, sitting up on a shelf, and she shook her head.

"I can't imagine saying no to that," she said. "But what if I kill someone?"

"One, you're not going to kill someone because they won't let it happen," Sasha said. "They've been around kids doing stupid things with magic for a long time. It just isn't going to happen. And two, if you know that you aren't going to say no, then you have to say yes. Don't you?"

"I don't even know if I should be here," Valerie said. "I'm putting everyone in danger."

Sasha sat back on her bed again, leaning against her own wall and putting her legs out in front of her, crossed at the ankle.

"Magic puts you in danger," she said. "That's why your mom ran away, I bet. She saw it more than anybody, what magic can do. But it's part of who you are. You aren't putting any of us in any more danger than we already were."

"I *am*," Valerie said. "You don't have people coming after you trying to kill you."

"It's a *war*," Sasha said. "Of course we do."

Valerie sat, silent and stunned for a moment, then Sasha folded her arms and shook her head.

"It's a *war*," she said. "And you're just finding out about it, like, today, but the rest of us have known it was coming for months now. Some of the upperclassmen might have known it was possible for years. It started just like the last one did, with everyone hoping that we could prevent it, but we *can't*. And that's why they need your mom. She's the one who knows how to *end* it."

Valerie looked at her knees, wanting to argue with this, but not able to find anything wrong with what Sasha had said.

"You have to do it," Sasha said. "If you say no, they won't teach you magic, and... Valerie, if you're dangerous, the only way to *stop* from being dangerous it to learn how to control it. If you're dangerous, *not* learning magic doesn't make you any safer."

"I never blew up anything before," Valerie said sullenly, and Sasha smiled.

"Yeah, but that was before. Now you're taking refuge at a magic school, and you're surrounded by magically potent objects. Imagine you sitting in here one day, fidgeting with some of my stuff, and accidentally forging a magic knife that cuts through all of the defenses and lets in everyone who wants to hurt us?"

Valerie looked at Sasha with a frown.

"That was oddly specific," she said, and Sasha grinned.

"I know. I was just imagining what trouble you could get yourself into with tell weed if you were really good at managing it and had no idea what it could do."

"And that's possible?" Valerie asked. Sasha nodded vigorously.

"I can actually build the spell in my head, but I'm not quite good enough with tell weed to get it to work, I don't think. If you were *good* enough... Yeah, it could happen."

"Then I have to say yes," Valerie said, and Sasha nodded.

"You do. You have to say yes."

Valerie sighed, standing and hopping down off of her bed.

"I'll go tell Lady Harrington, and then I'm going to make her let me talk to Hanson. I need to know he's okay."

"Are you like... together?" Sasha asked, and Valerie shook her head.

"No, he's just been my best friend forever, and if he got into trouble because of this..."

She shook her head, then waved.

"I'll let you know how it goes."

The office was locked and Mrs. Young was gone by the time Valerie got back there, but she could see a light on in an office down the hall, and when she knocked on the glass door, Lady Harrington came out of the office, coming to open the door for Valerie.

"Have you made a decision?" the woman asked, turning and leading the way back to her office.

"Yes," Valerie said. "I have to learn how to control my magic, which means I have to learn. It doesn't matter how hard it is."

"A commendable decision," Lady Harrington said, sitting back down at her desk and picking up a stack of papers and a pen. "I will let Mr. Benson known in the morning."

"I need to talk to someone back home," Valerie said, and Lady Harrington tipped the papers back down, adjusting her spectacles lower on her nose so that she could look at Valerie over them.

"Has anyone explained to you our policy on such things?" she asked, and Valerie nodded.

"Yes, but he is in danger," she said.

Lady Harrington set down her papers and dropped her glasses to the string around her neck, then folded her hands on the desk.

"What makes you think that?" she asked.

"When Roger came to get me," Valerie said. "Someone smashed the sidewalk, trying to hit me and kill me. It was…" She hadn't even been afraid at the time. It was surreal, remembering it, how she'd known that it was possible and been unfazed, even as she should have run screaming.

"Yes?" Lady Harrington prompted.

"They were trying to kill me," Valerie said. "And I'm afraid that they may be trying to kill Hanson, my friend who was with me, or catch him to use him as a hostage or…"

Lady Harrington nodded slowly, raising her woven fingers to rest under her chin.

"Miss Blake," she said slowly. "Any other year out of the past fifteen, I would have told you that you've been watching too many movies. This year, I'm glad that you are thinking cautiously, and I won't scold you, but I'm very sorry to tell you that Roger… He has a history. If he knew that you were not familiar with magic, I would not doubt that he would be quite happy to use his own skills to motivate you to cooperate, even if it meant intentionally frightening you. He is a very… pragmatic man. Firmly on our side, but… pragmatic."

"You think he might have lied?" Valerie asked. Lady Harrington sighed, looking down at her desk for a moment and nodding.

"Tell me what happened," she said. "As specifically as you can."

"He was asking me to get in a car with him, and I didn't want to," Valerie said. "I was going to walk home. And then the sidewalk… just right in front of, I mean *right* in front of me… it just… poom, like something huge, shaped like a gigantic baseball bat or something, hit it hard enough to shatter it, and there was

this… *dent*, but *big*, you know? *Huge.* There in front of us, and Roger told me that they missed, but that if we didn't get in the car…"

Lady Harrington swallowed and nodded, lifting her eyes.

"And from there he drove you directly to the building where you were staying with your mother?"

Valerie nodded. Lady Harrington lay her hands out flat on her papers and shook her head.

"I know that our foundation of trust is quite tenuous, just now, and I hate to challenge it by putting doubt in your mind, but I'd rather put your mind at ease and be the one who tells you the truth. I don't think that the Superiors were involved. The kind of magic that you're talking about, one that causes significant physical damage to the world around you, it isn't something that you cast sight-unseen. And if a Superior had been there when Roger was coming to get you, there is no way that man would have led them directly back to your mother. That is the *last* thing he would have done, in point of fact. I believe that your friend is quite safe, and that you were never in danger. Roger was simply motivating you, once when he came to get you out of a sense of his own importance and the importance of his time, and once again when he was trying to make your mother make the decision to return to the war. If you were in danger, your mother would be much more likely to cooperate."

Valerie felt her stomach turn sour and she looked away.

"I'm sorry," Lady Harrington said. "But it does at least mean that your friend is okay."

"I want to know for sure," Valerie said, and Lady Harrington nodded, picking up the phone handset from her desk and offering it to Valerie.

"Dial nine-nine for an external line," she said.

Valerie looked at it for a moment, then dropped her shoulders.

"I don't know his number," she said.

"Do you know why we are so careful with our phone usage?" Lady Harrington asked. Valerie bit back her first and second sarcastic responses.

"No," she finally said.

"Because a phone connects you to the world that is firm, traceable," the woman said. "Give me his name."

"Hanson Cox," Valerie said, and Lady Harrington nodded, taking Valerie's hand and wrapping it around the phone. Murmuring some words that Valerie didn't catch - very likely because they weren't English - Lady Harrington took Valerie's other hand, grabbing her index finger and poking the buttons on the phone base with rather more force than Valerie felt was necessary.

After a moment, the phone started ringing, and Lady Harrington picked up the papers off of her desk again to resume reading them.

"I assume I don't have to tell you not to tell him where you are," the woman said, and Valerie shrugged glumly.

"Not like I even know," she said, sitting back in her seat. Lady Harrington shot her a sharp look and Valerie nodded. "Yes, ma'am."

Hanson answered.

"Hello?"

"Hanson," Valerie said.

"Val," he said, his voice a surge of relief. "Where are you?"

Well, it got *there* fast.

"I'm okay," she said.

"Where *are* you?"

"The guy who came for my mom," Valerie said. "Look, I can't tell you what's going on. But I'm okay. And I wanted to make sure you were okay."

"Dude, I've been freaking out since you *went* with that guy," Hanson said. "I shouldn't have left. And my *mom* is freaking out. She went to file a missing person's report today, but they said that you were probably just with your mom, since both of you were missing."

"I'm not missing," Valerie said. "I'm okay."

"Are they making you say that? What's my jersey number?"

"Fourteen," she said. "I'm fine. Things are complicated right now, but... Do what you can to keep your mom from involving the National Guard, okay? I'm fine and my mom is... fine. Okay? Are you okay?"

Chloe Garner

"Why wouldn't I be okay?" he asked. She nodded.

"Okay. I'm going to try to get back to come see you as soon as I can, but I don't know when that's going to be."

"Where *are* you?" he asked. "Are you in witness protection? Did they come and relocate you? Do you have a new name?"

"No," Valerie said, though for a moment she considered that she should have said yes. It was a thorough explanation, apart from the sidewalk, which he appeared to be in complete denial over.

"Val," he said. "What's going on?"

Valerie looked at Lady Harrington, but the woman was at least pretending to be engrossed in her paperwork.

"I want to tell you," Valerie finally said. "But I can't. It's kind of dangerous, and so long as you're safe and I'm safe, I need to just… leave it alone."

"Are you sure you don't want the national guard?" he asked, and she nodded.

"I'm sure."

"Because my mom *will* get them out," he said. "You have to believe that."

"I know," Valerie said, smiling. "I miss you."

"Should I bring home your homework?" he asked, and Valerie froze.

This was it.

No going back.

"I'm at a new school now," she said. "I'm… I'm sorry, Hanson. I really am."

He sighed.

"You're calling to say goodbye, aren't you?" he asked. "Can I e-mail you?"

"Not right now," she said. "I don't have my computer, and they don't have internet here."

"There are like four places in the known universe that don't have internet," he said. "Whose phone number is this?"

She shook her head.

"Please," she said. "I'll be in touch when I can. I don't know when it's going to be, but it's best if you just let it be. You have to let me go."

"We've been best friends since we were eight," he said, his voice hard to cover over an edge there. "It doesn't work like that."

"I know," she said. "I didn't... It all happened really fast. And I would tell you, if I could. I swear I would tell you everything if I could. But I can't. There are good reasons, and... I'm sorry."

"Are you happy?" he asked after a minute.

"No," Valerie said easily enough. "But I'm working on it. I think I can be."

"And you *will* keep in touch with me?" Hanson asked. "You're not ghosting?"

"I swear, as best as I can, I will keep in touch," Valerie said.

"Okay," he said.

"I miss you," she said. "I'll talk to you as soon as I can."

"Bye, Val," he said.

"Bye."

She set the phone back down on its base and Lady Harrington glanced up at her.

"You understand that it will be some time before I can let you call him again," the woman said, and Valerie nodded.

"I don't understand *why*," she said. "But Mrs. Young made it pretty clear that it isn't something you just let people *do*."

"We spirited you away," Lady Harrington said. "When the Superiors hear that Susan Blake is back, the first thing they are going to do is come looking for you. We cannot allow you to leave traceable paths along which they can find you."

"All it takes is getting the phone number off of Hanson's phone and they can trace it," Valerie said. "You're talking about a *land line* like it's some kind of secure thing."

"Oh, that's not a land line," Lady Harrington said. "It's much more complex than that. But you are not well enough educated for me to expect you to understand it. And so, tomorrow you will see Mr. Tannis for the first of your potions tutoring sessions. He intends to test your capabilities on a number of concepts. I would caution you that he is very willing to see what happens, regardless of the more undesirable outcomes something might have. Work slowly, so that he has a chance to intervene at the last minute."

Valerie paused.

"You're serious," she said, and Lady Harrington returned to her paperwork.

"Completely," the woman said without looking up again.

Valerie went back to the room, sitting down on her bed and looking over at Sasha, where she had a textbook open and suspended over her face. Nothing magical about it, just a girl reading a textbook in a position where, if she fell asleep, it was going to fall on her face.

Valerie frowned.

"That doesn't look like such a good idea."

"What did he say?" Sasha asked.

"He didn't like it, but I don't think he's going to call the police," Valerie said.

"And what about Lady Harrington?" Sasha asked.

"She said I'm going to have to work really hard," Valerie said. "And that Mr. Tannis might not stop me in time to keep me from doing something dangerous."

Sasha nodded, still reading.

"He's known for letting students take their own risks." She twisted to look at Valerie. "Which is fine for upperclassmen, I guess, but I would hope he would warn you earlier."

Valerie gave her friend a glum look and lay down.

"So who is *Elvis Trent*?" Valerie asked. Sasha finally put her book down, using her forearm as a bookmark as she rolled over onto her side.

"He's a special upperclassman," Sasha said. "Graduated the School of Light Magic last year and decided to come here. His dad is on the Council, and he knows *everything* about the war because… Well, I don't know for *sure* how he knows, but there are a lot of guesses."

"He's older than twenty?" Valerie asked, and Sasha nodded.

"Well, he's right *around* twenty," she said. "And he's *hot*."

Valerie shrugged.

She hadn't missed that.

Still.

"Why is he hanging out in the cafeteria?" Valerie asked. "Doesn't have, like, cooler places to be?"

Sasha shrugged.

"Everyone eats in the cafeteria unless they're doing a part-load of classes and have time to go out to one of the cottages, or they have a teacher they're working for during lunch. A lot of the older class do one or the other, but Elvis has a full classload. Him and the other four of them who came from Light School this year."

Valerie tucked her arm up under her head.

"How do you know all of this?" she asked. "I mean... it was the first day of school."

Sasha shrugged.

"There aren't that many of us. We all kind of know what's going on with everyone else."

"*How?*" Valerie asked.

Sasha shook her head.

"I don't understand."

"You spent all day yesterday with me," Valerie said. "And before that, you just got here."

"We talk," Sasha said, frowning thoughtfully. "They aren't always talking to me, but everyone talks, and everyone hears. I knew when Elvis got in at Survival School the same way I knew when they put out the final list, day before yesterday, for freshmen. Someone called my mom and told her, and my mom checked that I'd gotten in and then we read the list."

"Do you *know* everyone?" Valerie asked. Sasha shrugged.

"I guess so," she said. "I mean, I'm not very *popular* or anything, if that's what you're asking."

"Why not?" Valerie asked. Sasha smiled and sat up.

"Were you popular at your school?" she asked, going to get pajamas out of a drawer and grabbing her shower kit.

"Maybe," Valerie said. "I mean, I had a lot of friends. I wasn't one of the *really* popular girls, but... You know. I had a lot of friends."

Sasha frowned.

"Don't you miss them?" she asked.

"Hanson," Valerie said.

"But not the rest of them?" Sasha asked, and Valerie considered this for a moment, then shook her head.

"Maybe I will, sometime, but…"

Huh.

She could go through her classes, her table at lunch, and she could make a list of all of the people she would laugh and talk with, but Hanson was *really* the only one she was going to miss.

Sasha shook her head, getting her towel off of the back of the door.

"I don't understand," she said. "I miss my friends from school. I'm going to write them letters tonight and just let them know how school is going."

"What will you tell them?" Valerie asked, sitting up.

"That I met my new roommate and I really like her a lot, and that I got into all of the classes I wanted and there are a couple of teachers I don't like, but my favorite teacher is awesome, and I can't wait to see them at the first break home," Sasha said simply. "Just leave out everything about the war and magic."

Valerie frowned.

"But what is there *but* magic?" she asked.

"Not a lot," Sasha said. "But it means they'll write me a letter back, and then I'll hear what's going on at school, still."

"Why did you come here?" Valerie asked. "If you know everyone here and *know* that they aren't your friends, when you have good friends you miss back home?"

Sasha frowned as though the question didn't entirely make sense.

"Because I need to learn magic," she said. "And my mom is a really good teacher, but she has a job, and it takes a lot of time. This is the best way."

"Why do you need to learn magic?" Valerie asked, and Sasha smiled.

"Because I don't already know it," she answered. "Can you leave the door open for me so I don't get locked out again?"

Valerie felt guilty, but she didn't know what to do, so she just nodded. Sasha picked up a book from the floor and put it between the door and the frame, waving over her shoulder as she left the room.

She started the next morning with Mrs. Reynolds class, but at the end of the day, Mr. Tannis was standing outside of her classroom door.

"And now the real work begins," he said.

Ethan

Ethan walked slowly down the hallway of the castle, aimless for the moment.

Castles all seemed so exclusive and glamorous from the outside, and so many magic users liked to call the things home, but at the end of the day, once you got inside, they were just giant stone buildings.

Drafty ones.

"Mr. Trent?" someone asked, and Ethan waited a full beat before he turned.

"That's me," he said, looking at an attractive woman in her early twenties.

"You aren't supposed to be here," the woman said. "You were supposed to wait in the library."

"There isn't anything in a library but books," Ethan answered. "I got bored."

"Your father expected you to be there, when he got out of his meetings with Madam Pelletier."

"Then he should have told me how long he was going to take," Ethan said.

"Please come with me," the woman said, annoyed without any real energy.

He shrugged and followed her back down the wide hallway. At some point, some rich king or noble or something had lived here and been quite proud of the place. Ethan couldn't imagine. No electricity, no plumbing to speak of, no light. The scars showed where it had been added in later, and it was all just weary and sad.

He followed the woman back to the library where they'd originally planted him, and Ethan went to go sit down in one of the high-backed leather armchairs, leaning against the side so his father got nothing but a slight profile of his face.

"Insolent boy," Merck Trent said. "You have some of the greatest opportunities a boy your age could imagine, and you wander and sulk."

"Opportunities," Ethan said. "I got into a second-tier school because of my stain, and you won't even let me start on time."

"You begin classes next week," Merck said, and Ethan sat forward.

It wasn't so much that he was excited to be in class as that he hated *traveling with his father. Politics bored him at their best, and this was the worst of them.*

Lots of closed-door meetings in out-of-the-way, secure locations, lots of secrecy and discretion. No teenagers.

Everyone looked at him sideways, wondering why Ethan was even there.

"You figured out how to use her then," he said, trying not to sound too interested.

"Apparently she's quite simple," Merck said. "Has no idea about any of this. Should be quite easy to convert and keep in place. The one thing Susan Blake will not do is abandon her daughter."

"Still can't believe you lost track of your own spy the moment she hit the field," Ethan said with a quiet snort.

"I have her daughter," Merck said. "That will be enough, assuming that you can keep her."

Ethan sighed.

"Have you ever seen a girl I couldn't entrance?" Ethan asked.

"No," Merck said. "What I doubt is your commitment to task, as always. I'm hoping she is as pretty as they say, at least."

Ethan grinned.

"She's pretty?"

"I'm going to give you all of the notes I got from inside of the school. I expect you to study them all the way and arrive prepared," Merck said.

"Anything to get me out of this purgatory," Ethan said.

"Your plane takes off tomorrow morning," Merck said. "Don't disappoint me."

They hadn't lied.

They ran her ragged.

For four weeks, Valerie worked from before the sun came up until well after it went back down again, memorizing and practicing, reciting and listing and identifying. Sasha helped as she could, but they didn't just bring everybody together at the school because they were too geographically dispersed to learn magic any other way. The School of Magic Survival was intent on using all of *everybody's* time.

And then, quite abruptly, the fifth week of school, Mrs.

Reynolds told Valerie that she was going to have to study on her own time.

Apart from Mr. Tannis, Mrs. Reynolds had taken the *most* interest in Valerie and her talents, and Valerie felt dismissed and rebuked, standing at Mrs. Reynold's desk at the end of the day.

The woman was poring over a list, marking it here and there with a red pen, when she looked up at Valerie once more.

"Is there a problem?" the woman asked.

"I don't understand," Valerie said.

"You're making fine progress," Mrs. Reynolds said. "I think that you've reached a point that, with the right reference books and some work on your own part, you can continue to make fast progress without being here in my classroom."

Valerie took half a step back, looking around.

"Did I do something wrong?" she asked. "I've been working hard."

Mrs. Reynolds looked up again and gave her a half a smile.

"The war," she said. "We try to keep the kids and the schools out of it, but sometimes when needs must, the teachers will help with magic prep work. Especially us. Magic Survival? They always end up calling on us for pre-packaged magic work to help keep our side alive, and things picked up a lot here in the last few days. So I need to get through this list so that I can start assembling kits tomorrow. We won't be doing any of it in class, but I can't do it with you here. I've been very impressed at your dedication, and I do sincerely believe that you'll be able to continue on your own with just some good guidance, but regardless, Miss Blake, I need to refocus my energy right now."

Valerie paused.

"Mrs. Reynolds, I have no idea what I'm doing. I'm just memorizing lists and… it's *boring*. I don't know what you expect me to do."

The woman frowned at her, and then gave her a wry smile.

"That's what magic *is* to most of us, Valerie," she said. "It's a long set of lists, words, plants, orders, placements, whatever it is that you're using to invoke the power, it's something that someone once wrote down and now you have it memorized. The fact that you can create it so simply out of thin air is nothing short of remarkable. Someday I would love to really inspect how you are doing it, but for now…" She looked at her list with an earnest frown. "For now I must be content that you won't blow us all up by mistake."

"Should I go see Mr. Tannis instead?" Valerie asked, and Mrs. Reynolds shook her head.

"You're welcome to, but it's my understanding that the list of *requests* they delivered to him this afternoon was twice as long and three times as complex. They assume the man can work miracles, and he's too proud to disabuse them of it."

"So I just…" Valerie said. "Read books and…"

"I will test you," Mrs. Reynolds said. "I will write a separate test for you and you will sit twice as long as the rest of the class to take it. I will *expect* you to maintain your rate of progress even as I am unavailable to work with you, because you have demonstrated yourself to be a capable student, and because…" She paused, looking up once more. "If I am going to be working extra hard to keep us all safe, I think that it's not unfair to expect the same of you. What do you think?"

"No," Valerie said. "I'll try."

Mrs. Reynolds nodded and returned to her work. Valerie stood for another moment, waiting. The woman didn't look up, but she did eventually speak.

"Did you need something else?" Mrs. Reynolds asked.

"Have you heard anything about my mother?" Valerie asked.

"Oh," Mrs. Reynolds said, laying her hands on the papers and looking at Valerie with a sad concern. For a moment, Valerie's world froze cold hard solid, a fear that she hadn't yet taken a moment to acknowledge, and then Mrs. Reynolds shook her head. "No. No one has heard anything about her, and I should warn you that we likely *won't*. Your mother's skill is in disappearing, looking for information that isn't being kept carefully enough, disrupting plans as they're being formed. I would call her a spy, but a spy implies a double agent, and that isn't how it works. More accurate to call her a magic sniper, I think."

"Sniper," Valerie said slowly. "Does she kill people?"

Mrs. Reynolds sighed, then shook her head.

"I don't know. There are a lot of people with very specialized skills that the Council called up to return to the war, but it's been a long time, and unless you *knew* them, personally, most of us don't remember the *exact* details of what people were doing during the war. I don't know. Your parents were… They were involved a long time before I graduated Light School."

"So if something happens to her, how will we know?" Valerie asked.

Mrs. Reynolds folded her hands and frowned.

"The field agents like your mom, they report back to the Council or someone who reports to the Council. When something happens, they stop reporting…"

"They go quiet," Valerie said. Mrs. Reynolds nodded. "She really never did know what happened to my dad, did she?"

Her teacher resettled in her chair, pulling the corner of her mouth down.

"I think that… I think that's a question you should ask her, when you get to. That's personal, and I wouldn't want to speculate."

Valerie nodded, suddenly overwhelmed. She picked up her backpack and went out the door, leaning against the wall and covering her eyes with her hand.

It was happening.

She'd been so preoccupied with trying to make it, to fit *in*, at the school, and she hadn't even considered that her mother was out *there* somewhere, risking her actual *life*. Doing something that had killed Valerie's dad fifteen years ago.

Somehow she'd managed to put her head down and *work* and not think about it, but that moment, the hesitation on Mrs. Reynolds' face, the *suggestion* that something might have happened…

She pressed her hand against her stomach, trying to make it stop hurting, then she went upstairs to Mr. Tannis' class. The door was locked.

Across the hallway, someone was singing.

Valerie went to look in Mr. Jamison's classroom, finding the man erasing the white board that spanned the entire front of the class.

"Mr. Jamison?" she asked. He looked over and smiled.

"Valerie," he said, then stopped. "Are you okay?"

"You were friends with them," she said. "During the war."

He nodded, setting down the eraser and coming to sit on the edge of his desk.

"I was. I considered the two of them to be some of the best friends I ever had. Still do."

"Is she going to be okay?" Valerie asked.

"She's the best," he said. "I can say that without hesitation. But the Superiors... I can't make you a promise, Valerie. I'm sorry."

She nodded, looking out the door at Mr. Tannis' classroom.

"Mrs. Reynolds told me that she can't work with me anymore," she said. "And Mr. Tannis... he almost lives in that room, doesn't he?"

"He does a lot of work to maintain all of the ingredients that they store in there," Mr. Jamison said quietly.

"He locked the door to keep me out," Valerie said.

"Not you specifically," Mr. Jamison said. "But he's... busy."

"I have no idea what I'm doing here," Valerie said. "I thought that I was doing well, making progress *toward* something, and that they were going to tell me what it was, like, later, when I could understand it. But they're just giving me busy-work, memory tests."

Mrs. Reynolds had been too kind to deserve it, but Valerie was frustrated and afraid, and it felt good to be *angry*.

"You're catching up for *years* of exposure to the concepts of magic," Mr. Jamison said. "And it isn't like they can get you involved with the hands-on work, after what happened the last two times. You need to know what you're doing before you can start rejoining your classmates in their class work."

She frowned harder, trying not to cry again.

"Is the point of this just to make more soldiers?" she asked. "Am I supposed to graduate and go off to war? Is that why Mom ran away?"

"I like to think that the war will collapse, this time," he said. "That the Council won't make some of the mistakes they did last time and let the Superiors get so far ahead of us in planning... I don't like to consider that the war might still be going on, by the time you graduate."

"Then what's the *point*?" Valerie asked. "It's not like I can apply to a college, based on all of this, and go get a *job*."

He laughed.

"The jobs that magic users can do are very specialized," he said. "And they tend to pay quite well, so long as you're clever or working *with* someone who is clever. I don't expect you'll have any problem."

"There's a big market for someone who can make plant-based magical neurotoxins?" Valerie asked.

"Bigger than I'd like to admit," he said softly, then shook his head. "We don't approve of those uses, but I know that the black market for spells is *very* lucrative. There are an unknown number of Survival School and Light School graduates who avail themselves of it."

"So that's what I'm supposed to do?" Valerie asked. "Mix potions and sell them?"

"Is that what you want to talk about?" Mr. Jamison asked. "Career paths? I can see why you would feel like you don't *see* it, but… It's an odd time, and I have requests on my desk from the Council right now, myself."

She scratched the back of her neck and turned away.

"No," she said. "It's fine."

She started for the door, then turned back.

"Mr. Jamison, how long did the last war go?"

"Nine years," he said. She nodded, angry. Oh, she was angry.

"And if my parents were both spy-snipers who only contacted the Council every once in a while to check in, how did my mom end up having me?"

He licked his lips.

It was the right question.

He didn't know.

"You think my mom cheated on my dad," she said.

"I know that your dad never doubted that you were his, not for a moment," he said finally. "But there were plenty of people who asked that question, at the time. They…" His nostrils flared at an old memory and he turned his face to the side. "They thought that it was worse if they had found a way to contact each other than if she'd cheated on him while she was out. The spies aren't supposed to have contact with anyone but the council, for their own safety, and if they *found* each other, they were risking operations that were critically important."

"Why didn't she ever tell me *anything?*" Valerie asked, not expecting an answer.

"They were hard times," Mr. Jamison answered. "She ran away to keep you safe from them. I wouldn't have *expected* her to tell you any of it. When wars go bad, people… They don't treat each other very well, sometimes. You really see what's at people's cores."

"Can't we just *kill* them all or something?" Valerie asked. "I don't *want* this."

He blinked, then shook his head and went to sit at his desk, drawing a tired breath.

"I know you don't mean that," he said. "But it's the philosophy that caused thousands of innocent civilians to end up dead. The fact that we didn't *want* a war, we ignored it, and we let it happen."

She didn't have anything to say to that.

"I'm sorry I bothered you," she finally said, turning away again.

"You're always welcome here," he said. "I'm never going to lock my door, because I want my students to come and talk to me when they need to. It's just… There's more work than *any* of us are going to get done, and if we don't get it done…"

"People die," Valerie said darkly. Maybe even her mom.

She shook her head.

"I'm going to go study," she said. She heard him sigh again, but she didn't turn back.

She went down to the dorms and let herself into the room, throwing her backpack on the bed and sitting down at her desk. Sasha was on her bed. It had taken a couple of weeks, but she'd finally managed to add enough magic onto the door so that she could let herself in, unless she was upset or distracted. Valerie had seen her walk chest-first into it just this week.

"Do you want to go eat?" Sasha asked.

"I'm not hungry," Valerie said.

It was true.

It was too early to go eat, yet, and she was too angry to actually want *food*. But the real truth was that Valerie was *over* sitting at a table by herself with Sasha, knowing that Sasha had people who would sit with her, so long as Valerie wasn't there.

There had been a lot of names, the first couple of weeks, once they'd figured out that Valerie wasn't going to get moved up to the upper classes. Civilian. Legacy. Charity case. Refugee. The one that had stuck was the Remedial.

They whispered when she came in the room, particularly at meals. Kids told her that their friend would have been the one to make it, if they hadn't given Valerie a spot. That she didn't deserve to be here.

At classes, the whispering mostly *stopped* as she came in the room, but it wasn't as bad because the teachers just started class. Yes, she had twice as much work as the rest of them, and Mr. Pallack often pointed out what *extra* stuff Valerie was supposed to be doing as he was assigning work to the rest of the class, but... Well, she could *deal* with that. It was the whispers and knowing that Sasha was bearing the cost of it right alongside her that she couldn't bear anymore.

"You're back early," Sasha said, checking her watch. "What happened?"

"The teachers are all busy," Valerie said. "I'm on my own."

"What?" Sasha asked. "What do you mean? How are you supposed to catch up?"

Valerie suspected that Sasha would once again play a significant role in that, but she didn't say it.

"I'm going to the library," Valerie said. "Maybe if I put up a big enough wall of books, everyone will just leave me alone."

Sasha gave her a concerned look, but Valerie didn't want to answer the questions, so she got her backpack and stood back up again, walking out the door and down the hallway.

The library was enormous, at the back of the school, two stories tall and three double-doors wide. There were dozens of tables in the middle, then the books.

Valerie liked the smell of the place.

Libraries had a dry, papery smell to them anywhere they were well cared for, but this one had an agedness to it that she adored. There was *knowledge* here. *Secrets.*

It was just up to her to go find them.

She wasn't ordinarily a book worm, though she enjoyed reading and she'd gotten good grades all along in school, but the library had become something of a sanctuary for her, here, because when she came here - in the few spare hours they'd been allowing her since the start of classes - she got time by herself to just *think*.

The plants from Mrs. Reynolds' class, the ingredients from Mr. Tannis' classroom, these were the only things she'd worked with in her own two hands, and it was like she could still feel them. Like they had a power in them that she hadn't even known about, at the time.

Her spellcasting classes were simpler, because she'd managed to avoid speaking in tongues and accidentally casting in a language she'd never before spoken, so she actually got to work with the class on most of what they were doing. She was behind three Romance languages, though, and they were delving into dead languages, now, so there she still had all of this *stuff* she was supposed to catch up on.

She didn't know how anyone expected her to do this. She'd been taking Spanish in school, but it wasn't like she was supposed to *speak* it. Not like the School of Magic Survival expected it. There, she was trying to remember vocabulary words well enough to sort of stumble through a conversation about what she liked to eat and how to get from here to there.

Now, she needed to have perfect diction and the ability to understand every word in a sentence, regardless of what kind of context it might have come up in, conversationally.

They expected her to be fluent in the language, skipping over conversational entirely.

It was so frustrating.

She took out her textbooks, then went wandering the shelves of plant-based potion ingredients, finding an encyclopedia that had been written well enough that she actually felt like she remembered what she'd read, from day to day. She took that back to her desk and sat down, paging through the encyclopedia to where she'd left off on her list from Mrs. Reynolds the day before.

Pall plants.

There were eight types, a vine, a bush, a grass, a tree, a succulent, an algae, a tuber, and a moss. Valerie saw nothing in common about any of them but that the book insisted that they go together.

Someone sat down across from her and she glanced up.

She didn't recognize him.

"Hi," he said cheerfully.

"Hi," she answered flatly, sensing a trap.

"I don't know you," he said. She glanced at him again.

"That's not funny," she said.

"No," he said. "It wasn't supposed to be. I don't know you, and I know everyone."

"Well, prepare to be disappointed," Valerie said.

Where had this *person* come from who was sitting in her chair and doing her schoolwork?

A month ago, she would have jumped at the chance for a distraction from what she was doing, given a friendly face, or - even better - an attractive guy she didn't know.

"I could go ask," he said. "But it's my experience that people who introduce themselves do a better job of it."

She sighed.

"It doesn't matter what I say," she said. She put her pencil down and looked at him squarely.

He was more attractive than she'd given him credit for, on first glance, and at the same time she saw exactly what she needed to see to know how pointless this was.

"You're related to Elvis Trent," she said.

He pressed his lips.

"So either you're in love with him or you hate him," he said.

"He hates me," Valerie said dismissively, going back to her work. "They all do."

"I don't," he said. "And, I mean, if I'm *going* to hate you eventually anyway, what do you have to lose talking to me *before* I figure out what a monster you are?"

"Wasting my time," she said.

"Didn't you just get out of class?" he asked, leaning across the desk to look at the book.

"They call me the Remedial for a reason," she said.

"Are you stupid?" he asked.

"No," she answered, kneejerk defensive. He shrugged.

"Then they're idiots," he said. "I'm Ethan. Ethan Trent. Elvis is my much-beloved big brother."

She put her pencil back down and crossed her arms on top of the book.

"Does this work for you?" she asked.

Who *was* she?

Of *course* it worked for him.

He was dark-haired and strong-featured, prominent cheekbones and long, straight jaw that came to a point under an expressive mouth.

He pulled his mouth to the side and shrugged.

"Okay," he said. "Sorry."

He stood and she put her hand out, palm down.

Why?

She'd just made him go away.

Why had she done that?

"No," she said. "Just a bad day. I'm sorry. I'm Valerie Blake."

"Blake," he said. "Do I know that name?"

"You might have heard of my mom, Susan Blake," Valerie said, and he nodded.

"The spy who went to ground after the war," he said. "Huh. So… Remedial? You not get ready to start here in time?"

"I don't know anything about magic," Valerie said. "Didn't know it existed until the day before school started."

He whistled, low, then frowned thoughtfully.

"Don't know how you catch up from there," he admitted, and she nodded, tapping the book with her pencil.

"Lots and lots of this, apparently," she said.

"Can I join you?" he asked.

"You don't want to do that," Valerie said. "My roommate is dealing with all the ostracism I can handle right now, sitting with me at meals. You don't… You just don't want to. I appreciate you

89

not being a jerk, but… There's nothing in this for you."

"Why do I have to have something in it for me?" he asked. "I'm just asking to sit at the same table as you in the library. Surely the world has not gone *that* crazy in the first month of school that I'm going to get branded somehow for doing it. Besides, I'm a Trent. I can do whatever I want."

She suspected that was true.

"Okay," she said. "You can sit here."

He nodded and started unloading his backpack.

"How have I not seen you before?" Valerie asked. Sure, she didn't *talk* to many of her classmates very often, but she knew them all by face, and it wasn't like there were that many places to hide. There weren't that many *people* around.

"I was out of the country for the last month," he said, opening a notebook and getting out a pen. "I've been keeping up with assignments from Europe, mostly."

"You have to be awfully special for them to let you do that, don't you?" Valerie asked.

"You have to be awfully special for Lady Harrington to let you in without a stitch of magic knowledge, don't you?" he countered.

She smiled. It was the tone. Friendly. Playful, even.

"You have friends here," she said. "Don't you?"

"Lots," he said. "I know all of the guys in the freshman class and most of the girls. My dad travels a lot to see the prominent families, and I get to meet people in person a lot."

"You know Sasha Mills?" Valerie asked.

"I know Bradley and Newton," Ethan answered. "Sasha and her mom… They don't stay in one place very much, so my dad hasn't ever gotten to go see them. It's like Ivory is avoiding him. We looked for her in California three weeks ago, but she wasn't there anymore."

Did Sasha even *know* where her mom was?

How had Valerie missed that?

Obvious question.

She'd been avoiding questions about moms.

He saw the look on her face and shook his head.

"Oh, no, it's nothing like weird or anything. Her mom is a

healer. She travels *a lot*, and she doesn't... Well, it's that she doesn't tell my dad or anyone else on the Council where she is. That's getting to be a big deal, right now. It's not, like, weird. Just political."

"Oh," Valerie said.

"You don't know about the politics at all, either, do you?" he asked, and she smiled.

"I'm learning pall-type plants just now," she said. "They're saving the complicated stuff for later."

"Don't eat Pall-moss," he said, nodding sagely.

"I'll write it down."

She was smiling again.

It felt strange on her face, after all this time.

"If you have to write down everything that you're *not* supposed to eat, I'm worried for you," he said, and she grinned.

"I've been a little unpredictable since I've been here," she told him. "Call it an abundance of caution."

He laughed.

It was a deep-chest laugh, and she wanted him to do it again.

Yegads, that had come on quick.

"Right," she said. "So, why aren't you at the School of Light Magic?"

"Elvis was here," he said easily.

"So?" Valerie asked.

"My dad wants us together for security reasons," he said.

He was a security risk, too? That actually made her feel immensely better.

"But you're going to the second-class school," she said. "Doesn't that like... I don't know, *diminish* something about what happens to you later?"

"My prospects?" he asked, his voice dark for a moment, though without any real brooding sincerity to it. "Kind of you to be concerned about them. My dad isn't. No, I get it. My dad is worried about us, and Elvis had already gotten in here, because they take the pre-graduated students first, so this was where I was supposed to go. It's fine. I can go to Light School next, if I want to."

"Do you?" Valerie asked.

"I still haven't had my first day of Survival School," he teased. "How would I know?"

She grinned.

"Well, I'd offer to help you, but I haven't got the first clue on any of this," she said. He put his chin on his fists and frowned at her, considering for a moment.

"No offense, but there's a war on. I get why you're *here*. If Susan Blake is out on the front again, they're going to come for her daughter, and this is one of the safest places to be. But why are they *teaching* you?"

"They actually told me I could take normal school by correspondence, though I can't see how, without any internet."

"Mail," he interjected, nodding, and she cringed.

"Anyway," she went on. "Um. I *made* things. In class. I made *stuff*, and she knew what it was and I didn't, and… Apparently they think I'm worth it."

"You're a natural?" he asked with a tone that wasn't quite disbelief, but lived right there on the border.

"I shouldn't have said anything," Valerie said. She *hadn't* told anyone, other than Sasha, and to tell the head of the Council's son just, boom, in conversation right off like that?

Unbelievable.

He smiled, and the chemicals in her stomach wanted to just forget skepticism entirely.

Stupid chemicals.

"You don't have to worry about me telling my dad," he said. "For one thing, one of the Council's firm rules is that they don't recruit magic users who are still in school. For another, I'd rather see my friends survive than march off to war. And for a third, Lady Harrington is required to tell him that kind of stuff, anyway, and the teachers are pretty reliable at passing on the reports that my dad wants to read. So. He already knows, and he knows that you're worthless for a while. Until you get your Pall plants straightened out, at least."

She closed her book.

It was playful, and he smiled, but she had no idea why she'd done it.

"Do you want to go get dinner with me?" she asked.

He raised his eyebrows.

"It was looking like you'd just started studying," he said.

"I'm hungry," she said. "And they don't have a problem with me leaving my stuff here for a while, as long as I come back for it."

"Fair enough," he said, putting his notebook back into his backpack and standing up, leaving the backpack. She shook her head.

"Look, you're nice, but you're going to want to take that. After you see what a big mistake you've made, hanging out with me…"

"I'm going to come back and finish studying," he said. "My roommate is using the most *obnoxious* music as a study aid tonight, and I'm not going back there."

"You're going to switch tables," Valerie said, and he grinned.

"If you say so," he said, motioning that he was waiting for her. He went to get the door and she went through, smiling again - again - as she led the way to the cafeteria.

She got a tray and went through the line, then went to sit down at an empty table, sitting quietly with her eyes closed, smelling her food and listening to the whispers.

Ethan sat down across from her, and the whispers got louder.

"You don't have to stay," Valerie said. "I expect you have friends you'd rather sit with."

"They're coming," he said, completely casual. She looked up and there were, indeed, four guys and two girls getting up from two other tables and bringing their trays over to where Valerie sat.

"You guys know Valerie?" Ethan asked. "Valerie, this is Shack, Milton, Patrick, Conrad, Yasmine, and Ann."

"Shack," she said. "I hear everyone call you that, but is that your real name?"

"It's what my dad's been calling me since I could walk," the boy said as he sat down. "I broke through the side of his tool shack in the backyard."

"Shack's a bruiser," Ethan said with a wide smile.

"Where have you been?" Yasmine asked. "Everyone kept expecting you. And Elvis said he didn't know."

"He didn't," Ethan said. "He and my dad are having a fight, so my dad told them not to forward Elvis' mail when it came in unless it was urgent."

A giggle went around the table and three heads turned to look at where Elvis was sitting at a corner table with three of his cottage roommates.

"So where *were* you?" Patrick asked.

"Recruiting," Ethan said softly, leaning over the table slightly. "They're trying to get the magic users in Europe involved early, but they still say there isn't a problem."

"But the Superiors are *killing* people again," Ann said. "How can they say that isn't a problem?"

"They say that the Council hasn't proven that it was organized Superior activity," Ethan said. "And that the Council only exists to perpetuate the myth of hostilities among the viewpoints. I'm not kidding, they used those words. Basically, if my dad doesn't have a war to general, he doesn't have any point."

"But *you've* said that," Yasmine said, and Ethan grinned.

"So? One thing for *me* to say my dad is pointless, another thing for a dude in France to say it."

"So what are you studying?" Milton asked Valerie.

"Plants and herbs," she said. "There's so much to memorize."

"My grandma used to take me walking in the woods, everywhere we went," Yasmine said. "She made me name everything that might *possibly* be used in potions."

"Which according to her was everything," Ethan said, and Yasmine grinned. Ethan picked up a finger to point casually at Valerie. "Her grandmother is one of the premier potion-based spellcasters for seventy-five-plus light magic potions. Wrote two or three of the books that they use as textbooks at Light School."

"I expect I'll read them at some point," Valerie said. "Mrs. Reynolds is very enthusiastic about how much reading and memorization I need to do."

"Mrs. Reynolds is the best," Shack said.

"Not like Mr. Tannis," Milton agreed. "She loves to do what she's doing, but she *also* likes teaching it. Mr. Tannis just can't leave the potions room."

"Like a hoarder," Shack said.

"I've actually been studying with him for several weeks now, and he's been as enthusiastic about what I can do as anyone," Valerie said. "He's really passionate and supportive."

They looked at her.

"What *can* you do?" Milton asked. She shook her head.

"I just mean how fast I can learn," she said.

Milton didn't look entirely satisfied, but Shack was the first to jump in.

"The first day," he said to her. "They made everyone leave the class for you to do something, and when you came back out, they said that some of the teachers looked scared. What did you *do*?"

"And can I learn how to do it?" Patrick asked.

"I just did what they asked me to," Valerie said. "And they figured out that I had no idea what I was doing."

"They shouldn't have put you here," Ann said. "No offense. I know that your mom is a big deal, and she got to do whatever she wanted to, when they called her back in again. But you should, like, be sleeping in the office or a cottage or something, and let a *real* freshman take your slot."

"They didn't give me a vote," Valerie said. "I would still be at home, if I got to choose. Wouldn't know anything about any of you. Would have gotten to see my best friend play basketball."

"Lady Harrington wouldn't let her stay if she didn't have potential," Ethan said. "You all know that."

Valerie lifted her head as Sasha came into the room, but the girl flushed and went through the food line as fast as she could, then went to sit at a small table at the edge of the room by herself.

"You have a friend who plays basketball?" Ethan asked.

"He had just found out he was going to be varsity when the guy from the Council showed up and tried to scare me into the car," Valerie said.

"Which guy from the council?" Ethan asked, and Valerie frowned.

"Roger," she said after a minute. "His name was Roger."

"Ah," he answered, like that made total sense. "Yup. He's one of my dad's attack dogs. Does exactly as he's told."

"I didn't like him," Valerie said, and Ethan nodded.

"Neither do I. You should have your friend come up for a weekend. There's a court here out by the cottages. We could play."

"I didn't know we could have guests come," Valerie said. "They won't let me talk to him on the phone."

"Oh, no," Ethan said. "You definitely have to write him a letter. But the school has a PO Box in the city that they use to send and receive mail, and it's pretty casual."

"I'm going to invite him to come visit my new boarding school by snail mail?" Valerie asked.

Ann snorted.

"You too good for our rules?" she asked, and Valerie shook her head.

"Look, I don't like being controlled, and it feels an awful lot like being controlled. But that isn't it. I just can't imagine saying 'hey, do you want to come hang out some weekend' and then putting it in an *envelope* and waiting a week to hear back. I mean, it'd take the rest of the semester to get it planned."

"Tell him that we have visiting weekends the second and third weekend in October, and that if he wants to come, there's a bus that leaves town at eight on Friday night and gets back Sunday afternoon."

"You think he'd actually get on it?" Valerie asked. "Because of a *letter?*"

"If he wants to see you, he has to," Yasmine said.

"Mrs. Gold is brutal about keeping the guys out after curfew," Ann said. "So if you're going to hide him in your room, you have to be *really* clever."

"I wouldn't want him in my room," Valerie said. "We really are just friends."

"Uh huh," Ann said.

"You guys seriously let non-magic people come here, though?" Valerie asked.

"Why not?" Ethan asked. "They sleep in the visitor cottages, we put away the stuff that just *screams* weirdo, and we maintain relationships with the outside world that don't involve magic."

"Things would get seriously weird if the *only* people we were around were magic," Shack said. "I mean, we're weird enough as it is."

One of the boys whose name had presently escaped Valerie elbowed Shack, and Ethan grinned.

"There aren't enough of us," Ethan said. "We *have* to keep the civilians around, just for company."

"How many magic users are there?" Valerie asked, and Ethan shrugged.

"Couple thousand families in the western hemisphere and Europe. The schools on this side of the Atlantic are all English-speaking, but there is a French one as well. We know that there are magic users all over the other continents, too, but they kind of do their own thing."

"If Hanson came, his mom would want to come, too," Valerie said. Ethan shrugged.

"So?"

"And she'd want to know where my mom is," Valerie said. The table quieted for a moment, then Ethan shook his head.

"Talk to Lady Harrington," he said. "There's got to be a story that they're using. It'll be simple and to the point, and you just follow their lead."

"How many of you have parents who are in the war?" Valerie asked.

Ann looked up and down the table, then shrugged.

"We're mostly Council brats," she said. "The washed-up ones who couldn't get into Light School."

"My dad is on the quick-strike team," Shack said.

"Of course he is," one of the brown-haired boys teased.

"What does that mean?" Valerie asked.

"He's on the cleanup team," Shack said.

"There are two," Ethan added. "The attack force and the cleanup force. Both of them have to be really quick on their feet with magic, but the cleanup force is more... humanitarian."

"Healers?" Valerie said.

"And defenders," Shack said. "That's what my dad is. He graduated from here, and he goes and tries to keep people alive while the attack team is fighting with the Superiors."

"Everyone is involved," Yasmine said. "Just not all of them are assassins."

Valerie blinked at her.

Assassin.

No one had used that word before, though maybe that was what Mrs. Reynolds had been dancing around, calling Susan Blake a sniper.

"Her mom isn't an assassin," Ethan said. "At least, she wasn't."

"Did she or did she not go behind enemy lines and kill people?" Ann asked.

"First, that stuff is still technically secret," Ethan said. "No one *actually* knows what either of the Blakes or the rest of the Shadows did."

Valerie only *just* managed to avoid asking who the Shadows were, realizing at the very last instant that she didn't want to admit out loud that she didn't know.

"Second, not everyone who goes behind enemy lines is an assassin. She sent back a lot of information, too, that helped keep people *alive*. And third, so what if she *is* an assassin? It's what the world needed most with Hitler, isn't it? Sometimes killing just the right guy saves thousands of lives."

"I think it's hot," Shack said, and Valerie gave him a withering look that he ducked with good grace.

She wanted to tell Ethan that he didn't need to fight her battles for her. The problem was that she *did*. She had no idea what her mom had been, what she'd done.

And it sounded like he did.

"She doesn't belong with us," Ann said after a moment, lowering her voice for Ethan's benefit but saying it loud enough to be sure Valerie heard.

"You're welcome to go," Ethan answered, turning his attention to his food.

Hands clapped down on Ethan's shoulders, and Valerie looked up at Elvis.

"Finally made it," Elvis said, slapping his palm against Ethan's face with what might have been affection.

"Elvis," Ethan said, a greeting.

Elvis looked over at Valerie and gave her a smile.

It wasn't a kind smile, but he was still witheringly attractive, even as the words formed to mock her.

"See that you wasted no time figuring out the worst way to slum it," Elvis said. "You know that she's *worthless* at magic. Only here because her mom's important."

"Make you feel better, pointing it out?" Valerie asked, standing.

"Does, actually," Elvis said, then smiled again. It was *almost* friendly. "See, the rest of us worked *hard* to get here. I'm on my second school, trying to master the craft and become someone useful to the community. Hoping to end up on the Council myself, someday. You took somebody's spot, and we all kind of resent it. Someone deserves to be here who isn't, because you're here instead."

"You're being a jerk," Ethan said. "And there's no point. She's here. Lady Harrington wouldn't have let it happen if there wasn't a point."

"They're having to teach her *everything*," Elvis said. "There's no way she graduates."

The entire room was looking at her. Valerie sighed, nodding.

"Look, whatever. You guys enjoy your dinner."

She picked up her tray, grabbing the cookie and the apple that she hadn't gotten to and walking for the door.

The room fell fully silent as she left, and she stewed all the way back to the library, where she hung out outside long enough to eat the remains of her dinner before she went back in to study some more.

A few minutes later, Sasha sat down beside her.

"The Trents are jerks," she said softly. "All of the Council brats are."

Valerie glanced over at her.

"I don't think I've ever heard you say a mean word about anyone," she said.

"I don't like to," Sasha said. "They all do what they do because they think they're right, and because... war is hard. But even when there isn't a war, they're doing things that *matter*, on the Council. Making sure that people don't abuse their magic or each other and… I don't know, keeping track of people, I guess. I think that's important, somehow, even though they've never really been able to say how. It's not that they're *bad* people…"

"Yes," Valerie said emphatically. "They are. They're snobs and they're cliquish and they aren't *real*. My mom asked specifically for me to be in a room with you. Can you imagine what my life would be like if I'd been with *Ann* the Council brat? I mean… I would have locked her out of the room and never let her back in, first opportunity. No question. You're a *good* person, and I don't care how *genuine* their motives are. They're bad people."

Funny thing was, she'd hung out with ones just like them, at school. Catty girls with lots of boyfriends and politics when it came to who they invited to what event.

Valerie was mostly immune to it - she was… well, she was *Valerie*, and everyone always invited her, because if she was there, it was cool - but she hadn't ever seen her friends act like *that* to someone. Not directly and not to their face.

Sasha shook her head and looked at the table.

"I just wanted to make sure you were okay," she said. "I guess you are."

"Who were the Shadows?" Valerie asked. Sasha looked at her and frowned, almost pained.

"I don't know," she said. Valerie pursed her lips, about to say something about how unhelpful that was, when Sasha waved her hands. "No, not like… Like, no one *knows* who the Shadows were. Or what they did. I don't even know if your mom was one, for sure, but if *anyone* was going to be one of the Shadows… She probably was. And your dad. They were people who did what they had to, to win the war. Ones that the Council didn't talk about what they were doing, and… There are just lots of rumors. Maybe they didn't even really do anything. My mom told me once that she thought it was possible the Council invented them to give the Superiors something to be paranoid about."

"That's smart," Valerie said, and Sasha nodded.

"That's war," the redhead said. "They have whole teams of people thinking up stuff like that. The tactics committees."

Valerie blinked at her, then shook her head.

"This is all too organized for me," she said. "Schools and councils and committees... What if I don't want to do it?"

"Then you don't," Ethan said, coming in the doors. "Hey, Sasha. It's nice to finally meet you."

"We met once," Sasha said, standing. "At a post-war ceremony for my mom. We were little."

He frowned.

"I don't remember."

"No," Sasha said. "You were too busy running around with a burning gwell lump on a stick."

He grinned.

"I do remember that. You were there?"

"Your dad gave my mom a medal," Sasha said. "My whole family was there."

Ethan frowned, sitting down across from them.

"Huh. Well. I'm sorry if I was a jerk little kid."

She shook her head.

"Just bored," she said. "I wanted to play with you, but I was afraid you were going to fling the gwell lump off at any second and it would hit me."

Ethan looked at the table, thinking.

"That's exactly what happened, isn't it?" he asked. "Ann came to yell at me and I turned too fast."

Sasha nodded.

"Yeah. My mom patched her up before your dad could give her the medal."

Ethan pulled his mouth to the side.

"She was angry at me for years about that," he said.

Sasha nodded.

"I'm going to go work on my homework," she said after a long pause. "Good night."

"You can stay and study with us if you want," Ethan said, and Sasha looked at him with cagey eyes, then shook her head.

"Tell your brother to lay off," she said, and he shrugged.

"If I could come up with a way to do it, I would."

Sasha looked at Valerie, as if expecting her to come, too, but Valerie motioned at the stack of books.

"I'm not allowed to take these yet. That's a junior privilege."

Sasha sighed and nodded.

Valerie watched her leave, then frowned.

"She's not going to be able to get into the room," she said.

"Why is that?" Ethan asked.

"I locked it too hard," Valerie said, watching after Sasha. "She can't open the door unless she focuses."

"You're serious," he said, and she shrugged, returning to her book.

"You locked the door so hard *Sasha Mills* can't open it, when she's your actual roommate?" he asked. She looked at him again and shrugged once more.

"I didn't mean to," she said.

"Geez, you really are a natural," he said. "I heard that the drain spell at her entrance test didn't even knock her out, that she put up a ward to protect herself from it in the *middle* of the protection cast."

"I have no idea what any of those words mean," Valerie said.

"She's the *best*," Ethan said, and she looked at him once more. He nodded emphatically. "Like, Light School was fighting to *make* her take the entrance exam there, just so that they could offer her all kinds of inducements to come there. She's *the best*. And you locked her out of her own room."

"And she really doesn't like you very much," Valerie said.

"She's right not to," Ethan answered. "I mean, I suck a lot less than I used to, but she wouldn't know that, would she? Her mom went tearing out of here after the last of the war stuff was done, and she never looked back. Sasha knows… Well, everyone knows *about* her, and I think there are a lot of kids who know her okay well because her mom would stay with them when she was traveling from one place to the next, but she *avoided* anyone from the Council. On purpose. So… she doesn't know that I'm not that same jerk kid that I was before, and now she's had a whole month with the rest of the Council brats to prove how much *more* awful we are now."

Valerie lifted her chin.

"This is game, isn't it?" she asked. He grinned, and she gave him half a smile in return, going back to her book, though she wasn't reading any of it anymore.

"Is it working?" he asked.

"Why?" she asked. "You just got here. Are you seriously so bored that coming to hit on the new girl is that exciting to you?"

"No," he said. "Hitting on Susan Blake's daughter, the one who was out in the cold but who came back and is working her *fine* butt off in the library trying to catch up? *That* is worth my time. I'd have flirted with you either way. I like to see girls smile. But... You see what coming from the center of power within the Council did to my brother. I woke up about four years ago, as Elvis was going to Light School, and realized that I don't want to be a prick the rest of my life. If I want *anyone* who isn't going to treat me different because I'm the Head Councilor's son... Gotta be you, right?"

"And you thought that all the minute you walked in here," Valerie said, still not looking at him.

"No," he said. "I thought 'wowza, who's the hot chick with all the books?'. The rest is since then."

She lay her forearms across the table, hand over hand in front of her, and she looked at him intently.

"Hanson could turn you into a pancake if he thought that you were just messing with me," she said. "And that's nothing on what *I* could come up with to do to you."

He grinned wider, and she smiled back.

"Why don't you tell them that you're a natural?" he asked after a moment, settling lower in his chair and digging into his backpack.

"It's none of their business," Valerie answered.

"It would make your life so much easier," he said. "I mean... I don't know if any of the Council kids are ever going to be okay with you being here... But a lot of the other kids would be nicer to you if they knew that you were *really* good at magic."

Valerie knit her eyebrows.

"Why would I want that?" she asked. "Sasha was nice to me from the very beginning, even before either one of us knew, and you... The jury's out, but if you can keep it up a while longer, I might actually buy into this reformation story of yours."

"I'll see how long I can hold out," he said, and she smiled again.

"But I don't see why I want to try to impress a bunch of pretentious jerks into liking me because I have some special power.

103

An idiot who likes me for what I can do isn't my friend."

"You're really smart, aren't you?" he asked, and she shrugged.

"I get by. But I lived…" She paused. The words as they had been about to come out of her mouth had been casual, and then she'd *heard* them. "I lived alone with my mom my entire life," she finally went on. "And she was *really* emphatic about learning everything I could, and figuring out how things worked, and knowing how to take care of myself. We used to sit at the table at night and just… *talk*…"

It hurt.

She nodded, swallowing.

"So. Anyway. High expectations. You know."

"I do know about those," Ethan said, glancing at his book. "Speaking of, I have a month's worth of schoolwork to catch up on."

"And I have sixteen years, apparently," Valerie answered. He smiled.

"You're going to shock them all when you get it," he said. "I just hope I'm there to see it when Elvis lands on his butt."

"Oh, I'm looking forward to putting him there," Valerie said with a nod. "In the meantime… pall-plants."

Valerie got back to her room a little after midnight, happier than she'd been since before Roger had shown up at her apartment in the city. Sasha appeared to be asleep, so Valerie grabbed her bathroom kit and went to brush her teeth and wash her face, then came back and changed into her pajamas in the dark, getting into bed as quietly as she could.

"The Trents are…" Sasha said after a moment. "When Elvis liked you, the first day, I thought that you were going to have an ally and I thought it was great, but they're just as fickle and unreliable as I thought they were. I thought maybe I was wrong, what I remembered about them. The way his dad talked to my mom at the ceremony, like he was only giving her the medal because he had to…"

"I don't think Ethan is like his brother," Valerie said.

"I hope not," Sasha answered. "I had all these *ideas*, what the

School of Magic Survival was going to be like, and then…"

"And then you got me as a roommate and it ruined them all," Valerie said.

"No," Sasha said. "No. That's not what happened. It's that they're all so stuck in *paying their dues* and *proving they belong*, none of them can even think about what you've been through, or how important the war is, or *anything*. Mom talked about the *terrible* things that she tried to help people get through, because one side or the other let the war spill out onto civilians. People died… *innocent* people, and our side killed them. Probably not as many as the Superiors, but plenty. Everyone's all excited about the war because they have *no* idea what it means."

"Are they?" Valerie asked. "Excited?"

"You don't know?" Sasha asked. "It's all anybody can talk about. They think that the Council is just going to sweep in and *destroy* the Superiors and it's going to be this big show of force… Anymore, that's what they think they're here at school to learn. War. It's the kind of thing that, if you let it keep going… that's what magic *becomes*. A tool of war."

"I don't know because no one ever talks around me," Valerie said. At least she knew that Sasha still had friends who were talking to her, when Valerie *wasn't* there.

"They're so immature," Sasha said. Valerie snorted.

"Sorry," she said quickly. "It's just strange to hear you say it. You're always so *positive*."

"I didn't like you with the Council brats," Sasha said. "They're the worst of the worst. They hope that the war lasts long enough for them to graduate, so that they can be a part of the big power grab when we win. They all just *assume* we're going to win."

"We are," Valerie said softly. "We don't have a choice, do we?"

Sasha was quiet at this for a long time, when a new thought occurred to Valerie.

"Hey, Sasha, how many people are there on the council?" she asked.

"Thirty," Sasha said.

Valerie frowned.

She'd been envisioning hundreds.

"How is it that there are *six* of them all born in the same year?" Valerie asked.

Sasha paused.

"There are eight that were born the same year as us," she said after a long consideration. "But five of them are cursed."

"Come again," Valerie said. She heard Sasha shift.

"They don't know which five of them, but there are five of them who are tied together with a curse that... Okay, I don't actually *believe* it, but it is hard to explain how *all* of them were born the same year. They say that there's a curse that was set by the head of the Superiors when he died. He was killed, but we don't know specifically how. Anyway, when he died, he launched a curse at the Council, and... They all had kids at the same time who were bound together, cursed with dark magic."

"Dark magic," Valerie said. Sasha shifted again.

"It's why they can't get in at Light School," she said softly. "They all have too much dark magic in them to qualify."

"Ethan told me he was here because of Elvis," Valerie said. She looked over as Sasha rolled onto her stomach and wadded her pillow up under her head.

"I think Ethan can do *some* light magic," Sasha said. "Maybe even enough to get in. I don't know. Maybe he didn't lie to you. Maybe it's all wrong. It's just what I heard."

Valerie lay lower in her bed, looking up at the ceiling in the darkness.

"It just felt nice to have a friend," Valerie said.

"I'm your friend," Sasha answered and Valerie shook her head.

"You've been more than a friend, but you didn't choose me. My mom chose us together, and your mom went along with it. You could have bailed on me, no doubt, but... Ethan was nice to me all on his own."

"Be careful," Sasha said, her voice drifting. "You can't ever guess what the Council brats want. It's all a game to them."

Valerie closed her eyes, letting the hour and the day weigh on her.

"You're a good friend," she answered to the darkness, not sure if Sasha heard her or not.

The Attack

Valerie was in the library again after classes - she had three with Ethan, and people just moved out of his way when he told them that he wanted to sit next to her - when Sasha came in with an alert expression, like a bird on a wire.

"Sasha, when do I get to learn actual defensive magic?" Valerie asked, exasperated at her book. "This is beyond boring."

"You need to come with me," Sasha said, picking at Valerie's elbow and looking around again.

"What?" Valerie asked. "What is it?"

"Now," Sasha said, her voice low. "Please?"

Valerie looked at her books, but Sasha was tugging at her with an urgency that suggested the packing up process was out of the question.

"What's going on?" Valerie asked as she followed Sasha into the hallway.

"You have to see," Sasha hissed. "But don't say anything to anyone."

Sasha dragged her back to the dorm hallway, where a small group of girls was growing in population even as Sasha and Valerie approached.

"Have you been doing magic?" Sasha asked as they were still out of earshot of the gathering.

"No," Valerie said. "I don't think so. How would I tell?"

Sasha frowned at her, then shouldered her way through the line of girls to look down at a scorch mark on the floor.

The way everyone was whispering, Valerie had no problem figuring out that this was not normal. The scorch mark was in the corner by a doorway, a big black mark on the floor, but a much more interesting shape up the wall, like the wall had split open, rather than just had a burn run up it.

The weirdest part was definitely that it was bleeding, though.

Valerie turned, going back through the girls as she passed Mrs. Gold in the hallway. The dorm matron was too focused on the girls and whatever else she knew of what was going on to stop Valerie, so Valerie ran upstairs to Mr. Jamison's room without interference.

His door was cracked, and she heard him speaking.

There was a rule to magic - spoken magic, especially - that you didn't interrupt it, because you risked breaking the cast.

But there was a bleeding scorch mark in the hallway where Valerie planned on sleeping that night, so she went in anyway, keeping silent as Mr. Jamison held up a finger at her, his eyes closed in focus.

Still unsure how important *either* of the things going on were, Valerie slid into a chair as noiselessly as she could to wait, and about a minute later, there was a sense of power, like the lights had brightened or the floor had vibrated, and then Mr. Jamison opened his eyes.

"What can I do for you, Miss Blake?" he asked.

"There's something downstairs you should see," Valerie said. He raised an eyebrow and looked around his room briefly.

"What is it?" he asked as he went to open a drawer in his desk and got out a small wooden box.

"Black scorch mark on the wall oozing blood," Valerie said.

He hesitated, then brushed past her at a faster walk than she'd used coming up.

Maybe she shouldn't have waited.

She followed him back downstairs, where virtually the entire dorm had turned out. Valerie passed Ethan and Shack as she waded through the students behind Mr. Jamison. Mrs. Gold was barking at the girls, demanding to know who had seen what.

"Please go get Mr. Benson," Mr. Jamison told her. "And Lady Harrington."

He knelt in front of the mark, looking back at Valerie.

"Who found it?" he asked. "Was anyone here when it was cast?"

Valerie looked back for Sasha, but she didn't see her. Ann the Council brat stepped forward.

"We think she did it," she said, pointing at Valerie. "We all know that she's out of control. She doesn't belong here."

Valerie was stunned. She hadn't seen that coming - the fact that she was capable of magic at *all* was still a secret within the school. The reactions of the students around Ann begged to differ, though. Shoulders turned toward her, eyes darted.

Sasha made her way back into view, but stayed out of the front ring of students, her eyes begging Valerie to forgive her.

"Were you here?" Mr. Jamison asked Valerie.

She shook her head.

"I was in the library," she said, her voice quiet. There was no way in hell she was going to get defensive because Ann the brat pointed a finger at her.

He nodded, then straightened, looking around.

"I need everyone to back off," he said. "The cast is still active, and I need to shut it down. Was *anyone* here when it happened?"

There were whispers, but no one spoke up. Valerie suspected that Sasha would know who had done it well before Mr. Jamison did.

"Valerie," Mr. Jamison said as she found herself entranced by the way the blood was oozing out of the wall. "Please take a step back."

She shook her head.

"It isn't blood," she said. "It's too thick."

"I know that," he said, putting his arm out, but it was like the oil and tell-weed on the back of the door. Valerie slipped around his hand, kneeling next to it.

It was...

It was blooming.

Opening up.

Like a bomb in slow motion, almost, but beautiful, floral in the way it unfolded, layer upon layer.

The flame had burnt the floor and the wall. That was unquestionable.

But it had germinated a seed of some kind, and that was what was doing the rest, first a long line of red... foam, dark past the point of crimson, and now a thread of silver erupting out from the foam, beading and reflective, growing up the wall...

Valerie put out her hand, touching the spot it was headed for, almost a foot above it.

"No more," she said. "Begone."

Mr. Jamison said something in a language that Valerie didn't know, still trying to pull her back, but the activity of the spell stopped and the silver thread cascaded down onto the floor like mercury.

He finished his cast and pulled her harder away.

"Valerie," he said.

"See, she did it," Ann said. "She's the one who shut it down, too."

Mr. Jamison looked Valerie in the face as she backed away, then Mr. Benson and Lady Harrington were in the way, and Sasha grabbed Valerie's elbow and pulled her into the crowd. It wasn't *much* cover, because the students split around her to avoid being too close, but it was something.

"I was in the library," Valerie protested. "I couldn't do that."

"I know," Sasha said. "It… They won't believe Ann. It's just her being petty. How did you *do* that?"

Valerie shrugged.

"I don't know. It just…"

"You used *verbal* spellcasting," Sasha said. "In *English*."

"So?" Valerie asked. Sasha shook her head.

"That's really hard… The force of *will* it takes to make English into spells…"

Valerie shrugged again.

"I don't know that I did anything," she said, though it was mostly a lie. If Mr. Jamison had turned around at that moment and told her that he'd been the one to shut down the silver line, and that it had just been coincidence that she'd spoken at the same time, she would have been relieved to believe him, but… Barring that, she knew better.

The four adults were talking, and Lady Harrington turned around to look at the students.

"Everyone is restricted to their dorm rooms tonight. We will come and let you out in shifts to eat your dinner, but you must go straight to the cafeteria and come straight back, after. No

110

socialization and no detours."

"My books are still in the library," Valerie said, backing away. She'd just run and get them…

"I need a word," Mr. Jamison said, striding through the crowd and motioning for Valerie to follow him.

Valerie sighed.

Her books were sleeping in the library tonight.

Mrs. Reynolds and two of the other teachers were hurrying down the hallway. The herbs teacher gave Valerie and Mr. Jamison an alarmed look as she went past, but none of them spoke. When they reached the end of the hallway, Mr. Jamison turned, dropping his head to speak to her.

"Why did you do that?" he asked. Valerie widened her eyes.

"I have no idea what I did," she said.

"You topped a silverthorn and spoke it out of existence," he said. "It was neatly and admirably done."

"Was it *wrong*?" Valerie asked.

"No," he said. "And it was a better job than I would have done. I would have spent the next five minutes working up a cast to go against the root, and you… You equated its growth with the main stalk of a plant and topped it, killing it. I didn't even know you could do it that way. Mrs. Reynolds is going to have a field day when she finds out about it, because she's been arguing that silverthorn has plantlike qualities for years, now."

"None of that sounds bad," Valerie said.

"No," he said. "But you didn't *know* that you were doing the right thing. It could have been like before, and you could have been building a poison or a *bomb*. You just did it, without stopping to think."

"You say it like I made a choice," Valerie said. He lowered his head a fraction further.

"What are you telling me?" he asked.

She shrugged.

"I didn't *decide* to go do it. I just did it. More like breathing than talking, not quite a heartbeat."

He blinked, looking back down the hallway. The girls were staring. Ethan was approaching with Shack.

"About time they knew what you could do," Ethan said as he went past. Mr. Jamison straightened, watching the two boys until they were partially up the stairs.

"You need to restrain yourself," Mr. Jamison said. "I don't know what you're capable of, and I don't know what's leading you to do what you're doing, but *you* need to figure it out. You put yourself and everyone else in danger, until you know what it is you're doing."

Valerie nodded.

"I'll try," she said. "I didn't *mean* to do it. It's just… It was like in class, or in Mr. Tannis' room. I just knew how to do it and I did it."

He pulled his mouth to the side, then looked up as Mr. Benson and Lady Harrington arrived.

"Looks like a prank," Mr. Benson said. "Are you sure she wasn't involved?"

"She says she was in the library," Mr. Jamison said. "I believe her."

Mr. Benson looked at Valerie for a moment.

"I don't know who did it, but we're going to find out. Magic has fingerprints to it, if you know what you're doing, and Lady Harrington is one of the best magic readers I've ever known."

"I hope you do," Valerie said, trying not to be so sarcastic that she got herself into trouble. "It wasn't me."

He nodded and glanced at Lady Harrington, who put her hands onto Valerie's shoulders and looked her in the eye.

There was an odd hesitation, then Lady Harrington shook her head.

"Her magic is tied up in this, but I can't be sure how. She was the one to shut it down. There is other magic involved, as well."

Valerie raised her eyebrows.

"You can actually tell that?" she asked.

"Are you accusing me of bluffing, young lady?" Lady Harrington answered. "You ought to go back to you room now."

"My stuff is in the library," Valerie said. "And I'm trying to get caught up."

Lady Harrington shook her head.

"We've been attacked," she said. "Tonight, you stay in your room. No wandering around, no getting yourself into trouble until we've figured this out."

Valerie frowned.

"Miss Livingston is going to be angry at me for leaving a mess," she said.

Lady Harrington raised her eyebrows.

"Then you can go get it before class in the morning. If she says anything to you about it, you may direct her to me."

Valerie twisted her mouth, wanting to argue that she had a hard enough time making it to class on time as it was, but it didn't seem like the wisest thing to say, and she ultimately managed to contain it.

She glanced at Mr. Jamison, a bit stung as she considered that he seemed to have actually been questioning whether she had done... whatever that thing was out in the hallway... but he had already moved on and so had Lady Harrington. Mr. Benson caught up to them, and Valerie turned, finding Sasha watching her from the door to their room.

"You can't get it open, can you?" Valerie asked.

Sasha shook her head.

"Not right now."

Valerie went and twisted the handle, then watched as the hallway continued to empty into the rooms. She closed her door behind her and went to sit at her desk.

"All of my books are in the library," she said. "I'm going to lose a night of studying."

Who was she?

"What did you do?" Sasha asked.

"I left them there when you came and dragged me out," Valerie said.

"No. To the cast in the hallway. I recognized the roseburn, but the way it was blooming..."

"You saw it too?" Valerie asked. "That's exactly what it was doing. Blooming."

"It's a technical term," Sasha said. "A roseburn should create a path for any number of magical elements to make their way through an otherwise hostile magic field, but I've never seen one that complex before."

"Hostile magical field," Valerie said. "First, you sound like a textbook. Second, what does that mean? The cast was meant to get around the school's security?"

"Warding," Sasha corrected. "The silverthorn couldn't have even *survived* if it hadn't been completely blocked from the school's warding by... whatever that stuff was. I wish I'd gotten to look at it more closely before you shut it down."

"Seriously?" Valerie asked. "Why is *everyone* on my case about that? I didn't *mean* to."

"Who was on your case?" Sasha asked. "I wish you'd shut it down *minutes* earlier. There's a hole in the warding big enough to grow a silverthorn in, and it's going to take *weeks* to repair, if they can find the time at all. They're all so busy with prepping war supplies."

"You noticed, too," Valerie said, feeling glum once more. "No one will even talk to me, anymore. They just send me away."

"And to just leave it like that," Sasha said. "With just Mrs. Gold to try to repair it? They should have made Mr. Tannis come down and look at it, at least. Maybe Mr. Pevins and Mrs. Lang." Valerie didn't know who they were. "At least. But to walk away? I'm half-tempted to go out there and try to repair it *myself*, and I'm a freshman."

"Why?" Valerie asked.

"Because someone has to," Sasha started, but Valerie waved at her.

"No, that's not what I'm talking about. Why would someone do that? Lady Harrington said they thought it was a prank, but what does it accomplish? She said they might have been trying to get into one of the rooms, but... That's a really elaborate setup to go in and shortsheet someone's bed."

"And you're going to get caught," Sasha said. "The alarms went off, like they're supposed to."

"I didn't hear anything," Valerie said.

"You weren't here," Sasha answered. "And it wasn't something you could *hear*. It was just, like, suddenly I couldn't focus on anything else. I had to figure out what was going on."

"That's what happens when the alarms go off?" Valerie asked. "Everyone goes running out into the hallway to see what's happening? Genius."

Sasha snorted.

"I expect it's supposed to be different, but that's what everyone *did*. And there it was, that great big red flame going up the wall… I thought it was going to try to burn the building down, but it went out really fast."

"So it was impossible to miss," Valerie said. "Why would you do that?"

"To put a hole in the defenses, I guess," Sasha said. "I don't know. Maybe they didn't know the alarms would go off?"

"If it was a student, I buy that," Valerie said.

"It had to be a student," Sasha said. "No one else can get in here."

Valerie looked back at her, then turned her chair to face the room.

"Okay," she said. "Prove it."

"I don't understand," Sasha told her.

"Prove that only students can get in here. That no one else could have been here."

"They'd have to come up the driveway," Sasha said slowly, shifting and holding out her fingers to tick them off. "They'd have to get up to the school. They'd have to come in the front doors. They'd have to make it to the dorm wing. And then they'd have to get past Mrs. Gold. I don't think any of those are possible."

"The driveway?" Valerie asked.

"You can't see it if you don't know it's there," Sasha said. "And there are a bunch of defensive wards on it, beyond that. The closer you get to the school, the harder it is to be there if you aren't supposed to be. We're really, really well defended. They say that they inscribed the sides of the bricks as they mortared them together, magic facing against magic, every single brick throughout the entire building. And then the war came and things really went crazy."

"Yeah, that's when they went crazy," Valerie said, looking at the externally-facing wall of the dorm room with new appreciation.

"It's just… it had to be a student. It had to be a *prank*, or, you know, like a fight between students. It was Trina's room that the fire was right next to."

"Is Trina in a fight with anyone?" Valerie asked. Sasha thought hard, then shook her head.

"I don't know. I don't think so."

"Who else was there at the very beginning?" Valerie asked.

"Lady Harrington and Mrs. Gold will figure it out," Sasha said. "This isn't *our problem*."

"My mom sent me here because I'd be safe," Valerie said. "If I'm not going to be safe, I need to figure out how to send her word, and then find a safer place to be."

"There isn't a safer place," Sasha said after a moment. "The schools are *closed*. I mean, maybe one of the back rooms of the Council, where they go to talk or whatever, but people come to the schools and they don't come or go. It's potent, having doors that close behind you like that. You can't find that kind of a defense just anywhere."

"Well, food has to come in and out," Valerie said. "And trash. And mail. There have to be weak points in the magic."

"Valerie," Sasha said. "That's *so* far over our heads. People who are *really* good at magic came up with these. We're freshmen and you…"

"I know, I'm beyond worthless," Valerie said. "I know. It's just… *Why*? I can't come up with a reason to do it."

Sasha shook her head.

"To create chaos and watch?" Sasha asked. "Practicing a cast that got out of hand? Because Trina said something mean that I haven't heard about yet? I don't know. But it couldn't have been someone *else*. It had to be one of us."

She remembered the feeling of breaking the magic, making it die. It had been satisfying. Like winning a game of chess, almost. The magic in the spell hadn't been… It hadn't been *malicious*, the way it had felt. It had just been *against her*. She had *needed* to destroy it, and it had had no defense against her, once she realized it.

Prank?

It hadn't seemed like a prank.

It had felt more like a test.

"Lady Harrington says she can find the person who cast it," Valerie said after a minute.

"I'm glad," Sasha said. "I don't like people using dark magic this close to where I sleep."

"Dark magic?" Valerie asked, and Sasha nodded.

"All of it was dark. Couldn't you tell? Couldn't you *feel* it?"

Valerie shook her head.

"What did it feel like?"

Sasha shook her head, shifting uncomfortably in her chair.

"I don't know. Like a shadow or cold or... Like a cave that you can't see into, and there might be something big and mean and full of teeth and claws watching you from inside."

Valerie shuddered, and Sasha nodded.

"You didn't feel it?" the redhead asked her again.

"No," Valerie answered. "No. It was just... there."

There was a knock on the door and Valerie startled. Sasha got up and opened it, finding Lady Harrington standing outside.

"You may go to dinner," the woman said, putting her hand on Sasha's shoulder for a moment. Sasha waited, then Lady Harrington motioned her on. The woman looked at Valerie with suspicion, but didn't get in her way as Valerie left the room.

"Classes are canceled tomorrow," Lady Harrington said. "You will be expected to continue to make progress at the topics you have been studying, and homework packets will be delivered sometime before lunch."

Sasha looked back, and Valerie could tell that something very important was afoot, but Lady Harrington moved on down the hallway, knocking at the next door. Valerie moved her feet quickly to catch up with Sasha, trying not to make extra noise or draw extra attention.

"What does that mean?" Valerie asked.

"It means that something *bad* happened," Sasha said. "And I don't think it was the cast."

"What could be worse than the cast?" Valerie asked. Sasha glanced at her.

Pity.

Oh.

"The war," Valerie said. "Something bad happened. Will they tell us?"

Sasha shrugged.

"None of the people who were in charge during the last war are even here," she said. "I don't know what to expect any more than you do."

Valerie thought that hard to believe, but she let it go.

They went to the cafeteria and ate together quietly. Ethan went past with the rest of the Council brats, but he didn't do anything more than meet her eye. The entire cafeteria was subdued, passing information along at a whisper.

Valerie felt like leaving, so that Sasha could at least capture the gist of what everyone else knew, but she was actually hungry, and one of the upper school teachers was standing guard at the doorway indicated there wasn't anywhere else they were going to let her be.

So.

They ate.

That cast.

The spellwork there.

Sasha knew *so much* about it, and Valerie knew *nothing*, and yet she had known how to stop it. Intuitively.

"English," Sasha said after a moment. "You did it in English."

They were both thinking about the same thing. Valerie shouldn't have been surprised.

"So?" Valerie asked. "Is it more mystical to use a foreign language?"

"No," Sasha said. "Well, I mean, it is more *cool* if you can do it in Coptic, but... no. Mr. Jamison explains it so well..." She drew a breath and nodded, glancing around for a moment, then settling over her tray. "English and Mandarin are fine languages for casting, because they've been used by *a lot* of people. The problem with both of them is that they're always changing. They haven't got *roots*. The words that you use and the way that you use them... they're invoking the power that a billion people put into them, but the way that *those* people use them are all different. There's a lot more resonant power in the *old* languages, the ones that were used for thousands of years, but the problem with *those* is that you have to use them the way that *those* people did, which, like with Sumerian, we've never heard anyone speak it, and no one *alive* has ever heard anyone speak it, so there's no way for *us* to draw on the historicity of the language…"

"Historicity," Valerie said.

"It's a word," Sasha protested, and Valerie nodded.

"I have no doubt," she said. "I asked why it was such a big deal I did it in English, and you just used the word *historicity* in your answer. I think an old person stole your body when you weren't looking."

Sasha sighed.

"My point is, it's *hard* to get any power into English. There are a bunch of intermediate languages that we use a lot more, because they're *older* and at the same time we know how to speak them well enough. I'd have been just as impressed if you'd done it in Sanskrit. Magically, at least. If you suddenly started speaking Sanskrit, I'd have you checked for every kind of magic Lady Harrington could think of."

Valerie snorted.

"Would you even recognize it?" Valerie asked.

"Sanskrit?" Sasha asked, nodding. "Wouldn't you?"

Valerie closed her eyes and Sasha laughed.

"I'm kidding, I'm kidding," the redhead said. "But I hear that Mr. Jamison reads it."

Valerie sighed, listening to the quiet around them.

"Dinner is over, ladies and gentlemen," Lady Harrington said. Valerie looked over at where the headmistress was standing in the doorway. "I need everyone to go straight back to their rooms so that I can let the next shift in to eat. No talking in the hallways, please, and no leaving your rooms for anything other than trips to the bathroom for your evening grooming. Mrs. Gold and Franky Frank will be supervising through the night."

Valerie looked at Sasha.

Supervising? she mouthed.

Sasha shrugged, and they got up to go throw away the

remainders of their meal.

"Library, one AM," someone whispered, and Valerie jerked, seeing Ethan walking away with Shack and one of the nameless guys.

"What?" Valerie asked.

"What?" Sasha asked her back.

Ethan looked back at Valerie for just a moment and gave her a small nod, then returned his attention to Shack.

"How do I get out?" Valerie asked.

"What do you mean?" Sasha asked. Valerie shook her head, taking everything in, now, that she might have missed under resignation of curfew.

Where was everyone?

How were they watching?

Why would she even meet Ethan?

Curiosity.

Silly question.

How would she get around them?

She scuttled back to the room with Sasha, then sat down on her bed.

"How do I get out of this?" she asked. "If I wanted to get to the library yet tonight."

"Valerie, I… I'm impressed by how hard you're working, but you don't *have* to study every single night."

"Not it," Valerie said. "Ethan told me to meet him there at one."

"In the *morning*?" Sasha asked. "We have… oh."

"Classes are canceled," Valerie said. "Something *big* is going on, and they don't even want us *talking* about it."

"They don't want us speculating about it," Sasha answered, sounding unsure. "Why would you go? What else did he say?"

"Just to meet him," Valerie said. "And I want to go."

Sasha frowned.

"I don't know," she said. "I think you should stay here. It's what Lady Harrington said to do."

"Do you always do everything everyone tells you to do?" Valerie asked, still trying to work it out. How was *Ethan* getting there?"

"Mostly," Sasha said. "What if he's just trying to get you into trouble?"

Valerie hadn't considered that.

"Then I'm going to have to be extra clever so that they don't catch me," she said.

Sasha threw herself onto her bed and planted her chin on her fists.

"What's the point?" she asked. "You don't know what he would tell you, even if he *was* trying to meet you there for a good reason."

"Maybe he knows something about the war," Valerie said. "Maybe he has a *cell* phone, and his dad texted him something about my mom or something."

"*I* have a cell phone," Sasha said, digging into a bag underneath her bed and getting it out. "They don't work here."

Valerie grabbed at it, anyway, resisting for a moment the urge to stand on her bed to see if she got a signal *up high*, and then doing it anyway.

"How do they do that?" Valerie asked.

Sasha paused.

"Magic," she said.

"Sasha, there's *something* going on. And it's *huge*. There was a fire in the hallway and… The teachers won't talk to us and they're all busy…"

"It's called a *war*," Sasha said.

Valerie frowned.

It was a valid point.

She sat back down on her bed and gave Sasha the cell phone back again.

"I miss my mom," Valerie said. "I wasn't *ready* for all of this."

"I wasn't ready for the war to come back," Sasha said. "And I knew it was. We all did. But it doesn't make any of us *ready* for it. They might make my mom come do healing for the fights, and the Superiors were known for targeting healers. She would write me a letter if it happened, but Merck Trent would sit on it as long as he liked, so that it didn't have any 'battle-critical' secrets in it. She could be out there right now and I wouldn't know."

"Out *where*?" Valerie asked. "I mean… Where *are* they? What are they *doing*?"

Sasha shook her head.

"I don't know. I really don't."

"Ethan might," Valerie said. "He missed the first four weeks of school. Maybe he knows a *lot* more than the rest of us. Maybe he decided he needs to tell me…"

"At one in the morning?" Sasha asked. "They won't keep us in our rooms *forever*. What's going to change between now and then?"

Once again, Sasha had a valid point.

They weren't changing Valerie's mind, but she appreciated having someone thoughtful and methodical talking her through it.

"What would you do?" Valerie asked.

"Mrs. Gold is *out* there," Sasha said, and Valerie shook her head.

"Wrong answer. What would you *do*?"

Sasha grimaced, then went to get her bag off of the back of the closet door.

"If they catch you, you invented all of this in a fit of manic inspiration," she muttered, and Valerie grinned.

"Magic," she murmured.

Sasha.

Sasha was a freaking *genius*.

Looking at the list of directions and the stacks of potions, the phonetic explanations of the verbal spells… All Valerie could think was that she hoped that Sasha was never on the *other* side.

Sasha went through it once more, making Valerie recite the spells in reverse, for fear that Valerie would accidentally trigger them.

"You have to do it *exactly* right," Sasha said at one point. "Since you don't *speak* the language, there's no room for error. Fluency helps so much…" She shook her head.

"Sasha, this is… This is absolutely incredible," Valerie said. Sasha gave her a dour look.

"If you're impressed by this, I hate to think of what you'd think of war spells. This is basic defense and evasion."

"How do you know all of this?" Valerie asked.

"My mom," Sasha said. "And, you know, I've been going to class for a while, now, too."

"I'm so behind," Valerie muttered. Sasha nodded.

"Now... please. Just... don't do it. Okay? It was a cool experiment to see if I could come up with a way to get you there and back, but... Please don't do it. Just stay here. Let him tell you whatever he's going to tell you *later*, if he was even going to turn up at all."

"I'm doing it," Valerie said, looking at the clock on the wall.

It was quarter to one.

She had her list.

She had a bag on her shoulder.

She had *magic*.

Freaking *magic*.

She went to the door and turned to look back at Sasha once more, who shook her head. Valerie flashed a grin, unable to contain it, then she took out the first spell, a paste, and marked her face with it, cheekbone to jaw, straight down, the way Sasha had indicated. It had an odd scent to it, and it made it feel as though her feet were a long way away and lighter, somehow.

Step one.

Eighteen steps to go, to get to the library.

Twenty-three to get back.

Sasha was concerned that Valerie did not pay enough attention to detail to get through this, and she had a valid point once more, but the bag on her shoulder all but sang to her, and Valerie was eager to go.

She was on a mission.

She made it to step fourteen.

So.

Close.

She was within sight of the library, but Sasha had noticed that there was a magic field here, just on the other side of the steps, that was designed to keep out people who might have come to raid the library, and it had a side-effect of notifying whoever had cast it - Sasha was guessing Lady Harrington herself - that someone had crossed it.

So Valerie had to disguise herself from *that* field, but not before she was out of line of sight of the main office, because the main office had the capacity to identify every student on the premises, and if it saw someone who *wasn't* a student or a member of the faculty, Mr. Benson would know immediately.

Valerie had wondered exactly what *about* the front office was watching her, but like an awful lot of Sasha's magic, it had seemed best not to ask.

At fourteen, she was supposed to slick the bottoms of her shoes with an oil-and-stuff mixture and read one of the spells, then mark the wall at the bottom of the stairwell with a short-term forgetting spell. Sasha said it wouldn't last more than fifteen or twenty minutes, so that was all she was going to get in the library with Ethan; she needed to be out of there after that.

The problem was, Valerie couldn't remember which was the wall-marking oil and which was the shoe-slicking oil.

They had been in a rack of vials, and she was supposed to just use them in order, but when Mr. Tannis had walked past at one point, Valerie had hidden behind a corner and jostled the rack, and they'd all fallen out.

She was kind of in trouble, getting back, but she was so close to the library, and there was no way she was failing before she at least *heard* what Ethan had to tell her.

So she took out the two oils and looked at them.

One of them had bits of green flotsam floating around in it.

The other one looked like Sasha had used two drops of red food coloring on it.

She opened them both and smelled them, glancing at the library again and wondering how Ethan was planning on getting in and if she couldn't just hang out here and wait for him to let her in.

Playing this guessing game…

The one was sweet.

The other was quite bitter, by scent.

Lofty, though, like smelling cold air after being cooped up in a humid classroom all afternoon.

She poured half of the red oil out onto her hand, ignoring how it dripped onto the ground, then she screwed the lid back on and stuffed it into her pocket. She took the flotsam one and held it up to the light, then sipped it - *why* had she done that? - and poured it onto her wrist, letting it flow down onto the red. The edge where one met the other was hot, but not uncomfortably so, and when they mixed…

She quickly slicked the bottoms of her shoes and put a handprint on the wall - there was no time for the intricate symbol Sasha had given her - then ran toward the doors of the library.

Steps fifteen through eighteen weren't going to make it. Either she was going to go now, or… Well, her hand was going to fall off.

Fall off?

Where had *that* come from?

And yet.

She knew it.

If she didn't go straight for the doors of the library, the mix of magics on her hand combined with the protections *around* the library were going to combust or acidify or something… whatever instinct it was that was guiding her wasn't being entirely clear on the details.

She backed through the doors into the library, hearing Sasha's vials clink around in her shoulder bag and wondering if there was any *hope* on her getting back to the room.

"You're late," Ethan said, and she shrugged.

"Had to hide from Mr. Tannis. Are they actually *patrolling?*"

"They didn't figure out who cast the spell in the girls' dorm wing," Ethan said. "Lady Harrington said that you were involved, but they think there's an upperclassman involved as well who knows how to cover his casts. Elvis could do that."

"Did you tell me to come here so you could accuse me?" Valerie asked, and Ethan grinned easily.

"No. Just. If they're grilling you, looking for who your accomplice was, you could point them at him, and they'd have a merry chase trying to figure out if it was him or not."

"You told me to come here," Valerie said. "And it took me a

lot of work to *get* here. Why?"

She went to go clean up her books to have something to do. It was likely the librarian would notice her stuff was gone, in the morning, but she couldn't just leave without it.

She couldn't.

She always cleaned up after herself.

"That cast," Ethan said. "I've seen something like it before, in Germany. And I think that there are some things that you should know that no one is telling you."

Valerie straightened, then sat on the desk, putting her feet on the seat of the chair.

"I'm listening," she said. He twisted his mouth to the side.

"It's stuff that I'm not supposed to know," Ethan said. "But I have a habit of wandering around where people don't... Why did it take you so long to get here, again? You should have been able to just walk here."

"What?" she asked. "How?"

"I reconfigured the defenses. I've seen the full schematic..."

He paused, frowning, then went to open the doors of the library.

"Stop playing," she said. "What did you *have* to tell me tonight that was so important?"

"That mark," he said without looking back at her. "It's distinctive magic. I don't know if you saw it but the shape of the scar on the floor... They aren't *ever* going to get it to come up. They're going to have to cast new defenses around it... Do you hear that?"

"Ethan," Valerie prompted, but he opened the door all the way, listening.

And that was when Valerie heard it, too.

Footsteps.

"Close the door," Valerie hissed. "They're going to see you."

"I reconfigured the defenses," Ethan said, his shoulders dropping. "Because I needed to talk to you. But they already did it..."

He looked over his shoulder.

"I just messed up big time," he said. "They might... Everyone is in danger. We have to go back."

"And do what?" Valerie asked, all the same hopping off of the table and walking over to him, past him into the wide expanse in front of the library. He followed her, letting the doors fall behind them.

"Do you smell that?" Valerie asked. Ethan shook his head.

"What do you smell?"

"Smoke," Valerie said after another moment as they both picked up pace. "Really... acrid smoke."

Ethan cursed and started to run. Valerie wasn't behind him more than a step, her backpack and Sasha's shoulder bag jolting back and forth on her back.

There was hissing and the sound of voices, ones that Valerie didn't recognize, and Ethan shoved her against a wall, listening.

"That's hellspeak," he whispered. "There are demons here."

Valerie thrashed.

"Sasha is there," she said. "I have to go help her."

"You just need to know going in," Ethan said. "They see you, they know you, and they are allowed to kill you, if they get an opportunity."

"Just tell me what to do," Valerie said.

He looked over his shoulder.

"You should go get Lady Harrington and Mr. Benson," he said.

"Nope, try again," Valerie said, pulling his arm down from where it was braced across her collar bones. "You can, if you want."

"You haven't got the first clue how to take care of yourself," he said.

"But they're *here*, and my only friend in the whole school is in there, and I'm going to go help her."

"*How?*" he asked.

She shook her head, pushing him back and away.

"I'll figure it out," she said, starting to run toward the dorm wing again. She glanced back once to see him watching her, then he held up a hand - good luck, it seemed - and he turned to run the other direction.

For help.

They only had to hold out for so long, and then the teachers would come and they would slaughter the demons.

Just for so long.

Valerie skidded to a halt at the top end of the hallway, seeing men and women, maybe half a dozen of them, tearing open doors and throwing girls into the hallway. Mrs. Gold was there, shrieking words Valerie didn't understand, and two of the strangers were in front of her, yelling things back. The air was thick with a dark gray smoke, and several of the walls appeared to be on fire.

Real fire, this time.

Valerie counted to her own door, finding that the doors on either side were open, but the door on her room was still closed.

Maybe.

It felt right.

She grabbed two girls on the way past, dragging them to their feet and pulling them up to her door. There was screaming as more girls came stumbling into the hallway. Valerie opened her door and shoved the two girls in, sticking her head in to look at Sasha.

Sasha was *ready*.

For what, Valerie would never know, but she was ready, and she had to hold back whatever it was she'd been planning.

"Hold this door closed," Valerie said, then - before Sasha could answer - she went back out into the hallway, pulling more girls to their feet and pushing them toward her room.

"Go," she yelled. "Go. In there."

There was a man yelling at a woman next to a cluster of five girls, and Valerie took the bag off of her shoulder, putting her hand into it and taking out a pair of vials. She knelt, pouring them on the floor in a pattern that was *similar* to what Sasha had shown her for disarming the library, but not at all identical, then Valerie stood again.

The two demons looked at her, and one of them took a step forward.

Halted.

"Go," Valerie yelled, walking cautiously around the wet markings on the floor and getting the girls up onto their feet. "In there."

"It's her," the man said. Valerie shuddered, backing away over her design on the floor. The two came after her, slowly, like they were having to fight their way, and Valerie turned her back and ran into her room, slamming the door and putting her back against it.

"Someone help me hold this," she said.

"It's magic," one of the other girls said. "It doesn't work like that. They broke all the locks on *our* doors."

"They won't get through that one," Sasha said. "Not in time."

Valerie closed her eyes and nodded, putting her hands out to the wall on either side of the narrow hallway that went from the door to the room, then pressing her back harder against the door.

The door thumped as the two demons outside reached it, and Valerie felt the door strain as though it was a part of her own body, but it held.

There was a pair of hands on her shoulders, and a soft voice.

"You've got this," Sasha said, marking Valerie's forehead with something. "Strength, focus, and power."

"We're going to get you, little girl, and then you're going to learn what magic can *really* do," the man said through the door. It was like he was whispering it to the back of her neck.

Her hair stood up as her skin prickled, and she felt Sasha mark her hands. The girls were whispering, terrified, but they kept their voices down as Valerie attempted to focus.

The door held.

They slammed into it again, and then it vibrated like it might simply fall apart, and then it burned against her back like her skin would blister and cook, but the door held.

And then.

And then something very strange happened.

It was remarkable what something had to be, for Valerie to consider it strange in that moment, but everything went calm and still and very quiet. Valerie opened her eyes, looking at the girls in the room, at Sasha mixing something new in a stone bowl, all of them frozen in time. The door was completely still. Valerie held it, anyway, suspecting a trick.

Instead, there was a knock.

"Valerie," a voice said. "You need to come with me, now."

"Not likely," she called back. "You can't come through."

There was a pause, and then a laugh.

"That's a good trick," he said, and the doorknob twisted and the door pressed against her back as it unlatched.

She pushed harder against it.

"Come on now," the man said. "Let's not let this become undignified."

"I'm not letting you in," Valerie said.

"They're going to kill you, do you understand that? That's what they came here for. I have one shot to get you out of here."

"The teachers are coming," Valerie said. "And they're going to kill all of you."

She didn't know if it was true, but she liked the sound of it.

"They won't get here in time," the man said. "But here's the trick. If you aren't here, none of this is worth it. They'll teleport out before the teachers even get here, because, as admirable a job as Mrs. Gold is doing holding the whole wing on her own, none of the demons want to face down Lady Harrington or Mr. Benson, much less Mr. Tannis, if he's armed."

"So I'm just supposed to go quietly?" Valerie asked.

"If you want you and your friends to live," the man said, pushing gently at the door again. Valerie looked in Sasha's frozen, unblinking face and shook her head.

"I would," she said, her voice lower now. "I actually would. But I don't believe you."

"Don't believe me what?" the man asked.

"That you'll leave them alone if I go with you."

"Oh," he said. "Yes, I see it now. No. I'm not with them. I'm here to *rescue* you."

"Why would I trust you?" Valerie asked. "You're here *with* them."

"Don't know if you've noticed, but I actually went to quite a lot of effort to get to you *before* they did, actually."

"You're late," Valerie said.

He laughed.

"Very good. Now. You need to come with me quickly. My spellwork isn't designed to hold forever."

"They're going to die, if I open this door."

There was a long pause.

"I give you my word that this door will not budge until Lady Harrington herself opens it."

"Who are you?" Valerie asked.

"Valerie, I'm your father."

Grant

The door opened.

Valerie wasn't sure if she'd opened it or if he had, but he…

If she hadn't been so animated from the fight, she might have fallen to her knees.

It was him.

Aged a good bit, with silvering hair that was much finer than it had been, back then, and with stubble on his chin where he'd been meticulously clean-shaven before, but she recognized him from the pictures.

There was no room for doubt at all.

"Dad," she said.

He put out his hand.

"I need to close this to cast on it, and then we have to move *really* fast," he said.

"Where have you been?" she asked, blinking. He drew her out of the room by her elbow - the demons on this side were just as frozen as the girls on the other side, and their absolutely-human facial expressions of violent range were terrifying. She looked closely at one of them as her father worked.

"Demons?" she asked. "How can you tell?"

"The fact that they didn't come through a door helps," Grant Blake told her. "After that, things get a bit tricky."

He finished a mark on the door and put his hand over it, and it hissed and sizzled and seeped into the door until it was invisible.

"That will hold," he said. "I don't care who they are. Between what you've got on there and that… Elsa Beth Harrington will be the only person in the whole *school* who can open it. They may have to replace the door."

Valerie shook her head, and he turned to her.

"I need you to be here and not here," he said. "After this, we move *fast*, okay?"

Her eyebrows went up, and he put his fingers along her jaw, his index fingers under her ears and his pinkies resting under her chin. He had cool, clean hands, by feel. He spoke words that she didn't recognize, then slid his thumbs along her eyebrows, lifting his chin.

"Yes. There. Let's go."

"No," Valerie said.

"I'm very serious about this," he said. "We have only a few seconds."

"Where have you *been*?" Valerie asked.

"I give you my word, I will answer that. Just not here."

Valerie looked him in the eye for a moment longer, then looked at the mayhem in the hallway.

Mrs. Gold appeared to have a three-tongued whip that she was using to chase down a demon who was fleeing her.

"She is scary," Valerie observed, and Grant Blake laughed.

"You have no idea," he said. "Come."

Valerie turned and followed him out of the school.

There was a low, sleek, black car parked out front, still running, and he opened the passenger-side door, looking back at the school as she got in.

"Can't believe she sent you to Survival School," he muttered as he closed the door and walked briskly around to the other side, getting in.

"Where have you been?" Valerie demanded as he put the car in drive and accelerated away. The force of it pressed her back into her seat for several moments.

"Doing my job, actually," Grant answered. "Which is more than I can say for your mother."

"What do you mean?" Valerie asked. "Don't talk about her like that. She thought you were dead. *I* thought you were dead. How are you not dead?"

"I was never dead," he answered simply. "I just found out that my handler at Council had multiple interests at play, and one of them was putting a lot of people at risk. So I went silent. No one ever said that meant I was *dead*."

"It's been fifteen years," Valerie said. "Fifteen, Dad. Where have you been?"

"Well," he said. "If you're asking why I didn't come *find* you, the biggest reason is the same as the reason that your mother ran away and hid. To protect you. The lesser reason is that your mother is incredibly good at what she does, and I never could find you."

There was a tone of humor, there, and he glanced over at her.

"I wish I had gotten to see you grow up," he said. "I can't tell you how bad I wish that. But after the first few years, honestly, you just accept it and get on with things."

"You didn't think about me," Valerie said.

"No," he said. "I did. All the time. But… I didn't think about *finding* you. I…" He sighed. "I don't think you'll understand until you have a child of your own, how much I missed you. But you were safe and with your mother, and I was trying to keep people alive."

Valerie sat lower in her seat.

"Mom thought you were dead. I know she did."

"I don't expect she did, actually," he answered. "She couldn't *know*, but we talked so many times, back in those days, about what it would be like if one of us died, what we would *do*, the things that were likely to kill us… It's war, honey. People *die* all the time. But your mother and I are nigh-on unkillable."

"Then why didn't she ever tell me you might be alive?" Valerie asked.

He looked over at her, pressing his mouth.

"You'll have to ask her that," he said. "I can think of lots of reasons, but I don't want to poison anything by putting them all out there. Whatever they were, I know she had good ones."

"Where are we going?" Valerie asked.

"Someplace safe," he said. "Going to be a couple hours, if you want to get some sleep."

"You think I can sleep after that?" Valerie asked, and he grinned, watching the road.

"I always could," he said. "And so could Susan. But you do what you like. The car is just about as safe as it gets, but I'm going to be pushing it all the way there to try to make sure that no one catches us. We have a lot to talk about, but it will wait for morning."

Valerie paused, shifting to put her head against the door.

"Would Mom be happy to know that I'm with you?" she asked. She was actually sleepy. Imagine that.

"I don't know," he said. "It's been too long. I genuinely don't know."

Her father woke her up to walk her into a small house in the midst of a forest. It smelled humid out, so she hadn't gone *that* far, and the house was lit, though not excessively. He took her to a bedroom with limited furniture, but it smelled clean - particularly the bed - and Valerie went back to sleep easily.

The next morning, she woke up confused, with violent dreams that had troubled her sleep all night.

It took her several moments to remember where she was, then she was out of bed, following the sound of food preparation in the small kitchen.

"Where were you all this time?" Valerie asked, going to sit on a stool.

"Doing my job," he said, not turning to look at her. "Good morning. Did you sleep well?"

"No," Valerie said. "What does that mean, doing your job?"

"It means lots of things," Grant said. "How do you like school?"

"They all hate me and wish I wasn't there," Valerie said. "When did you look for us?"

Her father turned around from the stove, pushing half a skillet of scrambled eggs onto a plate, then picking up a pair of salt and pepper shakers and putting the plate plus the shakers down in front of her. He went looking for another plate.

"The *last* time I went looking for you would have been about five years ago," he said. "There was a lull where they weren't watching everyone as close, and I could sneak out and back in again without them noticing. I never did find you, though. Why don't they like you at school? I would have imagined you would be very popular, if only for political reasons."

"Because I can't do magic," Valerie said, opening her mouth to ask her next question, but he put a sharp finger up.

"What do you mean you can't do magic?" he asked.

She shrugged.

"Mom never taught me. I didn't know it was even *real* until she sent me to school and disappeared."

He blinked at her, setting the skillet down on the counter.

"What do you *mean* your mother never taught you magic?"

Valerie shook her head.

"Don't know what to tell you."

"You *did* magic," he said. "I read it off the door. It was yours."

"I… Yeah, I kind of do that. Can you tell me what it means? No one really says a lot, other than calling me a natural and trying to make sure I don't make any more bombs."

"Bombs," he said flatly. "Your mother…" He shook his head, bracing his hands out on the counter to either side and letting his head hang. "You should have been one of the most gifted magic users the Council had. Why would she stunt you like that?"

"Don't talk about her like that," Valerie said. "You *weren't there.*"

"I wasn't…" he started with temper, then he shook his head. When he spoke again, his tone was much more even. "I don't know what she was thinking. Maybe by the time you were old enough for her to start teaching you, she'd made up her mind to raise you civilian. I don't *know.* What I do know is that you have an enormous talent, and they are *squandering* it at that school. Even Light School wouldn't know what to do with you."

"They're doing their best, Dad," Valerie said. "There is a *war* going on, you know. And you still haven't told me what you were *doing* all that time. I mean… You've been spying on the Superiors for all that time… Not ever talking to anyone on the Council? Are you even on our side anymore?"

"Sup…" he started, then closed his eyes as if counting his temper back down again. "That's what they're calling them, at this point? Superiors?"

Valerie blinked, feeling very sarcastic and defensive and very much wishing she knew more of what was going on.

"So?" she asked. "Isn't that what they call themselves?"

He sighed.

"There is a *faction* who call themselves *The Pure.* They believe that people shouldn't mess with magic because it's dangerous, unless they are capable of functioning at a very, very high level. There is a group who believe in non-propagation. That families that have magic should be allowed to continue to use it, but that we should not be teaching it to civilians anymore. There are the separatists… I swear, the Council are their own worst enemies. They've driven more families into our side than anything The Pure ever did…"

"*Our* side?" Valerie asked.

"Do you know what the Council does, Valerie?" Grant asked.

"Run a war?" Valerie asked, tart.

"They *control*," Grant said. "I don't approve of what The Pure are trying to accomplish, or what some of the non-propagationists are willing to do to help them, but the Council… They aren't the heroes in this story. They tell people who they are, where to be, how to act… They expect the magic community to report in to them any time they even change location, and they're working on a magic census where everyone is expected to report their specific *skills*, so that the Council can use them as they're needed. They draft people into a war that they don't have a stake in, and they expect them to *die* protecting civilians, even as they have their own families to think about. They *threaten* families… Tell me something, how did they ultimately get your mother back into the war?"

Valerie considered this for a full minute before she answered.

"Threatened her," she finally said. "Mom wouldn't go unless they put me into school."

He shook his head.

"Why on *earth* did she pick Survival School?" he asked, his tone different - less serious.

"Because Mr. Jamison was there, I think," Valerie said.

"Alan," Grant said. "Ah. Yes, that does explain it."

"Did you switch sides?" Valerie asked. "Are you and Mom fighting each other, now?"

He shook his head.

"No. Never. We just… We've seen different things. Has she had any contact *at all* with the magical community since she hid the two of you?"

Chloe Garner

"What do I know?" Valerie asked darkly, then shook her head. "I don't think so."

He nodded.

"Then she may not know the worst of it. I still fight against the really bad Purist tactics, but… It's about balance. They aren't *all* wrong. Sometimes they make some very strong points."

"But they're *in league* with *demons*," Valerie said, stumbling onto a strong point. He nodded, coming around to sit next to her. She wasn't sure if she wanted him there, but… That was her *dad*. Surely he wasn't *evil*, right?

"It's complicated, honey. I… I'll tell you the truth, okay? Promise. There are things I *can't* tell you, but I'm not going to lie. I *know* demons. I *like* some of them. They're… fun to be around… There are demons out there who are all blood and pain and fear, but there are others who just… It's better to be here than in hell. You know?"

"They're just glad to be here?" Valerie asked mockingly, and he shrugged.

"They've taught The Pure a lot… I mean *a lot* about magic… It's seductive. I can't deny that…"

"Do you do dark magic?" Valerie asked.

He nodded.

"Sometimes. When I need to."

Valerie shifted away.

"I don't even like that they've got ingredients that are more dark than fifty percent, there at the school," she said.

He tipped his head back and laughed.

"That's right," he said. "I hadn't… I'm sorry. I don't know what they've done to my daughter… Hidden her away somewhere or something, but I thought that *everyone* could see through that kludge at this point. It doesn't make *sense* does it? The whole percentage-dark-light thing? And… Debbie Reynolds is teaching the plant-magic there, isn't she? That's what I'd heard. I know for a fact that Debbie uses the light-natural-dark theory configuration in her casting, because she's always been *way* too effective at it. If it weren't for the fact that your grandmother is such a crotchety old witch…"

138

"What now?" Valerie cut in.

"What now what?" Grant asked, stabbing his eggs and chewing at them.

"Light natural dark Mrs. Reynolds, grandmother witch?" Valerie asked.

He sighed.

"You have... I can't believe she didn't teach you *anything*. The old-school way of evaluating magic and its components was on the light-dark scale. Anything that wasn't light was dark. And they were *forever* moving things up and down the scale, trying to weight certain components as more *significant* than others, in order to explain how spells worked out... It was a nightmare. Dozens of witches and sorceresses spent their entire lives categorizing things... And it doesn't *help* understand how things work. It's just an assignment of *value*, which means nothing to anyone except the old guard at the Council who think that anyone who dips below the fifty percent mark is *evil*, and some of the pretentious idiots at Light School."

"Okay," Valerie said slowly. "And what's the new-school thing?"

"There are three branches of magic," Grant said. "Light, natural, and dark. Natural can work with light or with dark, but you have to be quite clever to make light and dark go together. It's really unstable and reactive, when you do, and most of us use a natural magic buffer in order to get the three to play. This is one of the things that the non-propagationist crowd found out from the demons when we first started making contact with them, what forty years ago, now."

"You're learning magic from *demons*?" Valerie asked.

He hesitated.

"Yeah. Here's the thing. Demons only *rarely* lie. I mean, they lie *all the time*, but it's always leading up to some really big, important deception. And the way you get away with a *big* deception is by telling the truth *almost* all the time. There's an art to figuring out what's true and what isn't, when you're getting information from a demon. But. They know so much more about magic than we do."

"Dad," Valerie squawked. "You're learning magic from *demons*."

"Just how to *understand* it," he said. "And, objectively, the system makes more sense, doesn't it? People have aptitudes in the various *kinds* of magic... There's nothing *objectively* lesser about having gifts in natural magic instead of light magic, but the kids with light magic get to go to the best school, while the kids with natural magic go to Survival School or... *worse*... and try to get along with one hand tied behind their back by only using the subset of their components that have been rated 'less dark'. It's idiotic."

"What about *dark* magic?" Valerie pressed. He shrugged.

"That's up to you," he said. "I use it. It's powerful, and useful, and I'm fighting a war. Your mom would never touch it. Not for anything. But. Keep in mind that it's a *gift* to even be able to decide, if you can. Most of the magic community... most of the *world*... they only have the knack for one of the three. I don't even know if you're a mage. Could be you're stuck with natural like the rest of them."

"How would I know?" Valerie asked.

"Entrance testing," Grant said. "At any one of the Separationist schools. Any *one* of them."

"Okay," she said slowly. "And my *grandmother*?"

He nodded, finishing off his eggs and sitting back.

"I don't even know who *remembers* it at this point, but Lady Harrington is your mom's mom."

Valerie stared at him, and he grinned, lifting his head as a door behind her opened.

"Gemma," he called. "Come meet Valerie."

Valerie turned to find a stunning woman coming in through the front door.

"I told you this was a bad idea," the woman said. "You really thought you could steal her out from under Lady Harrington's nose. Now you've got *everybody* looking for you, and someone managed to track you here. We need to go. Now."

Valerie looked back at her father, who pressed his lips, then nodded.

"All right," he said. "All right. I'm not going to apologize. They would have killed her."

The woman looked at Valerie for a moment, then shook her

head.

"Better her than us," she said. Valerie raised her eyebrows.

"Who *is* this woman?" she asked.

"Don't talk about her like that," Grant said to the other woman.

"Look, I *get* the hope that this is going to be your happy little family again someday, I get the sentiment of it. But we're keeping people *alive*. She isn't. The world needs us more. And you... Dammit, Grant, you're going to get us killed."

"All of this is for nothing, if they kill her while I'm off saving the world," Grant said. "I thought you..."

"Nope," Gemma said, cutting in. "I'm not. We need to go. I'm serious. The wards on the house are jangling and I don't know how much longer they're going to hold."

Valerie looked at Grant, who frowned.

"All right. I'm driving."

Gemma sighed, but she nodded, going back out the door. Grant looked at Valerie and sighed, shaking his head.

"I have so much I've wanted to tell you over the years, all of these things I'd planned on telling you and teaching you... But it's never time, is it?"

"Who is she?" Valerie asked. "Do you have another wife?"

"No," he said. "That's your aunt. My sister, Gemma."

"I don't understand," Valerie said as they got into a huge black truck and drove out of the garage. "Mom never said you had a sister."

"Nice to meet you," Gemma said from the front seat. "No hard feelings about you being alive, right? It's a war."

"I don't know yet," Valerie answered. "I mean, you did say he should have let me die. Hard to get past that."

Had they really planned on *killing* her?

She'd had a hold on the door.

It hadn't felt like she was slipping, had it? Could she have held out until Lady Harrington or Mr. Benson got there?

She felt like she could have.

Right?

"Gemma is with The Pure," Grant said. "Close personal friend of Lan Wellington himself."

"May his body feed the magic," Gemma murmured.

"I don't know who that is," Valerie said. "Sorry."

"The first of us," Gemma said. "Leader of The Pure until his death pushed the resistance underground."

"The leader who cursed the Council kids," Valerie said with recognition, and Grant turned back to look at her.

"What do you know about that?" he asked.

"I know that they had an awful lot more kids all at once than any governing body should ever expect to," Valerie said, and Gemma snorted.

"We called them the council bunnies, there for a while. The bed swapping that was going on back in those days…"

Grant cleared his throat, and Gemma shrugged.

"She's a woman, Grant. Not your baby girl. Don't care what daddy lenses you're using to look at her through."

"I understand why my mom didn't ever mention you," Valerie said, and her dad laughed quietly.

"No," Gemma said. "We didn't get along. She never saw a problem she didn't think she couldn't fix it by killing someone."

Valerie's attention jerked back to her dad.

"So she *was* an assassin?" she asked.

Grant looked over his shoulder at her, then back at the road.

"I don't like that word for what she did," he said.

"What she's *doing*," Gemma said. "She's back in the game, isn't she? I *told* you."

"Why are you here?" Valerie asked. "Why are you *helping* her?"

"Because I'm the only friend you've got in the world," Gemma breathed, looking out the window. "You and the rest of the human race."

"*What?*" Valerie asked.

"You shouldn't hint at stuff," Grant said. "Not unless you're willing to back it up."

"I'm allowed to say whatever I want," Gemma said. "She's *your* problem. We just need to get underground. Now."

"What is she talking about?" Valerie asked.

"Stuff that you shouldn't know," Grant said, still gruff at Gemma. "Secrets."

"Why are you *helping* her?" Valerie asked.

The countryside whipped past outside; they were driving down two-lane country roads with huge trees and fields to either side of them.

"Who's coming for us?" Valerie asked.

"That's a valid question," Grant answered. "What did you hear?"

Gemma was silent for a moment, then turned to press her shoulders against the car door as she looked at Grant.

"I *heard* that they knew that Susan was out in the field again, doing her *thing*, and that that meant that your *spawn* would be unprotected. They've all been racing to come up with the best plan to be the first to snag her, as a weapon to use against your wife. And Vince's crew struck some deals and put it into action first."

"I thought it might be them," Grant said. "I might have recognized one of the demons."

"Did you kill them all?" Gemma asked. Grant snorted.

"If I had, they'd have known it was me."

"Yeah, because they *don't* recognize that it was you who came and snatched her out from under their noses," Gemma said.

"I used Pure casting," Grant said. "Old stuff, none of the new stuff."

"You're trying to cast doubt on the Old Guard," Gemma said with some appreciation.

"Why didn't you stop it?" Valerie asked. "If you knew? People were in *danger*."

Gemma snorted, glancing back at her.

"Because I didn't know long enough in advance to lay a plan," she said. "I just barely gave your dad enough heads up to be there before they filleted you."

"So that's it?" Valerie asked. "He walks in the door and takes me out, and neither of you even *care* what happens behind us?"

"I care," Grant said. "I just know that you have to play the long game, not the short game."

"And *students dying* is okay, in your long game?" Valerie

demanded.

Gemma sighed at her.

"You have no *idea* the tradeoffs we have to make day-in and day-out, child. Don't speak that way to us."

"Where are we going?" Valerie demanded. "I want to go back to school."

Maybe her dad was one of the bad guys.

Maybe he was *lying* to her.

He was her father. She *knew* him. But she didn't know him. Had never actually known him.

"I need some time," Grant said. "I need to know that you're going to be okay, going back to them…"

Gemma interrupted him with laughter.

"You think you can protect her from *all sides* wanting her as leverage with a couple of days of daddy-daughter tutoring? We can't *keep* her. You know that as well as your wife did. She's a liability out here. And that school can't keep her *safe*."

"Lady Harrington is a powerful woman," Grant said. "I think she can do it."

"Failed once," Gemma said.

"I still don't see *how*," Grant said. "They teleported in eight demons. How did they get them in?"

"Something was burning," Valerie said. "In the hallway. It left a mark on the wall, and there was a silver… thing… growing in it… *silverthorn*. There was a silverthorn growing in it, and I killed it. Or stopped it. Or whatever."

Gemma looked back at her, twisting hard in her seat.

"They *grew* a silverthorn in Survival School?" she demanded. Valerie shrugged.

"Unless everyone got it wrong. Or I'm remembering it wrong."

"You're remembering it wrong," Gemma said. "There's no way."

"Susan didn't teach her any magic," Grant said. "She's doing her best."

"She *what*?" Gemma asked, twisting again. "Grant, we can't keep her. And you can't teach her enough to survive them… I'm sorry, brother. I really am. But we… More merciful to just drop her off a *cliff*."

"She's a natural," Grant said, sitting up to look at her in the rearview. "Think carefully, Valerie. The silverthorn. Describe it to us."

"Like a pea plant," Valerie said. "Growing up in the middle of bright red blood foam. Made of mercury."

Gemma put her hand over her mouth.

"How did they get a silverthorn to grow?" the woman asked.

"How did you stop it?" Grant asked.

"I told it that that was enough," Valerie said. "I think. I don't remember the exact words."

Ethan had seen something just like it in Europe. She thought about telling them that, but she still wasn't sure what side either of them were on, nor whether Ethan had told her in confidence.

"You told it…" Gemma started, and Grant grinned.

"I told you," he said. "She's a natural. You should have felt the lock she had on the door when I got there. Would have done better trying to go in through the *wall*."

"What happened when you stopped it?" Gemma asked.

"It kind of wilted and died, and then the teachers came and sent us all to our rooms."

Gemma and Grant exchanged glances, and Valerie sat forward in her seat.

"Something happened," she said. "Didn't it? What happened?"

Gemma looked back at her.

"The Pure," she said. "They went to a shopping mall in the middle of flyover country and they killed about three-hundred people. The Council didn't have enough people there to try to fight it, and it ended up getting about a dozen magic users on the Council's side killed. They can't afford to lose that many people, and they're on their heels. The Pure think they can strike a decisive blow against the Council itself and end the war before it even gets going again."

"Was mom one of them?" Valerie asked.

"Your mother doesn't do battle front," Grant said. "If there's a fight *everyone* knows about, she won't have been there. No one will know, the day something goes wrong with her."

"She's going to die alone and no one will *ever* know," Gemma agreed, sitting back against the door again.

"She's unkillable and you know it," Grant answered.

"Why do you hate her?" Valerie asked, and Gemma looked at her innocently.

"Me? Oh, how about the fact that she *abandoned* me to the dark side and never cared if I lived or died? How about that she turned her back on *everything* that we were fighting for in order to protect *one* child? How about she never even *looked* for your father, never asked how he was doing, just took you and disappeared one day?"

"She thought he was dead," Valerie said.

"No she didn't," Gemma said. "She might have lied and told *you* he was dead, but she knew. She knew that if one of The Pure got hold of him, they'd torture him for a year, more, before they'd even consider letting him die. He knows too many valuable things."

Valerie queased, squeezing herself against the seat back, and Grant looked over at Gemma.

"I think I'm about done with you," he said. "If you want to stay in this truck, I think you're done talking."

"Just saying the things no one else is going to tell her," Gemma said, then turned her face away again.

"Where are we going?" Valerie asked.

"A cave network," Grant answered. "We used to use it for cover, a long, long time ago, but at this point almost everyone has forgotten it exists. So we use it to hide out as a last resort. It's not very comfortable, but magic doesn't work right there, so no one uses it for fear of hurting themselves."

"And what then?" Valerie asked.

"A very good question," Gemma said.

"Well, Gemma is going to go back to work," Grant said pointedly, "and we're going to train."

"Train at what?" Valerie asked.

"Self-defense, mostly," Grant said. "A little bit of test magic, to make sure that if something happens, you have the best chance of seeing it coming. Maybe some offensive magic, if we get going."

"You think she's going to be ready?" Gemma asked.

"They don't let me *touch* potion ingredients at school, because of what happened," Valerie said.

"And what happened?" Grant asked.

"I made a neurotoxin and a bomb," Valerie asked.

"Simultaneous or separate?" Gemma asked, looking at her with interest once more.

"A neurotoxin bomb?" Valerie asked. "No. They were separate."

"Oh," Gemma said with a shrug.

"Not surprising that they have no idea what to do with you," Grant said. "Teaching a natural is notoriously difficult."

"How are we supposed to train if we're inside caves that make it impossible to do magic?" Valerie asked.

"There are holes in the effect," Grant said. "Your mom and I mapped them, a long time ago. If you don't know where they are, you'd never be able to find them on the fly, but I know where we'll be safe."

The casual mention of her mom... of a time before Valerie had even been born... It hurt her chest. She still didn't trust him, though.

"I think I should just go back to school," she said.

Gemma snorted, but kept her thoughts to herself.

"I understand," Grant said. "That's where your mom put you, and I'm basically a stranger. But you have *my* magic. And no one is going to know how to train you to use it like I will. And I'd love to say that, if you insist, I'll just take you back to school, but I'm not taking you back until I know that you have *some* chance of surviving it. That's just... how it is."

"Your daddy is kidnapping you," Gemma said cheerfully.

"Are you enjoying this?" Grant asked, and Gemma nodded. "Immensely."

"Are you evil?" Valerie asked.

Gemma looked at her sideways, not hardly as bothered by the question as Valerie had hoped.

"No," she said. "I just know what it looks like."

Grant turned off of the little road onto a strip of gravel that wandered through thick, overgrown forest. Eventually he pulled

Chloe Garner

off of that and turned off the engine.

"You have supplies?" Gemma asked, and Grant nodded.

"I keep it topped up, here," he said. "Checked it a month ago."

"All right." The woman leaned across her seat to hug Grant with real affection, then Grant looked back at Valerie.

"We're here," he said. "We need to let Gemma get back before someone notices she's gone."

Valerie looked at the woman, who gave her an odd look.

"I know you think I'm just... terrible. I'm not. It's just... hard... It's hard to do the right thing when it means people are going to die. You don't *come back* from that. And the longer you do it... the less you recognize yourself in the mirror. I get why your mom ran away. I just... I thought that she would be out here, doing the right thing, long after the rest of us gave up. Shook me, down deep, that she'd do it when things were... They weren't *easy*, because it's never easy, but... It was as close as we ever got. And she gave up and ran away... For you."

Grant came around to open Valerie's door as Gemma slid across the front bench to sit at the driver's seat.

"You're just going to let her drive away and leave us here in the middle of nowhere?" Valerie asked.

"Way it has to be," Grant answered. "She'll come back as soon as she can."

"When will that be?" Valerie asked.

"Probably a couple of weeks, at least," Gemma said. "Have to wait for everything to cool down again before I sneak off."

"Weeks?" Valerie asked, but Grant had already shut her door and Gemma was backing back onto the road again. "Weeks?"

"How long did you think it was going to take to train you?" Grant asked. "An afternoon seminar?"

"You... No," Valerie said. "No. Make her come back. Call her. I can't *be* out here for *weeks*. I have classes and homework and studying to do. And... That's where Mom sent me. They're good people."

"They are, actually," Grant said. "I know a lot of them personally, though it's been a long time."

"They're going to be worried about me."

148

He grinned.

"There, you underestimate me," he said. "Come on. We need to get underground before the shade deserts us."

Valerie followed him, feeling more exposed and alone than she had even the first day of school.

Was her father crazy? Was that why her mother had let Valerie believe he was dead?

Was he on the wrong side?

Was he going to hold her here forever, just stretching it a little bit at a time, letting her believe he would let her go *soon*, just not now?

He glanced back at her once, but the undergrowth was thick and the trees overhead covered the ground with roots that would take you out if you lost focus.

Eventually they came to a glorified hole in the ground, dark and the size of a large animal den. Grant knelt, looking down inside it, then nodded.

"It's just the way I left it," he said. "Come on."

"Are you sure this is a good idea?" Valerie asked, but he was already moving, crawling on hands and knees down into the earth. Valerie squatted, then leaned back to walk on her heels and her palms, scooting down the steep entrance.

After the bright light outside, even in shadow, the dim of the cave was blindingly dark.

Grant pulled her up onto her feet, putting his hand on top of her head.

"It's still a little low here," he said. "Don't stand up tall until you're sure you don't have something above you."

He spoke a word, and a small gold flame appeared in his palm that lit the entire room.

For a moment, Valerie was devastated that his 'cave system' was just a dug-out little hole in the dirt, that her father was delusional and dangerous, then she saw the small gap in the dirt, there in the floor, and she followed him over, sliding once more down a steep floor and into…

One of the most beautiful places she'd ever seen.

The gold of the flame turned slightly silver and choked off, but the light was still enough to reflect on a room of solid blue crystals. The floor under her feet had once been a part of them, but it had been walked to dust. All around them, the walls, the ceiling, the floor were covered in the blue crystal growths, and they radiated an energy that Valerie didn't have words for.

"Wow," Valerie breathed.

"Welcome to the dark gardens," Grant answered. "The Pure think that all magic is the same, that there are those who can use it and those who can't. And that those who can't are inferior to those who can."

"The Superiors," Valerie said. He sighed.

"Yes. It's such a simplified view of their philosophy, though. They think that those who have the ability to do magic, who actually *cultivate* that ability… that they are the only ones who deserve it. That embracing magic is what *makes* them superior. Not that their superiority makes them able to embrace magic, you see?"

"Maybe," Valerie said, still taken with the crystals. Grant began walking once more, looking around.

"I have things to tell you that I need to know aren't going to make it back to Lady Harrington or anyone else at school, and particularly not to anyone on the Council," he said.

"Why?" Valerie asked.

"Because the Council leaks like a sieve, and ever since Lan died, The Pure have been devastatingly thorough in documenting who knows what and who thinks what. If the wrong thoughts reach the Council, those thoughts will *immediately* go to The Pure, who will know what path they took. Does that make sense? Almost anything I tell you that isn't common knowledge amongst the resistance could be the thing that gets Gemma killed."

"Gemma," Valerie said. "Why her?"

"She's my spy," Grant said. "My agent. I send her in to them every single day in hopes that we can avoid or prevent the shopping mall incident from yesterday. If we can find out in time, we can get the Council to send the right people, or we can derail it from this side and make it so that it isn't worth doing."

"What went wrong yesterday?" Valerie asked.

"I didn't find out in time," Grant said. "And I was kind of

already en route to come get you, by the time Gemma knew for sure that it was happening. They're getting *faster*, these days. They all still think Gemma is loyal, but... we're having to do three times as much work to figure out how to route information so that it isn't clear who sent it. There are only so many scapegoats you can use without getting them all slaughtered."

Valerie followed him through a narrow gap in the crystal room, like leaving a geode, and into a much more run-of-the-mill wet-walled cave.

"Anyway, all of that to say that The Pure admire where magic takes root and spreads in a way that validates its primacy. The Dark Garden is a Pure name for that cave. The magic is what's growing the garden, not the light..."

He went to a cooler sitting on the ground against a wall and opened it.

"It isn't cold, but it's clean," he said, getting out a bottle of water. Valerie drained it without having realized she was thirsty.

"You keep enough food out here for *weeks*?" Valerie asked.

"I do," he said. "For ten or fifteen, depending. This is my refuge. I want it to hold up as long as I need it."

Valerie went to sit on the cooler, looking around.

When he closed his hand and the flame there went out, it was going to be pitch black.

"This is where I live now," she murmured.

"It isn't *that* bad," he said, flicking his hand toward the wall. The orange flame in his palm stretched across the gap, finding a torch there and lighting it, and then leaping again to another torch some way down the wall from there.

"No, that's much homier," Valerie answered. "They're going to be worried about me."

He came to stand in front of her.

"They aren't, actually," he said. "Well, the next couple of weeks are likely going to be very strange for a lot of them, but at the end it's all going to work out."

"What does that mean?" Valerie asked.

He nodded.

"I have a gift with time. It's a tricky magic to master, and that's why I went after it. You can't *freeze* time. It won't go that far. But if you're clever, you can make it not go and then go, and you can change how fast it's going here compared to there, as long as it all catches up in the end."

"Okay," Valerie said.

"That's how I got you out," he said. "And it's how I'm going to fill in the time you're gone. When you get back, it'll all go at once, and you aren't going to feel like you *did* all of it, but you'll remember it, and so will everyone else."

"That makes no sense," Valerie said, and he shook his head.

"Not intended to. Just informing you that you don't have to worry about what Lady Harrington or Mr. Benson or anyone else is thinking, right now."

Valerie shook her head.

"What side are you on?" she asked. "I don't know how to trust you."

He narrowed his eyes for a moment, then looked around.

"As long as you're here, you're welcome to take a torch and go exploring. If you get lost, just put the torch out, and I'll come find you. You can do whatever you want with your spare time. But we're going to train. Because you are weak and alone, and I won't stand by for that. You can trust me or not trust me about anything I *say*. I can see that now, that it's not going to be possible to just jump in, like that. But what I care about *most* is that you can defend yourself, and *that*? You oughtn't need to trust me for that part."

Valerie nodded slowly.

"Okay," she said.

He waved her forward.

"Then let's get started."

The first couple of days were very much like her self-defense classes as a kid. How did she stand, how did she move, how did she block and defend against various kinds of magic attacks.

The thing was, her body was *made* for magic. The more she did, the more she could see how true it was. She could block a fireball with her palms, and if she spoke the right word, it wouldn't even touch her. Her father could try to rip her apart or blind her or any of a dozen other things to hurt her or disorient her, and she could block each one of them almost without thinking.

All he had to do was give her the clue to what it was she needed to do, and she *could* do it.

This wasn't like learning the kinds of pall-plants, where she had to work so *hard* to get the information to stick in her brain.

No.

No, all she had to do was think 'leg drops back, deflect not absorb' and half of his casts just dropped to the ground, broken or deflected or whatever else it was that happened to magic energy that was cast and never landed.

He barely had to speak a word to explain the difference between one type of cast and another. They just felt *real* and *easy*, like she'd been learning in a foreign language her entire life and now someone was finally speaking her *native* language.

They worked for hours at a time, few words, lots of magic, and then he'd let her loose while he rested and made plans.

He said that casting was always more energy-consuming than defending, and that that was the power of the School of Magic Survival - if you focused on survival, you always put yourself at the advantage.

Valerie had asked how the advantage of surprise weighed into that, and he'd sent her out on a walk.

The cave system just went on and on, twisting and splitting and reconverging. She hadn't gone far, the first time, but each time he gave her a break she wandered further, watching the shapes of the walls and the ceilings and the floors, the path of water through limestone for an era.

She came back on the afternoon of the second day - it *felt* like afternoon, though she hadn't been up to check the sun and neither of them wore a watch - and sat down across from her father.

"Lady Harrington," she said. "How can she be my grandmother?"

"She's your mom's mom," he said, looking up from a pad of paper. "Back when we were in school, she was the headmistress at Survival School, and there was this *thing* about Susan going to Light school even though Lady Harrington was the headmistress at Survival School, but… You know, people just forget. You stop saying anything about it, stop bringing it up, they stop thinking about it… I know everyone on the council still remembers, but the younger magic users, even the ones who were *at* school with us… They mostly don't even know."

"Why didn't *she* say anything?" Valerie asked.

"Because she's Lady Harrington, I expect," he said. "She didn't want anyone to think that she was biased, concerning you."

Valerie frowned.

"You don't like her," she said.

"Never much mattered," he answered.

Valerie fidgeted for a minute.

"Tell me about the curse?"

"What do you think you know?" he asked.

"That they can't get into light school because their magic is too dark," Valerie said.

He waited.

"Is that it?"

She shrugged.

"I guess."

He shook his head.

"They buried that one good and deep then," he said.

"What does it mean?" Valerie asked.

"In demonic mythology, groups of five have importance. Their powers are amplified by each other, and they have fated significance. The five children of the Council are cursed with dark powers, it's true, but the cast wasn't entirely dark. The person who killed Lan mixed their magic into the cast, and those five are also likely to be the only ones who can win the war."

"What?" Valerie asked, thinking of the table of kids she'd sat with. "*Them?*"

"I don't know if they even know," Grant said. "Don't know what their parents might have been telling them all these years. Maybe just that they're touched with the darkness and nothing more. But that's the understanding I had, from way back in the day."

"Why aren't they being trained, then?" Valerie asked.

"They're at Survival School," Grant told her. "What else do you expect them to do?"

"*Tell* them that they have to go win the war," Valerie demanded. "Tell them how important it is, and make sure that they're actually working hard so that they'll be able to."

He shrugged.

"Don't know what to tell you. The Council has never really been marked with *wisdom* in my book. Just bossiness and a lot of resources."

"They're supposed to win the war with *dark* magic?" Valerie asked. "That doesn't seem right."

"The world isn't all light-and-dark in an eternal struggle for domination," Grant said. "Sometimes dark fights dark and sometimes light fights light. Though, I'll admit, there isn't much *light* magic running around on the Separatist side. A few, but mostly natural magic."

"Was Mom the one to kill the old Purist leader?" Valerie asked. He shook his head.

"No, but I know she was there," he said. "I don't actually know who did it. The story about the curse is third-hand at best."

She sighed.

If her mom was going to be an assassin, the least she could be was the one who took out the leader of the genocidal maniacs.

"There are a lot of things you would be better off knowing," Grant said after a minute. "But I can't tell you, because if you let on that you know them, they'll know that you've been talking to someone with Separatist knowledge, and I don't want to open up that can of worms."

"Then why do you keep mentioning it?" Valerie asked.

"Because it bothers me that you aren't asking the right questions," Grant said.

"All right," Valerie pressed. "What should I be asking?"

"Why do they want to kill everyone?" he asked. "And why are they so bad at it?"

Valerie paused.

Considered.

"Yeah," she said. "I mean, there are people *everywhere*, and they have to all show up at once to kill them?"

He shook his head.

"You've fallen for war propaganda," he said. "You're willing to see the opposition as stupid, mindless killing machines with various degrees of competency. Some days I'm pretty sure the Council has fallen for their own line. But The Pure aren't like that. They don't *want* to kill civilians."

"Okay," Valerie said slowly. "Are you telling me that the mass casualties are because of collateral damage? That they were all just there at the wrong place at the wrong time?"

He shook his head.

"No, you aren't *thinking*," he said. "*Think*."

She sat down finally, closing her eyes.

"If I was a psycho killer, what would I be doing it for?" Valerie asked.

"Why is the right question," Grant said.

"I'm really *good* at killing people. Poisons and neurotoxins and bombs are really *easy* to make, and then you just… send them out and let them do their thing. Killing *lots* of people is hard, though, without getting caught. So am I practicing? Trying out different weapons to kill people, looking for the one that I can deploy fast enough to wipe out the entire civilian population? But then why would I want to do that? Because I'm an egocentric jerk who believes that people without magic don't deserve to live…?"

"You might have found two people who ascribed to that, during the last war," Grant said. "But not the hundreds it took to do what they're doing. Keep going."

She opened her eyes.

"I don't *know*," she said. "Stop playing with me."

"This is part of your training," he answered. "You have to learn how to *think*, because casting is all about knowing who your enemy is, what his weaknesses are, and what you *want* to happen. If you can't see down the road at least that far, your spells aren't going to *do* what you want them to."

"So I'm not an egocentric jerk who likes watching people die," Valerie said. "Why do I kill them?"

"You *must* ask this question any time you're looking at the potential of fighting someone. Why do *they* want to kill *you*, and why do *you* want to kill *them*? If you don't have an answer, you're only fifty-fifty, betting on dumb luck that you're on the right side."

That actually made an awful lot of sense, to Valerie.

"They don't deserve to live," Valerie said. "I kill them because they don't matter. But why go to such *lengths* to kill them? Why be so *organized* about it? Why not just curse people as they go by on the street, and get on with my life? Is it so important that it's worth a *war*?"

"Good," Grant said. "Now. They don't *mean* to kill the people they kill."

"How do you know?" Valerie asked.

"If they did, for one, they'd stick around and finish the job. Instead, they come, they curse, they fight the Council when the Council's fighters show up to try to stop them or to try to lift the curse, but they don't double down and make sure people die."

"I'm not impressed," Valerie said. She heard Grant laugh.

"How about this?" he asked, then. "How about I asked Gemma why they're doing it."

"She's your sister," Valerie said. "You might trust her, but I don't, and not just anyone has access to a sibling who is on the other side."

"And as well-positioned as she is," Grant agreed. "I started trying to convince them, long ago, and that was part of how I figured out that my liaison to the Council was compromised. No one ever heard anything I had to say about it, and they started looking for a mole."

"Why does Gemma say they're doing it?" Valerie asked, opening her eyes. "Killing people at random."

He shook his head.

"This is the big secret, Valerie. If they find out that you know it, Gemma will probably end up dead."

"She didn't really like me very much anyway," Valerie said, and he gave her an exasperated look. "Fine. Okay, fine. I won't tell them."

"That none of *them* seem to ask bothers me more than

anything," he said after a moment, then folded his arms across his chest and drew a deep breath. "They aren't *trying* to kill anyone. What they're trying to do is separate people from their native magic ability, so that the magic users who presently exist will *truly* be the only magic users out there."

"And that's worth going to war over?" Valerie asked, and he shrugged.

"Depends on how you feel about it. A lot of the Separatists just want to be left alone, but The Pure think that they ought to be *choosing* who is able to use magic in order to make sure that they aren't dangerous to the community, and the non-propagationist crowd just wants to stop *all* new magic."

"Why?" Valerie asked. "I mean, how many people are we *talking* about, who are learning new magic? Is it just the students at the schools?"

He shook his head.

"Any person out there in the world is going to have *some* latent magical ability. It's inborn, and there isn't a lot you can do to change your own potential. It's that very few of them are ever going to find someone with the ability to awaken that potential and teach them how to use it that keeps them from becoming magic users, themselves."

"So *Hansen* could learn magic?" Valerie asked. Grant sighed.

"Without even knowing who that is, categorically, the answer is yes."

"Why do they care?" Valerie asked. "What business is it of theirs?"

"Magic is dangerous," Grant said. "Everyone agrees on that. It's why we have the schools. A long time ago, a group of magic users got together and established places where young people could come and learn their magic from dedicated professionals who have a vested interest in them doing so safely. The world is *full* of magic users who didn't graduate from one of our schools, though, and even the ones who do… They become *dangerous* people, with skills that the average person can't combat, can't defend. There's no Hippocratic Oath to magic. Once you know what you're doing, it's between you and your conscience and what the rest of the magic community is prepared to stop."

"Okay," Valerie said. "So why are they killing everyone instead?"

"There you go," he said. "Because it turns out that separating a person from their magic ability kills them."

Valerie paused.

"Okay. Then why keep trying?"

"Because they've had limited success on individual cases, where they used highly-targeted magic or did something clever to hide away the ability rather than remove it. But every time they try to weaponize it, instead of getting a silent epidemic, they get a very sudden mass murder."

"Why have I never heard about this on the news?" Valerie asked.

"Magic," Grant answered. "A lot of work and a lot of magic, trying to keep everything underground. And they stopped for... a long, long time because one of their key scientists accidentally destroyed her own magic and then died about eighteen months later. And the war took away a lot of their resources. But with the Council cracking down and driving more Separatists into the fold, The Pure think they have their window to go for it, and they've... Well, they've done it."

"Why didn't you stop them?" Valerie asked.

He looked toward the cave entrance for a moment, considering.

"That's what's hollowed Gemma out," he said. "Not being able to fix it every time. This is one where she found out too late, and we couldn't get the information routed to the Council in time."

"And a lot of people died," Valerie said, not accusing. He nodded.

"A lot of people died."

"Because they failed. Again."

"Because The Pure failed again," Grant agreed.

"Why doesn't Mom stop it?" Valerie asked. Grant snorted.

"She's always had it in her head that she *could*," he said. "I'm not certain that she wasn't the one who caused the accident that ultimately killed the Separatist scientist. I don't know what she's doing. No one has heard from her since the whole thing started."

"You don't know how to find her and ask?" Valerie asked. He laughed at this.

"No one knows how to find your mom when she doesn't want to be found," he said. "There's no telling what resources the Council used to track her down, with you."

"How did you find each other before, when I was conceived?" Valerie asked.

He hesitated.

Tipped his head at her.

"Now there is Susan Blake's daughter," he said. "I don't know if it would work, but I could probably try. Seeing as she might think I'm dead, the odds go down, but it's an interesting tactic."

"How did you find each other?" Valerie asked. He shook his head.

"That magic is over your head, just now. You need to practice."

She sighed, and he grinned.

"Defend yourself."

She was learning *so* much.

Her father was right - he understood how she thought so much better than anyone at school, and he trusted her to try things and that her mistakes wouldn't kill the both of them. She was picking up some languages for spoken casting, and her mixed potions were... She could actually *choose* what some of them were going to be in advance.

It was the procedural magic, though, the ritualistic and pattern-based stuff that was really coming home for her.

It was fun.

If she'd been willing to admit it, it was the most fun she'd had in as long as she could remember. Magic was *real*, and it was a field for her to play in. Her father didn't constrain her by what she was doing or how, so long as it worked, and he often sat and watched her casting with an odd expression on his face that she'd come to recognize as an affection for the memory of her mother.

Mostly, though, she resented being here.

There was nothing to do when he got tired of her during the

afternoons, and there was no one to commiserate with when he lost his temper at her or mocked her mother for failing to teach her anything of importance.

There were only so many times that Valerie could stand up for her mother before it became pointless and frustrating for both of them.

Sitting down at their evening meal one night almost two weeks after he'd taken her out of the School of Magic Survival, he handed her a bag of trail mix and a bottle of water.

"I need to tell you that I'm not the man your mother married," he said, sitting back against a wall and propping his heel up on his toes.

Valerie looked at him benignly for a moment, then raised her eyebrows and shook her head.

"All right," she said. "Who are you, then?"

"I certainly used to be," he said. "But your mother... She has sort of a marvelous stabilizing influence on everyone around her."

"The assassin," Valerie said. For weeks, maybe even months now she'd been feeling like maybe she'd *never* known her mother.

"Yes, the assassin," he said. "But that *really* isn't what she does. Anyway, no, I don't think she would even *love* me, anymore, if we didn't have history. Maybe she wouldn't love me at all. I was never... I'm good at magic. At Light School, that's all anyone tends to see, that you're better than everyone else. It made me into the golden boy, right up with her, king and queen of the prom, if you will. But I wasn't even really ever that guy, even back then. And... There weren't a lot of people who knew it, but your mom was one of them. And she didn't care. She saw what was *good* in me, and she loved me for it."

He shifted, looking down at his feet for several moments before he spoke again.

"I always wanted to be the man that she thought I could be... I got close, there for a while. We fought the war, we had you... we were powerful. But..." He shook his head. "You shouldn't judge her for what I am now. I'm not who I was. And I can blame the war, to everyone else, but I have to tell you the truth. It's because she isn't there anymore."

He looked Valerie in the eye again, and she blinked, looking at her knees.

"I loved her," he said. "I want you to know that. I still do. But whatever you may think of me, don't put that on her."

"I feel like I never knew her at all," Valerie said. "She never talked about anything that happened before I was born. I mean, at all. I had the pictures of you, but she didn't even talk about that. Everything was a secret and I never had any idea at all."

"She was protecting you," Grant said after a moment. "I can see it now. I thought... Well, nevermind what I thought. She could see the future for you, the way it was, and she took you out of it. I'm thinking that maybe I never looked at it from her perspective, how you would have grown up. I still can't believe she didn't teach you a stitch of magic, but... Getting you away from the council... I'd have done it, now, but back then I never would have gone along, even if I'd have been there to discuss it with her. She did right by you."

Valerie was about to say something - she really was - though she wasn't ever going to find out what.

"Get down," Grant shouted, leaping toward her and shoving her to the side as something very loud and very hot went past.

Valerie scrambled off of the ground, trying to get her feet under her without getting up as a face disappeared around a corner.

"Defend yourself," Grant growled, working his thumbs over his fingers as he stared at the doorway.

Valerie ran to the table of casting ingredients, her hands finding things - some of which she'd used and some of which she'd never touched before - and she started mixing.

Crush, strip, drown, mix, and then she was looking at a rapidly-congealing ball in the bottom of the mortar and pestle. The vanny powder had desiccated the genua oil, leaving a sticky lump that was holding all of the rest of the ingredients together.

And she didn't know what to do with it.

It felt, for a moment, like playing mud-pies in the back lot with Hanson, having pulled together all of the various things available to mix with the mud, it really left little to do with it but start over.

On a reflex, she fished the mass out of the mortar and tossed it behind her, reaching for a stack of ben reeds. She would split them along their fibrous axis and take the individual hairs out...

Something behind her lit off with a whoosh of flame, and Valerie turned to find an arc of purple flame that ran from floor to ceiling in the red-rock cave. Grant was shouting, and there was a fight going on, on the other side of that wall, but it put out enough noise that it was hard to hear specifically what was going on, and she could only just see it in the occasional gaps in the flame.

It was a gorgeous purple.

She'd never known anything would burn that color.

Struggling *not* to be distracted by it, she returned to the... the reedy thing there whose name she had *just* known, stripping fibers out of it and...

... tying bows.

Tying freaking bows.

Why?

Like anyone was going to tell her.

She tried to ignore the violence of noise going on behind her and continued to work.

Defense?

Maybe.

She wasn't *quite* ready to give it that much credit, unless you went with the 'good offense' version of the idea, but she'd kept them away from her as her father fought.

She marked her arms, back of the wrist to the outside of her elbow on both sides, with a bluegreen paint that she'd made, as Grant looked over his shoulder.

"You need to get out," he said. "Now."

"And go where?" Valerie asked, putting a hand up and speaking the four words he'd taught her to stop heat-based magic. The paint on her arm sizzled, but it held.

"Up and out," he said, grabbing something off of the table and starting to mark the floor with it. There were words from around the corner that Valerie couldn't make out, but Grant lifted his head to listen for just a moment.

"And *then* what?" Valerie asked.

"If you stay down here, you will die," he said.

"I thought that using magic down here was impossible," Valerie said.

"Supposed to be," he answered. "We're standing in one of the biggest holes in that rule, and apparently these guys don't know the risks they're taking, casting so close to the cave's affect. Either way, I need you out of here so I can take care of just myself."

"I'm doing my job," Valerie protested and he nodded exaggeratedly.

"The gusset flame was impressive. I'll give you that. And you… I'm proud of you. But you have to get out. I'm going down there, down that way, and they aren't going to see you. They'll think you came with me. You sneak out behind them and you just *run*, okay?"

"No," Valerie said. "I'm staying with you."

"No," he said, shaking his head and very quickly reaching up to take her chin between his thumb and the crook of his index finger. "No, you're going to *live*, because that's what we're good at. And the way you live is…" He pointed. "That way."

He continued working, smashing two sets of ingredients together in his palms, then listening for another moment.

"Five seconds," he said. "Then you move. And you go as fast as you can. Okay?"

"Dad," she said.

He gave her a quick smile, then nodded.

"Trust me," he said, putting both hands on the ground in front of her feet. "Don't move until the time is up."

Four.

Three.

Two.

The men came around the corner and Grant took off like he was unprepared. Valerie only just managed to stifle the instinct to go after him, as the men gave chase, a blue electricity crackling among them.

One.

Zero.

They took another second to make it out the other doorway into a narrower section of cave that led to a section that had some beautiful white crystals growing along the corners. Valerie watched after them, then bolted the way they'd come.

She hadn't been out of the caves since she'd come down with Grant, but she had a pretty good idea the path back out, as she'd covered almost all of it every day since she'd been there.

She hit sunlight and threw both arms across her face, even as she knew it was only dusk.

"Over here, kid," a voice called, and Valerie squinted to find Gemma sitting on the hood of the hug black truck. Valerie looked over her shoulder.

"You have to help him," she said. "They're chasing him…"

The ground shook and Valerie stumbled.

"Over here," Gemma said again flatly. "It isn't for us to help him fight. We just sit up here and wait to see who survives. Like always."

Valerie walked away from the cave entrance backwards, watching it as a plume of dust shot out of the earth.

"Where's their car?" Valerie asked.

"Apparently they didn't know *exactly* where the cave was," Gemma said. "They parked about a mile away, back that way."

She motioned with her thumb.

"And you were just going to sit up here and wait?" Valerie asked. "Why didn't you warn us?"

"You think you get cell reception down there?" Gemma asked. "You're lucky I found out about it at all. I've only been here about a minute and a half."

There was another large explosion that Valerie felt with her feet more than she heard it, and she looked at Gemma with urgency.

"Please," she said. "Please go help him."

"Not my job," Gemma said. "If he loses, somebody has to go back and keep an eye on The Pure and let the Council know when they're about to go kill another stadium full of people."

Valerie let her shoulders drop.

"You'd let him die for that?" she asked.

Gemma gave her a hard look, then shook her head.

"I'm no good to him. Didn't train at spellcasting like he and your mom did. What I'm good at is politics and reading lies. It's exceedingly hard to lie to me. Makes me everybody's favorite person, once they're up high in leadership. Makes me pointless in combat." She paused. "But if they kill him, I will kill you myself, for putting him in this position."

"No," Valerie said after a moment. She went to climb up onto the hood of the truck next to Gemma. "No, you won't. Because that isn't who you are. You might leave me for *them* to kill me, or just leave me to certain death from exposure, because that's *fate* killing me, or whatever. But you aren't going to kill me. You still think you're one of the good guys."

Gemma looked directly at her for a moment.

"Think you've got it all figured out, don't you?" she asked. "You've never been betrayed by someone you love, and you've never *betrayed* someone you cared about. Maybe you're right about me killing you by negligence rather than with a weapon, but that smug happy idea that you've got the world on a string is going to be all the more painful when you lose it for how certain you are of it."

"How did they find him?" Valerie asked. "I thought no one knew about this place."

The truck rocked back and forth.

"From the way they're going after him, they *don't* know about this place," Gemma said. "Best guess is that they tracked you. You've got something on you that they got a hook into, and it took them this long to resolve the magic down to where they could find you. If they've got the right magic and actually stopped to *think* before they went charging down there, they'll have figured out it was your dad who took you, and he's dead, whether or not he walks back out of that cave, right now."

Valerie shuddered.

"You need to hear it like it is," Gemma said. "Been protected too long in the bubble your mom made, and then again at school. This idea that students can just *be*, can just blithely go about their days like nothing is going on out here? Those days are coming to an end, and *fast*."

"Is that how it was before?" Valerie asked, and Gemma shook her head.

"The Pure have their game together. Took a long time for the

Council to form, the first time, so they think that they're a long way ahead, compared to last time, but The Pure know what they're up against, and they know where the weak points are. *You* are a weak point. They are going to come for you, they are going to come for the sons and daughters of every man and woman fighting them. They believe that hard that magic is a danger to humanity and that it should be purged from the latent population. You are just the collateral damage required to distract and disable your mother."

There was another shudder and Gemma slid off the truck, standing with her shoulders up, alert, and watching the hole in the ground where a slight kick-up of dust followed the unheard explosion.

Valerie had very little available to her to defend herself with, at this point, but she went to stand a few strides away from Gemma, braced. If they beat her dad, they at least had to go through her.

"Tell me again why we didn't run?" Valerie asked.

"Because if they know that your father is alive, they know that I'm a traitor, and I'm dead no matter what happens next," Gemma said. "And because if he needs me, I will be here."

There was a howl from underground, a man's voice triumphant, and Gemma relaxed.

"Now that is something you don't get to do every day," Grant said, climbing up out of the cave and shaking off his shirt.

"Should have left her to die," Gemma said. "You've compromised *both* of our major safehouses."

"I have more," Grant said, grinning. He had blood rolling down the side of his face from a cut up at his hairline, and little pockmarks on the other cheek like something had exploded near his face, but he was happy.

"None so readily available at need," Gemma said.

"You need to take her back to school," Grant said.

"I'll do no such thing," Gemma said, taking half a step back.

"Yes, you will," Grant said. "Because I need to clean up here and finish the spell to close out the time loop, so that they stop looking."

Gemma sighed.

"You take such risks," she said. "She isn't *worth* all this."

"And yet, I'm the one who gets to choose," Grant said, brushing dust and debris out of his hair. "I'll see you in Macon."

Gemma sighed.

"I can't drive up to the school," she said. "They'll know I was there. I don't have your warding."

"The truck will make it," Grant said.

"I don't know where it is," Gemma said, as though it was a trump card.

"Valerie does," Grant said. "Stop arguing. This isn't negotiable."

"Less and less is, it seems," Gemma said, then shook her head and turned to go back to the truck.

"Wait, no," Valerie said. Grant looked at her expectantly and Valerie paused, wondering if this wasn't *really* what she wanted, anyway. To go back where her mother had put her, where she trusted the adults and she wasn't in the middle of a war.

Well...

She hoped she wasn't in the middle of a war.

"Why won't you take me?" Valerie asked.

"I can't go back, darling," he said. It was the first time she could think of that he'd used a term of familiarity like that. He was still radiating enthusiasm from the fight. "Lady Harrington will have fixed the holes I used to get in, the first time. Gemma can, because her magic is so much *quieter* than mine, but once she lets you out of the truck, you're going to have to move fast. Things are going to be collapsing behind you. Best if you run, actually."

"Wait," Valerie said more emphatically. "When will I see you again?"

He paused.

"Wasn't sure if you would," he said.

"You're my *dad*," she said. "I've thought you were dead my entire life. I want to see you again."

He shook his head.

"Then come fight," he said quietly. "Only way I come back is if the war is well and truly over."

He held up a hand as Gemma laid on the horn.

"I'm not going there after dark," the woman yelled out the

window. "Not even for Grant Blake."

Valerie looked over her shoulder at the truck, then turned back to say something else to her dad - she didn't even know what - but he was already underground again.

She sighed and went to get in the truck.

Gemma was quiet for a long time.

A very long time.

Long enough that Valerie had long begun to wonder if the radio was broken, because that much silence had to be uncomfortable for *anyone*.

"It will be… strange… when you get back," the woman finally said to her.

"Okay," Valerie said. "Lots of new secrets to keep, training with my dad to disguise…"

"Oh," Gemma laughed. "That's *normal*. The strange part will be that you never left."

Valerie started to respond to that, then closed her mouth again and frowned.

"Okay," she said slowly. "Clearly I did."

She'd totally forgotten to try to get in touch with Sasha to let her know that she was okay.

Felt bad about that.

"No," Gemma said. "You'll even *remember* what you did while you were there. You never left. Whatever story your father invented for everyone to believe, you've been walking around there at the school from the night he took you. No one will ever know that you were gone unless they intentionally go looking for magic."

Valerie felt her mouth fall open.

"That's not possible," she said.

"Technically, you're right," Gemma said.

Valerie waited.

And waited a bit more.

"But…" Valerie prompted. Gemma snorted.

"Don't try to get me to explain it to you," she said. "I'm just a human lie detector. I haven't got useful or interesting magic, when it comes to being out here in the field."

"I'm going to *remember*?" Valerie asked.

"You are," Gemma said. "And you'll have to deal with having dual memories for the rest of your life. At some point, you'll probably lose some time, minutes here and a few hours there, as your brain tries to work it out. It's a very delicate instrument, your brain. Doesn't like knowing two things were true when it's only possible for one of them to have been true."

Valerie frowned at this, pressing her shoulder against the car door.

"Has it happened to you?" she asked.

"Only reason I'm alive," Gemma said after a moment. "Several times over."

"Does it hurt?" Valerie asked.

"Not for me," Gemma said. "Can't say, for you."

"But I wasn't *there*," Valerie said. Gemma shrugged.

"Gotta deal with it for yourself," she said, then went silent again.

She didn't speak again the entire rest of the trip.

"You have to tell me where the driveway is," Gemma said as the sun began to set off to Valerie's right.

"I don't know," Valerie answered.

"I know it's on this road," Gemma said. "But I can't *see* it, and you can."

Valerie sat forward, pointing.

"That one? Maybe?"

"More specific," Gemma said, slowing.

"You can't see it?" Valerie asked.

"I know within a mile where it is," Gemma told her. "I'm going to drive off the road on your say-so."

"Okay," Valerie said. "Um. Slower?"

"Gotta be specific," Gemma said. "If you get me stuck, everyone is going to die."

Valerie glanced at her.

"You say that a lot," she said, and Gemma shrugged.

"It's true more of the time than people want to hear."

"Why didn't Dad bring me?" Valerie asked. "Slower. It's right... right there, that... by the tree."

"Lots of trees," Gemma said, the truck at a crawl. "He had to clean up the caves. Undoubtedly they tried to use magic against him and fried themselves. Bodies and cave-ins to fix."

"There," Valerie said. "The... bendy tree... Yes, there from... no, on the other *side* of the bendy tree."

"Not helping," Gemma said.

"Doing my best," Valerie said, all the way up against the dash board now. "Okay, turn a little harder and... Stop. No. Stop. Back up. You went too far."

Gemma put the truck in reverse and Valerie marveled at the tree-lined sand driveway that Gemma couldn't see.

"It's just right there," she said.

"You aren't making this any easier," Gemma said.

Valerie pointed.

"Just... that way."

This time, Gemma managed to get the truck onto the driveway, and Valerie had a fleeting moment of doubt that perhaps she shouldn't have helped the woman find it.

She was giving The Pure a direct path to the school, through this woman.

What if she was a double-agent?

What if she really did hate Valerie and all of the rest of the people on this side of the war and was willing to see them all die in order to end it?

What if Valerie's dad didn't understand at all?

It was done.

A moment later, Gemma nodded.

"I can see it now. We're past the warding."

Valerie sat back in her seat, watching the school come into view around a bend, there on top of a hill.

It was a beautiful building.

"Was everyone okay, after the attack?" Valerie asked.

"How would I know?" Gemma answered. "You'll know for yourself, soon enough."

She rolled the truck to a stop and looked over at her.

"Once your feet hit the ground, keep moving. The magic is going to clean up all of the evidence that you ever *weren't* there. That's your prime timeline, after this. Don't let it erase you."

"Erase me?" Valerie asked. Gemma nodded.

"Totally possible. Apparently it happened to me once. Don't remember a thing. And... I know I seem callous, but you being alive is better than you being dead, all things being equal."

Valerie frowned at her.

"You're the weirdest grown-up I've ever met," Valerie said, and Gemma laughed.

"You don't get out much," she answered. "Go. I can't stay here any longer."

Valerie got out of the truck, pushing the door closed behind her, and immediately there was a sense of pressure between her shoulders, like she was being crushed between a pair of hard foam rollers.

She ran.

Her back was pressed against the door, the demon thumping at it with a pressure that threatened to overwhelm her, but she held.

She held.

There was shouting in the hallway, and hissing, voices she didn't recognize, couldn't even place what language they were speaking, and then sounds of enormous violence.

Valerie looked at the girls in the room and drew a slow, deep breath.

"I think it's over," she said.

Several of them were sitting on Valerie's bed crying, but Sasha just let her arms drop and nodded.

"You did it," she said. "You held them out."

There was a knock on the door.

"Valerie?" Mr. Jamison asked. "Is everyone in there okay?"

"I think so," Valerie called back. "Is everything... done?"

"They're gone," he said.

Valerie looked at Sasha for guidance, and the girl shrugged, twisting her mouth.

"I don't know if they can fake a voice," she said.

"Can you prove it?" Valerie asked.

"I was there in Mr. Tannis' room the first day of school when you demonstrated that you aren't like any other student in school," he said.

The girls looked at Valerie, and Valerie nodded, opening the door.

There was dust, dark gray and drifting, all down the hallway of the dorm wing.

"I need you to all stay in there," Mr. Jamison said. "I just need to see who's there and check to make sure that you're all okay."

"What happened?" Valerie asked, sticking her head out into the hallway.

"Mrs. Gold held them off and the rest of us came and finished them," Mr. Jamison said.

"Is everyone okay?" Valerie asked, a lifting sense of hope in her chest. He pressed his lips, looking past her into the room.

"We need to make sure we know where everyone is," he said. "Lady Harrington will make any announcements that need to happen."

Something about his face.

Something was wrong.

Something was really, really wrong.

Yasmine was dead.

Valerie pressed her back against the door, just the way she had that night, her heart racing.

The demons had managed to kill her before she'd gotten away, along with two other girls, sophomores whose names Valerie hadn't known.

"What are you doing?" Sasha asked from her bed.

What had she just been doing?

She'd been running down the hallway at a full sprint, but…

Everything.

She could remember all of it.

She'd written to Hansen; he was coming next weekend to visit.

She'd practiced and memorized and they'd cleaned up from the attack, and she'd told everyone how she'd held the door over and over again, without even knowing. She remembered the parents coming, the loud arguments just behind a door, people crying.

She had feelings for Ethan Trent.

Not just flirty, what's-going-to-happen feelings.

Real, where-is-he-now feelings, and he smiled when he saw her in the hallways.

He thought she'd been dead, and it had changed things.

And she *remembered* all of it.

It just...

It wasn't real.

Was it?

Which thing had actually happened?

School was crazy, sure, but her dead father coming and teaching her magic?

Surely that was just a wish-fulfillment dream of some kind.

One that had felt awfully real, okay, but she'd been at school the whole time.

She knew she had.

"Sorry," Valerie said. "I think I forgot my shampoo. Going to take a shower."

"Forgot your towel, too," Sasha said, laying back on her pillow again to continue reading.

"Right," Valerie said. "Sorry. Mind was somewhere else."

"Mind was off being moon-eyed over Elvis Trent's little brother," Sasha said, then looked at Valerie like she hadn't intended to say anything out loud.

Valerie laughed.

"Oh, so that's how it is, is it?" she asked, and Sasha ducked her head behind her book again.

"You're cute," the redhead said. "It's just... I don't know. He's a *Trent*."

"Yeah, I get it," Valerie said.

Valerie got her towel off the back of the closet door and went to get her shower caddy from under her desk - what had she been thinking, heading out without *anything*...

She still had sneakers on.

She pushed them off with her toes, stripping her socks and tossing them in the hamper in the closet, then got her flip-flops and picked everything up again, walking down the hallway to the bathroom.

She passed the spot - which Mr. Jamison and Mr. Tannis were still attempting to block the magic from the mark on the wall - and she frowned at it.

Spoke words in Aramaic and Greek scolding it for being there, then put her hand up at the spot where she'd first touched it to kill the silverthorn.

It hissed and sputtered and bubbled, but retreated down toward the floor until it was just a black pop-mark.

She frowned harder at it, but she couldn't make *that* go away. Not without more stuff.

More stuff.

She wondered what Sasha had stashed away in the room that she might be able to use on it, continuing on to the shower.

It was Tuesday.

Hansen would be there on Friday, straight out of school.

He said that his mom wasn't coming - huge shock for Valerie, given that she didn't think Hansen had ever traveled without her, even for sports stuff - but that she sent her love and was glad to hear that Valerie was okay.

The letter was sitting on Valerie's desk.

She turned on the shower, feeling very strange, and on an impulse she ran back to her room, picking up the letter from Hansen and taking it back to the bathroom with her.

She hadn't read it enough times to memorize it, but she had read it enough times to know everything that was in it.

Hansen had such under-developed, cramped handwriting. He was a smart guy. Did better in his classes than most anyone, but his handwriting looked like he'd failed second grade.

He was coming this weekend; he'd meet the bus downtown after school and bring his overnight bag. Couldn't wait to see her and hear what had actually happened that day.

That day.

Valerie shuddered at the thought of it, going through the cover story from Lady Harrington once more.

The opportunity had come up at the last minute, to go to the Prestigious Global Learning Academy - she wasn't sure if

Chloe Garner

Prestigious was part of the name or not, but she always capitalized it, now - as part of a sponsorship through a job that Susan had taken. It had all been now-or-never, and they'd agreed to jump at it, but Susan had been very busy with work, and didn't have an international cell phone worked out yet for the section of Africa where she was, and GLA had a strict no-phones policy for all students.

It impeded learning focus.

Hanson was going to have questions.

Questions that the cover story hadn't addressed.

And Valerie was going to have to lie to her best friend.

Oh, how she didn't want to do that.

She loved Hanson too much to lie to him.

But.

Magic.

She'd *just* experienced what being involved with magic could do to you, and she had no intention of putting that on him.

Maybe better if she hadn't invited him at all, but Ethan had encouraged her, said that having a friend from back home come visit would help her get past what had happened with the demons.

The bodies in the hallway.

She'd seen one of them, just a glimpse that Mr. Jamison hadn't successfully blocked, and… she was having such a hard time figuring out what she was supposed to feel about it. It was all a muddled mess in her chest and her stomach…

She just wanted to see Hanson.

To hear about how things were at school and in the neighborhood and with basketball…

That was her strategy. If he got to asking questions that were too hard, she was going to ask him about basketball. He could talk about that for hours.

Yasmine was dead.

Violently.

Ann was devastated.

She'd stayed in her room for two full days, and she really wasn't speaking to anyone, even now.

It was…

That wasn't supposed to happen.

It wasn't supposed to be *real*.

Valerie washed her hair and wrapped herself in a towel, carrying her clothes back to the room and getting dressed in her pajamas.

It was a little early, but there was no point getting back into her regular clothes.

Which desperately needed to be washed. She added them to the laundry bin.

And shook her head.

She'd worn them for multiple days.

But there was Hanson's letter in her hands, same as every other time she read it.

Her father was alive.

She knew he was.

She spoke languages she'd never heard before because he'd taught her.

She couldn't just *forget* what he'd taught her.

It didn't matter how badly she wanted it to not be real.

Except she *did* want it to be real. He was *alive*.

"Do you know where the teachers hang out after class?" Valerie asked Sasha.

"There's a teacher's living space up on the second floor by the library," Sasha answered. "They all live in cottages, but if they're still in the building, that's where they'll be. Unless they're working in their classrooms still. Why?"

Valerie shook her head.

"I think I'm going to go talk to Mr. Jamison," she said.

"All right," Sasha said. "How much homework do you have left tonight? You want to play a game?"

"I... Yeah, I think I have time. Let me go talk to him, and then I'll see."

Sasha smiled at her and rolled onto her stomach, getting out a pencil and reaching up onto her desk to write something down. Valerie got her flip-flops back on and put on a long sweater - it wasn't quite *cold* out yet, but the school felt open and empty during the hours that most of the students were in their dorm rooms, and the sweater made her feel safer and more comfortable.

She walked slowly down the hallways, finding a set of stairs that would take her up on the right side of the building, thinking very carefully about whether or not she should talk to Mr. Jamison at all.

Maybe Mrs. Reynolds, instead.

But her mother had trusted Mr. Jamison.

What about Lady Harrington?

Her father had been intentionally *avoiding* the woman.

It would be a breach of trust to go straight to her.

But she had to talk to someone.

Didn't she?

What about Sasha?

She knew she would inevitably talk to Sasha, though she might leave out the part about her guru being her father - that was still a deep, dark secret - but…

Mr. Jamison would have *advice*.

She hadn't been back an hour, and she couldn't keep her mind straight. It kept switching back and forth which timeline it believed, but it didn't ever manage to get *rid* of the idea that the other one was fully true, as well.

It made no sense, and she thought she might scream.

Mr. Jamison.

Her mother had trusted him.

And Valerie had to trust *someone*.

She found the door with the Staff Living Space marking next to it, and she knocked.

One of the upperclass teachers answered, and Valerie took a step back.

"Is Mr. Jamison here?" she asked.

"Alan?" the man asked, looking off to the side and behind him. "You've got a student here looking for you."

Mr. Jamison appeared, and he frowned.

"Come in," he said, holding the door as the other teacher went back to whatever he'd been doing.

Mr. Jamison escorted Valerie back to a small table in the far corner of the room, where they had some privacy, and he sat down.

"What can I do for you?" he asked.

Valerie opened her mouth, then realized that she had no idea what she was actually going to say.

She swallowed, and Mr. Jamison waited.

Did she tell him about her dad?

No.

She was going to try to tell him what had happened without bringing that *specific* point up.

"My mom trusted you," she started, and he nodded.

"I still consider her one of my closest life friends," he said. "I'd trust her with my life today, if that was what I needed to do."

Valerie nodded.

"Something happened," she said. "And I don't know how to explain it. I have two memories for the time since the attack, and… I don't know how to do it. It's… It's making me feel crazy."

He lifted his chin to look at her, then nodded.

"I wasn't sure if you'd tell me," he said. "If you'd tell anyone."

She licked her lips and considered.

"You know," she said, and he nodded.

"I do. I swept the entire hallway for existing magic signatures, trying to make sure that the bloom we all knew about was the only thing that someone from the outside had cast, trying to get in… The magic you did that night to get to the library… I'm very intrigued by it, but I'm not going to ask. You got away with it fair and square. But I did find… *your father's*… mark on your door."

He whispered the part about her father, and she bit her lips between her teeth.

"You know," she said.

He nodded again.

"Not certain on the particulars, but I remember what an odd skillset he had. And that he was willing to use it out at the edge of safety because he was certain it would never go wrong on him. How do you feel?"

"Crazy," Valerie said again.

"Physically," he said. "Any weak muscles, feeling of fever or fatigue, headache, numbness?"

"Those are possible?" Valerie asked.

"They're symptoms of much more important things having gone wrong," he affirmed.

Valerie swallowed harder, then did an evaluation of her body.

"I think I feel normal," she said.

"Where have you been?" Mr. Jamison asked, leaning in so he could speak more softly.

"I don't even know," Valerie said truthfully. "I learned a lot, and now I have to figure out how to pretend not to know any of it."

He gave her a sympathetic half a smile.

"Yes, you do," he said. She gave him an exasperated look.

"You're supposed to tell me not to worry about it, that I'm safe here, that my secret is safe at school."

He shook his head.

"Not even close. Any one of these students could have a parent who sympathizes with the Superiors, and *anything* that hints that your father isn't dead? It could be very dangerous."

"That's what they kept saying," Valerie muttered. "I just wanted everything to go back to how it was. At least that was a level of crazy I could deal with."

"Not possible," he said, looking around the room for a moment. "The Superiors are making open attacks, now, and the Council is drawing in all of its resources. There are going to be kids finding out that their parents have gotten involved with the war every day for a while, now, and the expectations they're going to put on the school are going to keep getting higher. They may even have upperclassmen doing work for them, by the time the semester is out."

"How did they get in, Mr. Jamison? It wasn't me."

"I know it wasn't," he answered. "Had to have been a student, I think, or a member of the faculty, though that's hard to imagine. I've known everyone here for at least ten years, and a lot of them since I was a teenager."

"How do I *do* this?" Valerie asked. He shook his head.

"I can't help you unless it's with physical symptoms. You've got to figure it out, though. The stakes are too high."

"But I *know* things," she whispered. "I cast on the mark in the girls' dorm hallway and I shrunk it."

"You did what?" he asked, standing. "Show me."

The other teachers looked over, clearly curious what was going on, but Mr. Jamison just walked out of the room, Valerie following.

She walked down to the dorm wing with him, going to stand in front of the black dot against the wall.

"You did that," he said.

"I did," she answered.

"With magic you learned in the past couple of weeks," he said.

"Yes."

He scratched the top of his head.

"*How?*"

She repeated the cast to him as carefully as she could - she knew she was probably getting conjugations wrong, and a lot of the enunciation felt flat compared to how it had been the first time, but it was close as she was going to get.

He blinked at her.

"Your father taught you *that?*" he asked.

"No," she said slowly. "He just taught me a bunch of words in languages that I might find useful and told me to go nuts."

"Go nuts," he said. "That man…"

Valerie looked around quickly.

"He was hiding from Lady Harrington," she whispered. "Why?"

"Could be a lot of things," Mr. Jamison said. "Not the least of which that she hated him and mistrusted just about every decision he ever made."

"Can I tell Sasha?" Valerie asked.

"Up to you," Mr. Jamison said, scratching the top of his head again as he looked at the spot. "We tried *everything* on that thing."

"How do I know who I can trust?" Valerie asked.

"There are three courses in life," Mr. Jamison said. "The most extreme on both ends, and somewhere in the middle. I think that trusting everyone would be foolish, and I think that trusting no one would kill you inside. So you do something in the middle. If I hear anything that seems relevant, I'll let you know… Your father came here to save you. Did he think the attack was *about* you?"

"That's what he said," Valerie answered.

Mr. Jamison paused, pinching his mouth tight as he considered that.

"They're talking about the curse again, aren't they?" he asked.

"He talked about it a little," Valerie said. "And Sasha said something before that."

He nodded.

"Inescapable, with all of them going to school this year..."

He looked at her with a new thought, but shook his head and looked away again.

"What?" she asked.

"Nothing," he said. "Just... I don't believe in it, for what it's worth."

"What has the curse got to do with me?" Valerie asked.

He gave her a hard look and shook his head.

"I don't believe in it," he said. Mrs. Gold came out of her room, down the hallway.

"Alan Jamison, what do you think you're doing down here, this time of night?" she asked.

"Valerie just told me that the mark here had shrunk," he said. "I came down to see. That's all. Mr. Tannis and I will come take a look at it tomorrow."

The woman came to stand next to Mr. Jamison, scowling down at the mark.

"Good riddance," she said. "Sooner that door closes, the better."

She looked at Valerie.

"Should you be in your room, then?"

"Yes, Mrs. Gold," Valerie said. There wasn't a curfew on, but it wasn't ever in Valerie's best interests to antagonize Mrs. Gold. She glanced at Mr. Jamison, who was still frowning at the mark on the wall.

"Good night, Mr. Jamison," Mrs. Gold cued, and he nodded.

"Right. Good night, Mrs. Gold."

He walked past Valerie, his attention somewhere else, and she went into the room, throwing herself on her bed and looking at the ceiling for a long time.

"Everything okay?" Sasha asked.

"Yeah," Valerie said. "It's fine."

Return

"I can't go with you," Martha Cox said as she sat on the end of Hansen's bed while he packed. "Someone there will recognize me."

"She's going to ask why you aren't there," Hanson told her. "You never miss anything."

"If she's going to try to get away with saying that Susan Blake just dropped her at a boarding school on her way out of town, you are going to tell her that I was hopelessly busy, and she'll believe it."

"Not how it works, ma," Hanson said. She gave him a dour look.

"It doesn't matter how you think it works," she said. "Just keep your head up and pay attention. I need to know everything that's going on there. Who her friends are, who she confides in, where her mother actually is. Anything you can do to get her to start telling you the truth is best."

"She's going to try to keep me from figuring it out," Hanson said.

"You're her best friend in the world," Martha told him. "Use it."

He put the last of his clothes into the bag and zipped it.

He didn't like it.

He didn't like any of it.

But that hadn't ever mattered, had it? What he liked and didn't like.

They had a job to do, and his mother had devoted his entire life to doing it.

He looked down at the bag for a moment, then at his mother again.

"I just…"

She nodded.

"You just want to pretend like none of this ever happened," she said. "You like your life just fine. I know. I even get it. But this is important. You know that."

"I know," he said, glum. "I just hate spying on Valerie."

"That's why she trusts you so much," Martha answered.

Yeah.

He knew.

"Magic is a constant learning process," Mrs. Reynolds was saying, drawing things on the board and referencing them as though they meant something. "You have an impression that once you graduate from the School of Magic Survival, you're going to have a handle on things, but you need to understand now that you won't. We'll teach you as much as we can in four years - and with your undivided attention, that's quite a lot - but you're going to spend the rest of your lives figuring out what all of this *meant*, and everything else besides."

"Then why are we even here?" a boy named Geoffrey asked.

"Because you lack so much *knowledge*," Mrs. Reynolds said. "And this is the time that the Council and the first headmasters of the schools have chosen and reaffirmed over and over again as the best time for you to build that foundation of knowledge. You come in feeling like you know quite a lot, but how to actually *cast*, what responsibilities you're taking on by doing it… Those are things that we are growing in you as fast as we can, here, so that we can get you into the specializations as quickly as possible, where you'll get your depth of magic. My Seniors are learning the second family of botanic healing magic, this nine weeks, and I can put my hand over my heart and say that at least some of them are going to save *lives* someday."

Valerie had been daydreaming, and she'd failed to catch what had set Mrs. Reynolds down this path.

"Valerie, what are you doing?" Mrs. Reynolds asked, and Valerie jerked, not sure what she *had* been doing.

She looked down at her desk where she'd been running her fingertips along the smooth wood quite aimlessly for as long as she could remember.

There was a blacked mark on the wood. One with a very distinct shape.

"What is that?" Mrs. Reynolds asked, coming to see.

"I don't know," Valerie answered.

She'd done it again.

She didn't even mean to, and yet.

She kept doing it.

"Geoffrey, can you go get Mr. Jamison, please. Tell him that I have a language consult I need from him."

The boy stood and, casting a curious glance at Valerie that might have been only *just* this side of hostile, he left.

"Do you know how to purge it?" Mrs. Reynolds asked, and Valerie shook her head.

"I'm sorry."

She'd been thinking about training with her father. How there had been so few lectures and so much of him just throwing random magic at her and seeing what she would do.

It had been fun, in its antagonistic way.

Mrs. Reynolds cared about her - Valerie believed that - and wanted her to succeed, but Grant Blake had actually *made* her succeed, whether or not it had felt like care at the time.

She'd been getting *better* at this stuff. At knowing what she was doing and why, and sometimes even creating casts on purpose to do what she wanted them to do.

That night after she'd come home, when she'd cast on the mark on the wall, that had been the last time she'd *intentionally* cast magic, and she'd only done it accidentally a few times, since.

Two weeks of solid magic, and then two weeks completely devoid of it.

It was beginning to wear on her, and she thought about drawing another symbol on top of the one she'd already done, because her finger was itching to do it, and because screw them and their rules and their fear. They were stifling her and making everything worse for her, not better.

Mr. Jamison returned with Geoffrey and looked over Valerie's shoulder at the symbol.

"What language is that?" he asked, and she shook her head.

"Don't know," she said. "Didn't mean to cast it."

The class whispered.

"What does it do?" Mr. Jamison asked.

Valerie closed her eyes.

She could feel it, actually.

The cast had power in it, power that was sourcing from deep in her chest, and that - *that* - was something that she did own.

"It's protection magic," she said after a minute.

She'd been thinking about her father throwing firebombs at her, and how she had gone through every manner of magic he'd taught her, one after the next, deflecting, absorbing, returning them directly at him.

He'd been proud of her for that one.

"It's *fire*," Ann said from the front row of desks. "She's using *demon* magic. I bet it's dark and that's why Mr. Jamison doesn't know about it."

Valerie wanted to get up and yell at Ann that she would *never* use dark magic, but the problem was that she didn't *know* that for sure.

It was actually possible.

"Protection from what?" Mr. Jamison asked.

Valerie shook her head, trying to force the feeling in her chest to talk.

"Fire," she said after a moment. "Hard fire. The kind that's really... *hot*."

There was a soft giggle that went around the classroom, and Valerie stared hard at her desk.

Yes, she *knew* that all fire was hot. It was that this was different.

"I know what you're talking about," Mr. Jamison said. "All the same, we had better take the desk to Lady Harrington, and you need to avoid doing that again."

Valerie stood as Mr. Jamison started to edge the desk into the aisle to carry it away.

"There's another symbol," Valerie said quickly, and he looked back at her, then at Mrs. Reynolds.

"Go on," Mrs. Reynolds said. "But come back quickly. We're having a quiz yet this morning."

Valerie nodded, going out into the hallway after Mr. Jamison.

"All right," he said. "Show me. Carefully and slowly. I don't want you to arm this thing and set it off."

"It's a protection spell," Valerie argued, and he nodded.

"I believe that's what you think," he said. "But I don't know that symbol, and there's no telling what it actually *does*."

Valerie sat down in the desk, resting her elbow on the peninsula of wood along her side and tracing her finger along the smooth veneer, waiting for the inspiration of the idea to hit her once more.

It wasn't like the cast she'd done on the mark, recalling something that no longer had power in it.

When she remembered the symbol she'd been wanting to cast, it came to her with clarity that was inescapable, and she drew it over top of the first symbol like they'd been made to fit together like that.

Mr. Jamison watched with hawkish attention as she finished the figure the first time and started going over it a second time. The wood was beginning to char under her fingertip, and he motioned for her to quit after the third time.

"I can see it," he said, indicating he needed her to get up. "I'll see if Lady Harrington knows what any of it is. Is that it?"

Valerie ran her thumb over her index finger, as if priming it to keep going if it wanted to, but there was no more desire to doodle.

"That's it," she said. He jerked his head toward the classroom.

"Go take your quiz," he said.

"Mine is harder than everyone else's," Valerie told him. "Because they get points for demonstrating that they can *do* the magic, and I just get more technical questions."

"You know some of your classmates would kill for the natural skill you walked in the door with? They're struggling to get basic casts to work."

"Then why are they here?" Valerie asked. "I thought this was only the best of the best."

He looked over his shoulder, then sighed.

"In our circles, money is cheap. But *connections* talk."

She frowned, and he shrugged again.

"Anyway, some of the kids who made it have *got* it, they just have to figure it out. You're all still just freshmen, after all."

"I still think of myself as a junior," Valerie answered, and he grinned.

"And if you could tell me *what* this was and what it did, I'd consider it junior level work, if it ever applied to one of your classes. Go on. Go take your unjust quiz. I bet you ace it anyway. You work harder than any two of them combined."

"I have to," Valerie said after him as he headed to the office.

She turned and went back into the classroom, feeling quite sorry for herself. Ann looked over as Valerie took the empty desk in the front row next to her.

"You took somebody's spot," Ann hissed. "You ought to feel terrible for that."

"You did, too," Valerie answered, cutting herself off before she could accuse Ann of having cheated off of Yasmine to get this far.

She actually thought it was true, but that was below her.

Way below her.

The quiz was partially written and partially casting, as always, but Valerie was shocked to find ingredients on her desk as she sat back down. She looked up at Mrs. Reynolds to tell her that she'd made a mistake, but the teacher was watching her and gave her a little nod.

She was up.

Time to prove she could control her magic and make it do something intentionally.

Great.

She really was working her butt off, trying to catch up on a lifetime's worth of exposure that the rest of the students had, but she was getting closer to being able to match them, when it came to test knowledge.

She could still blow everybody up while her mind wandered, and she was more than a little surprised that Mrs. Reynolds would give her a shot at it *right* after she'd cast something on her desk that no one had even recognized.

There was only one word on the written part of the quiz that Valerie didn't recognize, though she could guess at what it was from the other elements on the list.

She tested well.

But the back of the paper was just a very generic list of instructions with the ingredients. Prepare the lafia leaf. Blanch the pell-seed. Measure out the vant dust.

Valerie gritted her teeth and looked at the pile of *things* on the other side of her desk.

She only recognized half of them, but she didn't doubt that Mrs. Reynolds had done that on purpose to the entire class. They were going to think that the pell-seed was the pile of pellets there, but

Valerie happened to know that pell-seed was actually a cubed preparation of a root. They would actually propagate like that. The pellets, though... Possible that was the dust, but there was a vial of gray dust that looked like a shoo-in for vant.

She worked her way through identifying the ingredients, finally getting them settled in her mind for which was which, as best as she was going to. There were still three of them that were best guesses, and which could have gone in any combination.

She glanced at the clock, finding that she was not just *behind*, but *way* behind. She needed to get the cast finished before the end of class to get any credit for it at all. Better to try and fail than not have finished it.

Mrs. Reynolds reminded them often.

Though.

She also reminded them that they were working with volatile biology that could be dangerous if mishandled, and they were responsible for their own safety and the safety of their classmates every time they worked with them.

So it kind of went both ways.

Valerie took out the prep kit that she'd been carrying in her backpack since Mrs. Reynolds had issued it and set to work cutting, cubing, scraping, measuring.

And then.

Well.

It was like listening to a television in the next room. Right up until the moment that it clicked, it had only been a background noise, but then quite abruptly she could hear the voices distinct from the music and understand every word of it.

Of course.

Of *course* you mixed the vant dust with the green quell gel. That was just where it *went*, if you wanted to create an effect that had any geographic coverage at all. And the pell was there to stabilize everything, because half of the ingredients were becoming volatile even as she prepped them, and while some of them would combust, most of them would simply fail to do *anything* if the pell seed wasn't there to keep them from expiring early.

She didn't just have to work quickly because class was going to end soon. She had to work quickly because the ingredients demanded it.

As she worked, students around the room were beginning to finish their casts, and multi-colored bubbles exploded into existence around them. Ann finished hers and got a light blue bubble that came all the way to the side of Valerie's desk. The girl looked over at Valerie with a sort of smug satisfaction and leaned back in her chair.

Valerie continued working.

She was close.

There were whispers as other kids finished the cast and nothing happened.

Trying to keep her eyes down, Valerie couldn't see how many, but from the sound of the bubbles, she was one of the last ones still working, and at least two had failed.

Drizzle.

Valerie took a slow breath, knowing that there was a *knack* to drizzling. It was never just that simple. You wanted to start at the center of the cast, where the magic was going to start working, and then work your way out, covering as much of the cast as you could without going back over a section that was already in the process of working.

A spiral was the recommended method, though there was a zigzag pattern that Mrs. Reynolds said some users preferred because it was easier to do without overlapping again.

Not as potent, but slightly less likely to fail.

Valerie steadied her hand, still aware that the potency of the cast was fading for every moment she waited, then tipped the stone jar and began to pour.

Her blood just went cold.

Not fear, not dread anticipation.

Just.

Emotionless.

Stony.

It was *easy*.

She'd never done it before, but she was *fearless* that she knew exactly how to do it.

The drizzle went in an easy loop around the center, flowing smooth, her hand steady. She ran it slowly, letting it seep down into the cast as she went, feeling the build of power like a pressure in her chest.

Confident.

She hit the edge of the cast and set the stone jar to the side then, waiting on the cast to finish mixing, she reached up to her head. Acting on sheer instinct, she pulled a strand of her hair, cutting the entire cast in half with it.

There was a dull explosion of power from inside of her chest, and a vivid red bubble expanded rapidly around her, in a blink, encompassing the entire classroom.

Mrs. Reynolds was watching her with an inscrutable expression.

She'd cheated.

She'd used an ingredient that wasn't provided for the quiz.

On the other hand, she'd clearly won the game.

Valerie had no idea which would count for more.

"Freak," Ann muttered.

"Loser," Valerie answered quietly.

The bell rang and Mrs. Reynolds stood, going to the front edge of her desk and sliding her thumb along it, leaving a faintly gold streak there on the wood.

The protective bubbles all burst.

Save Valerie's.

"Mmm," Mrs. Reynolds said. "Miss Blake, I need to have a word with you. The rest of you may turn in your papers and go on to your next class. I'll return scores at the end of the week."

Valerie stayed at her desk as the room cleared, and Mrs. Reynolds leaned against the front desk for a long moment.

"You did very well," she said after a moment. "You're a virgin, then."

Valerie gawped at her, eyes bugging, unable to find anything to say to that. Mrs. Reynolds nodded.

"Virgin hair has certain magical properties to it that are unique, and most potent in your own casts, doubling down when it's protective magic. Just so that you know, if you try that trick again that it wouldn't have worked, otherwise."

"Um," Valerie said. "I just… I had an idea."

Mrs. Reynolds nodded, still watching Valerie closely.

"I value promptness, so I won't keep you long enough to make you late for your next class. I appreciate your instincts and your intuition, but you also need to demonstrate that you can follow instructions and do what you're told. I haven't decided *which* I value more, in this context. Do you know how to shut down your cast?"

Valerie looked at it for a moment, then split the pile of ingredients in half using her thumbs and poured what remained from the stone jar down the center gap.

The bubble faltered, collapsing in for a moment and then just vanishing. Mrs. Reynolds nodded.

"Well executed. Go on to your class, but come see me at the end of the day."

Valerie grabbed her backpack from the chair and threw the prep kit into it, dashing out the door.

She was elated.

It wasn't Mrs. Reynolds reaction. She might have just failed the cast.

It was that she could *do* magic. Not just have it happen to her.

She was absolutely *ecstatic*.

She almost ran straight into Ethan.

He'd taken to walking her from the herbology class to her ritual calisthenics class, and he was still waiting outside of the door.

"You get in trouble?" he asked.

"I don't know," Valerie answered. "But I just cast a protection spell, and it was *awesome*."

He laughed.

"She *let* you cast something?" he asked, and she nodded, grinning.

"It was part of a quiz, and… I *killed* the cast. I just… Well, I didn't do it the way it was on the paper."

He glanced over at her.

"That's really dangerous," he said.

"What, all of the magic you've ever used has been exactly the way someone taught you?" Valerie asked, and he gave her a deep nod.

"*Exactly* the way I was taught," he said. "Without deviating."

She frowned, then shrugged.

"That's not how I do it," she said.

"You're going to get in big trouble, like that," he said, his brows knit. "Bad things can happen if you mess up a spell. Some of them are a lot more dangerous than others, but it's about precision. Doing it exactly the right way."

"How did we get these spells?" Valerie asked. "Did aliens leave them inscribed on a wall somewhere?"

He gave her an exasperated look.

"The Council has researchers who know what they are doing, who figure out new magic. It's our job to just learn what there is. And, I mean, you couldn't learn *all* of it in a lifetime. That's why people specialize. So they can at least get to the really intense, niche stuff in *one* focus."

She sighed.

"I don't know what to tell you. I don't think that's how I work. That's not how Sasha does it, either."

"Sasha knows the rules," he said. "You can change one thing a little, and get the outcome you want. I guess I shouldn't be surprised that she's that far ahead of me. But I still think she's working off of a specific spell that someone taught her."

He frowned again, but they'd been walking quickly in order to get to her class in time for him to make it to his.

"See you at lunch?" he asked. She nodded, smiling again.

He made her happy.

"See you at lunch."

She went into the ritual magic room and was about to set down her backpack when she noticed Mr. Benson.

Waiting for her.

"We need to see you in the office," he said. Valerie didn't look at the rest of the class as she followed him out of the room and down the hallway to the main office.

Mrs. Young gave her an I-knew-it look, and Valerie looked at her shoes.

It wasn't supposed to be this hard.

Her mom had deprived her of *years* of learning and practice, and then just threw her in, in the middle of it. What had anyone expected?

This wasn't her fault.

It wasn't.

She went into the larger conference room, where they'd moved the central table off to the side to make room for her desk.

The marks felt like something she'd seen a million times, like something on the inside of a door, or a tattoo on her own skin. If she'd sat back down, she had no doubt she'd start fingering over them again the moment she lost focus.

"I'd like to hear your explanation, first," Lady Harrington said.

Mr. Tannis and Mr. Jamison were there.

"Don't you have classes?" Valerie asked.

"They're being covered," Mr. Benson said. "And they are none of your concern. Lady Harrington asked you a question."

In point of fact, she hadn't, but Valerie kept this to herself.

"Um," she said. "I don't know what you want me to say," she said. "I just *did* it. It's what I do."

"No," Lady Harrington said. "You make bombs out of horticulture. This is something entirely different."

"She did *speak* to the silverthorn and kill it," Mr. Jamison said, and Lady Harrington gave him a sharp look.

"You aren't here as an advocate," Mr. Jamison," she said.

"Aren't we *all?*" Mr. Jamison answered. "She's a student at the School of Magic Survival. It's our job to do the best we can to teach her and help her grow as a magic user."

The woman pressed her lips and looked at Valerie again.

"I reserve the right to eject a student from this school at any time, if they are endangering others with reckless spellwork."

"It's a protection spell," Valerie said.

She was almost certain.

"That is not a human language," Mr. Jamison said quietly. "I know or recognize every documented human language."

The words were… She hadn't ever considered that *possible*. Valerie was deeply impressed, though she knew that she was supposed to consider the statement a warning.

"Where did you learn them?" Mr. Tannis asked.

"I didn't," Valerie said.

True.

Whatever those shapes were, her father hadn't taught them to her.

"We understand an intuition with spellcasting ingredients," Lady Harrington said. "But that? And, yes, I *know* what that *is*. That is not something that you can just luck into by touch and guess."

"What is it?" Valerie asked.

"I won't discuss it with you," Lady Harrington said. "What I want to know is who showed you how to do it."

This just made her more curious.

"We were talking about protection spells and how they work, and I just started doing it," Valerie said. "It was like doodling. I wasn't *thinking* about it."

"You just *casually* created perfect forms of some of the most potent spellcasting characters on the planet?" Lady Harrington asked.

If they were that *potent*, why weren't they teaching them? Why didn't Mr. Jamison know what they were?

Valerie looked at the four adults, then pulled her shoulders up to her ears.

It was cheeky.

But they were taking it so *seriously*.

"It wasn't *wrong*, though, was it?" Valerie asked. "I did it right."

"Propagation of this language is incredibly tightly controlled," Lady Harrington said. "Whoever taught you has broken *significant* Council rules and needs to appear before them."

Her father *hadn't done it*.

She didn't have to tell Lady Harrington anything about him.

Not even if she *wanted* to tell the truth.

Door.

Inside of a door.

It hadn't been a random idea in her head, the way the symbols showed up on chestnut wood… and skin…

"My mom," she said finally. "And she didn't teach me. I just remembered." She nodded toward the desk. "She had a… *thing*…

on the inside of our door at home that *was* those shapes."

And a tattoo of it on the inside of her forearm, but Valerie didn't have to tell Lady Harrington anything about that, either. Not *Grandma*.

Mr. Jamison looked at Lady Harrington and shrugged.

"I could believe that," he said.

"You were in Mrs. Reynold's class last period, weren't you?" Lady Harrington asked. Valerie nodded.

"That desk belongs to her," Valerie said.

"The desk belongs to the school," Lady Harrington said. "Please go and get her."

She addressed the order to Mr. Benson, who shifted.

"I actually have some *academic* work that I needed to get to today," he said. She pressed her mouth, and Mr. Jamison stepped forward.

"I'll do it," he said. "Won't be a minute."

"Please remain with her class while she's here," Lady Harrington said, and Mr. Jamison paused, then nodded.

"Sure."

Valerie wanted to tell him to stop, that she *needed* him to be here, whatever was going to happen next, but he was moving quickly and out the door before she found the beginning of words.

They sat, waiting for Mrs. Reynolds, who really wasn't more than a minute or two, though it felt like a decade.

"I'm in the middle of a lecture," the woman said. "I have a carefully-planned syllabus that is completely packed out."

"I won't keep you," Lady Harrington said. "I noticed an odd spike of magic during your last period class. Can you tell me what happened?"

"Of course," Mrs. Reynolds said. "We were testing a run-of-the-mill shielding spell, and Valerie amplified hers."

"Significantly," Lady Harrington said.

"Significantly," Mrs. Reynolds agreed. "I haven't decided if I'm going to mark her down or up for having gone off of the cast directions, but it was an impressive piece of work."

Lady Harrington glanced at Mr. Tannis, then nodded.

"Thank you, Mrs. Reynolds. That's all I needed from you. You can release Mr. Jamison back to his own classroom, please."

Mrs. Reynolds touched Valerie's shoulder, then left.

"Do you need me?" Mr. Benson asked. "You got your answer. Susan Blake taught her how to do it unintentionally."

Lady Harrington nodded.

"You're right. I'm sorry to keep you from your work."

He held up a hand and left. Lady Harrington looked at Mr. Tannis again.

"Well?" she asked.

He sighed.

"I hate to take help," he said.

"You need it," Lady Harrington answered. She turned to address Valerie once more. "Miss Blake, you need to learn to control your magic, and you need to make more prudent decisions. I don't like rewarding poor behavior, but I don't feel I have a choice in this matter. You have a gift, and we need to use every tool at our disposal, in the present situation. In addition to him being your academic advisor, you will be reporting to Mr. Tannis after class each day, Monday, Tuesday, and Friday, and you will spend at least two hours of your lab day on Wednesday in his classroom. You will be his research assistant through to the Christmas break. Is that clear?"

"Doing what?" Valerie asked.

"Whatever he asks you to," Lady Harrington said. "You are endangering the students at my school with your behavior, and I don't care if your mother *is* Susan Blake, I will expel you if I decide that continuing to foster your skills is not worth the resources I am spending to keep you and the rest of the students safe from your magic."

What did that mean?

Was she casting protection spells *intentionally* for Valerie?

Valerie bit the inside of her lip and nodded.

Lady Harrington gave her an encouraging nod.

"Mr. Tannis is one of our most gifted teachers, magically, and you have no better mentor than him to learn how to control your gifts. What adds even more value is that you will be helping him with *very* important work. If he needs you cleaning beakers, you'll clean beakers, but it's in the interest of saving *lives*. I'm not putting you to work pushing a broom or digging a ditch. The outcome of his work is of vital importance."

Valerie nodded.

"Okay," she said.

Lady Harrington nodded firmly and looked at the desk once more.

"I'm going to have to destroy this," she said. "I need you to not do it again."

Valerie felt like she couldn't make that promise, but she nodded anyway.

"Good," Lady Harrington said. "Please return to your class. You'll start working for Mr. Tannis this afternoon."

"What do you know about thrown casts?" Mr. Tannis asked that afternoon as Valerie walked into his classroom and sat down her backpack.

"Um," Valerie said. "We haven't studied them. Do you just, like, throw a handful of *stuff* or something?"

He sighed, getting up from his desk and coming around it.

She *had* learned how to throw a cast from her father, but it had been odd… It had felt natural, easy even, but the *method* of it had always felt like if she thought about it too hard, it wouldn't work anymore. She certainly couldn't teach it to someone else, or explain it.

"The ingredients, if there are any, stay with you. It is the *magic* that you are throwing. Do you understand?"

She hesitated.

No.

"Yes."

"Very good. I want you to summon a heat energy in your palm."

Valerie blinked at him.

"Any way I want?" she asked.

"Can be flame, can be literal heat, can be scalding water for all I care," he said.

She nodded slowly, looking around the room.

Red powder in a glass vial.

That looked good.

She went to get it, opening the vial and smelling it, then checking Mr. Tannis with her eyes, she sprinkled it into her palm.

Words.

Greek ones.

Potent.

An energy circulated above her palm, kicking up just a bit of the red dust in a cyclone pattern, and then it lit off in a bright burgundy red.

"Good," Mr. Tannis said over the whooshing sound of the flame. "Now. Send it at me."

She raised her eyebrows, too focused on keeping the flame alive to be able to speak to him.

He sighed.

"I assure you that a freshman is not going to be able to *harm* me with magic," he said. "I am able to defend myself."

Valerie looked hard at him, and he raised his eyebrows.

"Whenever you feel confident enough," he said, pursing his lips.

She turned her attention back to the storm of fire and rolled her jaw to the side, considering it.

It *lived* on her palm.

Just like that.

She could kick it up a bunch, maybe add a bunch more powder if she was careful and, I don't know, shout at it?, and see if she could get it to go *big*, but that wasn't *throwing* it. And she liked her eyebrows, thankyouverymuch.

She needed to find a way to lift it *off* of her palm and... shift it. Over to him.

Did it have to cross the entire classroom to do it?

No.

No, that didn't seem to be in the rules he'd given her.

Okay, *maybe* it was implied by the word 'throw', but... Well, if he wanted her to follow rules, he was going to have to be more specific about them.

She put her left hand out, letting it settle level with the cyclone, feeling the magic power of it, then she snapped, jerking her hand down. The flame extinguished and in the same moment, she flung the *magic* of it at Mr. Tannis, opening her hand.

There was nothing there.

Nothing to see.

Not for the half a second it took to get to him, but then it sprang back to life right at his chest, a ball of flame now rather than a twister. He spoke a word as it smashed into his chest and spread across the flat of it, tendriling out over his shoulders. It died off, but not without tracing a black mark where the hottest of it had been.

He looked down at his shirt, then nodded.

"Good," he said. "I can work with that. Let's get to work."

The next day at lunch, Valerie shook her head.

"I don't know if I'm supposed to talk about it," she said.

"You told Sasha, didn't you?" Shack asked, indicating the redhead who now sat with them occasionally, down at the end of the table as far away from Ann as she could get.

"Of course I did," Valerie said. "If they expect me not to tell *her* something, they should *tell* me. But everyone else? I mean. What if what he's doing is secret?"

"But you told Sasha," Shack said.

"You think it's for the war," Ethan said. She twisted her mouth to the side, then nodded.

"I think it might be."

He frowned, working his jaw for a moment.

"Students aren't supposed to be involved in the war," he said. "Elvis is a graduate from Light School, and he's not allowed, since he's enrolled here."

"Would he want to?" Milton asked.

"No," Ethan said. "No, I think part of the reason he came *straight* here was to avoid getting involved in the war. But they can't say to my dad that his son is avoiding it, because he's *literally* not allowed. The upper schools got really competitive last time, because there were so many people trying to *use* that rule." He looked at

Valerie. "They better not have you doing war work."

"If it saves my mom's life?" she asked. "I don't care."

He pursed his lips at this, then turned his attention to his lunch again.

"I like Mr. Tannis," Sasha offered after a moment. "He's really smart, and he's good at explaining things."

"Is he?" Valerie asked. "Mostly he just makes demands and expects me to figure it out."

"That's your super-power," Ethan said without looking up, then jerked like he'd said something insulting. Valerie raised her eyebrows.

"What's that supposed to mean?" she asked.

"I just..." he said. "All of this is against the *rules*. You're supposed to go by the book, learn the basics and advance to the harder, more detailed stuff. You don't just... *do* magic."

"Look who cares about the *rules*," Ann said.

"What?" Ethan demanded, and she laughed.

"You showed up to school a *month* late," she said. "And I guarantee that you weren't just off on some diplomatic intercontinental trip on behalf of the Council. What did you *really* do with all your time in Rome, Ethan?"

"Shut up," he said, as though she knew something.

Valerie wondered what it was.

"Visit weekend next weekend," Shack said, either oblivious or incredibly kind.

"Hanson is coming, isn't he?" Sasha asked. "You heard back."

Valerie nodded, swallowing an unchewed bite of food to speak again.

"Yeah, he said his mom can't make it, but he's coming weekend after this one. I can't wait to see him."

"You two have a thing?" Ann asked, and Valerie shook her head.

"No, he's just my best friend going all the way back."

"You can't just be friends," Ann said. "It doesn't work like that. One or the other of you is *always* going to get a crush on the other one, and then the friendship is *weird* and it doesn't work anymore."

Valerie stared at her for a moment, then looked at Shack again.

"My birthday is next week, so it's going to be for my birthday. He said he'd bring cupcakes or something to celebrate."

Shack grinned.

"Happy birthday," he said.

"Early, moron," Milton said. Shack shrugged.

"We celebrate birthdays all month at my house," he said. "Because one day just can't fit it all."

Valerie grinned.

"I like it," she said. "More presents."

"You have no idea," Ann said passively, watching something across the room. "His parents *love* giving presents."

Valerie tipped her head at Shack, and he grinned.

"It's a thing my mom does," he said. "She likes coming up with stuff that no one else has and no one else has thought of. So she tries everything."

"Magic stuff?" Valerie asked.

"One year, it was a basketball court in the back yard with a scoreboard and a concession stand."

Valerie paused, then nodded.

"Wow."

He grinned.

"Eventually my dad - my dad's *really* competitive - he decided he was going to outdo her, and they've been competing at presents ever since. Some of it gets kind of crazy."

"I bet," Valerie said. "You're rich, then?"

Basketball court in the backyard. Who would have put *that* together?

The whole table went still, and Ethan looked at her.

"Magic users usually are," he said.

"I guess," Valerie said. "Time and resources to pursue it."

He shook his head.

"No... It's that magic is *very* lucrative. Even if you're only using it for small stuff..."

"I want to use it to grow flowers for a nursery," Sasha piped up, and he motioned at her.

"Like that. She would have the best nursery in the region and she could charge whatever she wanted for the plants she was selling,

202

and she'd be one of the richest…"

"Nursery owners," Sasha supplied, and he nodded again.

"Nursery owners around."

"Well, I'm not rich," Valerie said.

"Do you even know how much it costs to *go* to this school?" Ann asked, on the edge of her seat still as she watched a table in the corner of the lunch room.

"No," Valerie said. She'd thought it was free, something the magic community just *did*.

Shack ducked his head, glancing over at Ann, but Patrick wasn't nearly so shy, and he told her.

It was a year's salary, most places in the country.

Valerie's chin dropped.

"No," she said. "I've got to be on scholarship, then. My mom doesn't have that kind of money."

"Scholarship," Ann scoffed. "You think you have *academic merit?*"

"I have *need*," Valerie said.

"Your parents are rich," Ethan said softly. "I'm almost certain of it. They may have graduated into the war, but the Council pays really well for the people on the front line, and more for the ones *behind* the front line, figuratively speaking. And they were both deep in behind what was going on. I wouldn't be surprised if your mom let all of that money stay where it was, for fear of someone using it to track her down, after she disappeared, but…"

Sasha nodded.

"Two parents with handlers to the Council?" Sasha asked. "You're probably richer than…"

"No one at *this* table," Ann said, standing and walking briskly away. Shack glanced at Valerie.

"If you *needed* the money, maybe you could talk to someone about getting it," he said.

"I don't," Valerie said, short not at him but at this idea that *everyone* knew things about her that she'd never even guessed at. "Why would I need money? I'm at boarding school."

"Better spellcasting ingredients to study with," Ethan said, not looking directly at her. "Books. A lot of the girls wore magically-inclined jewelry."

Sasha dug a necklace out of her shirt and held it up.

Valerie gave her an exasperated look and she put it away again.

"I don't *need* anything," Valerie said, standing. "I was happy with my mom the way we were."

"No one's saying that you have to be some spoiled rich kid," Ethan said, looking up at her. "Just... there's probably money if you want it."

Valerie shook her head.

"I don't."

She threw away the remainder of her lunch and went to sit by herself at the library until her next class.

History

"Don't think of it as a magic wand," Mr. Tannis said, stepping away from her. "Think of it as a way of focusing your magic."

"That would make it a magic wand," Valerie said dryly, looking at it.

It looked nothing short of twiggy, the appearance of twisted, aged wood and bits of splinter sticking out, but the moment it had hit her palm she'd been able to feel that it was different.

Like a continuation of herself in a way that she'd never known how to measure.

"You got it?" he asked.

"Yeah."

"All right. I'm looking for heat that is invisible that doesn't have to come from you to me. You just cast it *at* me, like throwing, and the first I should be aware of it is when it hits me."

She looked at the onyx twig in her hand and frowned.

"You want me to cook your heart," she said.

"You overestimate yourself, Miss Blake," he said. "I want you to *try* to. Whatever means you choose."

"And what if I hurt you?" Valerie asked. "Lady Harrington will kick me out. And there are people out there who want to kill me."

"I think you substantially overestimate your tactical value to anyone," Mr. Tannis said. "Regardless, Lady Harrington knew what you were going to be doing and she agreed to it. In the impossible case that you managed to incapacitate me, she would be aware and see to it that you did not face consequences."

"I don't like being the attacker," Valerie said. "This is supposed to be survival school."

For a moment, Mr. Tannis eased, and he came to sit down on one of the broad worktables that his students used as desks.

"That, Miss Blake, is a perfectly reasonable point. And I'll admit that what I'm asking you to do does not fit into the curriculum anywhere but boot camp."

"That exists?" Valerie asked, and he tipped his head.

"If you want to hear my earnest point, you will refrain from commentary," he said. "We teach this type of thing, but not in a focused manner. It is not something that *any* of the schools wish to adopt as curriculum - the art of taking life. You are specifically correct that *this* school is concerned with the *defense* of life. Yours or others. So what I am about to tell you must remain perfectly secret. Your speculation up to this point doesn't concern me; it isn't anything but teenagers making the stories of their lives bigger than they are. But you deserve to know this.

"About four weeks ago, there was a major Superior attack. Multiple of the fighters representing the Council died in that attack, and a number of civilians that I don't have at its latest figure, though it was much larger than a hundred. Normally, our fighters are reasonably evenly-matched against the Superiors, and they retreat quickly, leaving our *school's* graduates the time and space to try to help the civilian survivors.

"This time was different. The Superiors stood their ground and fought our people, and they had a new style of cast that our people were unprepared to defend. This is precisely the thing that I have been tasked to develop - a defense against a cast that flash-cooked our fighters as they were going to help injured and dying civilians."

Valerie thought about Gemma, standing next to a man or a woman giving the order to go kill people, to go *hold their ground* as people died... And it didn't make sense.

If they were just trying to separate people from their magic...

"Was my mom involved?" Valerie asked.

"No one knows," Mr. Tannis said. "But I can tell you for certain that if she had died, they would have notified you within days. If she had died *there* at the fight."

"What about going quiet?" Valerie asked. He closed one eye, then shook his head.

"That may be months or a year or more," he said. "I don't even know how the Council will treat it, this time. That's just what I remember from last time."

Valerie sighed, looking at the wand in her hand.

"So if you can figure out how to defend from a cast like that, it might save my mom's life?" Valerie asked.

"I think the odds are exceedingly slim that she would be in one of these fights," Mr. Tannis said. "But I do think that you will have helped save someone's life. Potentially Mr. MacMillan's father."

Shack.

"All right," Valerie said. "Are you sure I can't hurt you?"

"I am much stronger and much better-trained than you are," Mr. Tannis said. "And even if that weren't true, this room is warded to within an inch of its life. Damaging magic is extremely muted unless I put a hole in the wards for a purpose. We do too many dangerous things for it to be otherwise."

Valerie nodded, looking around the room.

So many boxes and bins and bags to choose from.

Where to start?

The rules were too specific.

She'd been working for an hour, going through all of Mr. Tannis' stuff to try to find something that would do what he asked her to do, but it wasn't the same. Many of the ingredients called to her, but for other things.

What was nice was that she could at least *tell* that that box of metal ball bearings was only interesting because she wanted to build an alarm system that would trip if someone tried to cast across it.

Mr. Tannis had eventually gone around his desk and started grading papers, only glancing up at her from time to time. She felt like apologizing, but at the same time she refused to apologize for *not* attacking him and trying to cook his organs.

Seriously.

She sat down cross-legged on the floor and closed her eyes, waiting for something to occur to her.

Was there something that she *knew* that she could use to cue her ability? Or was she simply not *able* to hurt things? She wouldn't have minded if it was true, though the neurotoxin the first day belied it.

And a bomb.

She still remembered how to build the bomb. Knew where the ingredients were, on the wall.

A bomb.

Now that was an interesting thought.

All she had to do was get it to go off inside his chest, and to be heat rather than explosion.

Could she do that?

She stood, going to get the things that she'd used in the first bomb and sitting down at a desk to consider it.

If she replaced a couple of the ingredients with a specific configuration and a placement order ritual…

There was a language, deep in the back of her throat, one that was pressing to get out even as she put together the order in her head for the rest of the cast.

Her hands were already working, preparing ingredients and placing them, feeling the way the power built up around them. She pushed them around with the wand, getting them into straight lines and sometimes letting the wand touch more than one ingredient at a time to let the power between them neutralize.

What a useful tool.

The words just came all on their own, though they weren't proper *words*, so much as sounds.

Angry ones.

It matched up well with the magic of the cast, actually, and the intent.

Mr. Tannis was watching her with interest, but when she spared a moment to look at him, he nodded encouragement.

She kept working.

The entire cast took about twenty minutes to complete, and then she held up the wand like a lightning rod, drawing the energy of the cast up and off of the desk. She slowly stood, sensing that she would be more powerful on her feet, and she pointed the wand at Mr. Tannis.

"Go," she said simply.

He grabbed his chest and his eyes went wide.

"Mr. Tannis," she said, dropping the wand and running over to him.

He held up a hand and shook his head, coughing and leaning out over his desk.

"That was *marvelously* done, Miss Blake," he said. "I am uninjured, though my pride may be a bit stung. The odds of that being the exact cast that the Superiors used is infinitesimal, but it is exactly what I need to work against for defense magic. I wasn't able to come up with a way to do it, and you have. Now I can defend. We'll start again on Monday. You'll be doing that cast a lot, as I work, so get used to it."

Valerie went quickly back to the desk, scuttling the cast and picking up the wand.

"May I keep this?" she asked.

"Some of your teachers will consider it cheating," he said. "But I'd like you to practice with it whenever you get opportunity. It will make your casting better, here."

Valerie really wasn't interested in making her attacks stronger, but she did like the wand, so she stuck it into the side pocket of her backpack and hefted the pack up onto her shoulder. He raised a hand and straightened - finally.

"Enjoy your weekend. I understand you have company coming."

She smiled.

"I do."

He nodded.

"Be careful. But have a good time."

She gave him a tight smile and left, going downstairs and to her dorm room, where Sasha was writing a paper.

With pen and paper.

How strange.

"What time does the bus come this afternoon?" Sasha asked.

"Should be in the next thirty minutes or so," Valerie answered. "I'm going to go take a shower and then wait in the cafeteria. Want to come with?"

Sasha grinned.

"Am I invited?" she asked.

"Of course," Valerie answered, then stopped. "You know that there's no way I would have survived all of this without you, right?

I mean, just none."

"That's not true," Sasha answered, looking back at her paper. "You're really strong and really smart. You would have been fine."

"Um, no," Valerie said. "I would have gone nuts and burned the entire place down. You should be there to meet Hanson, because my two closest friends should know each other."

"Is Ethan going to be there?" Sasha asked, still looking hard at her paper, though the pen had stopped moving.

"No," Valerie said. "I mean, I'm sure he'll be around this weekend, and stuff, but I didn't ask him to come to the cafeteria to meet Hanson."

"Are you sure that they're going to be okay, together?" Sasha asked. Valerie raised an eyebrow.

"Oh, come on, not you, too," she said. "Hanson is just my *friend*. Seriously. Nothing more."

Sasha shrugged.

"Ethan has a temper."

"I've yet to see it," Valerie answered, getting out her shower caddy and towel. "I don't want to talk about it anymore."

Sasha nodded.

"He likes you a lot," she said.

"Is that a problem?" Valerie asked, and Sasha looked over at her quickly.

"No. I just… I'm jealous of the way he looks at you."

"Do you have a crush on Ethan?" Valerie asked, feeling wretched that she had missed it.

"No," Sasha said. Too quickly. She was lying.

"Really?" Valerie pressed. Sasha laughed, looking away for a moment and then back at Valerie.

"No. Not Ethan. I just wish *any* boy would look at me like that. Like the whole room goes fuzzy when you walk in."

"Oh, my gosh," Valerie said. "Wow are you a romantic."

"He *does*," Sasha protested, blushing.

Valerie grinned.

"Then we're going to have to find you a boy," she said.

"Have you had boyfriends before?" Sasha asked.

"You haven't?" Valerie countered, and Sasha shook her head.

"I didn't stay in the same place very much, in the last five or six years. I had my friends at school, but I didn't do anything outside of school because I was traveling with my mom. Before that, I thought boys were icky."

"Most of them still are," Valerie said. "Seriously. Shower, and then we're going to talk."

She hurried down the hallway, checking her watch, and showered quickly, going back to the room to find something to wear.

She was ridiculously excited to see Hanson, but at the same time, she didn't know how to feel.

She really wasn't the same person who had left a couple months ago.

She was.

She *was*.

But she knew about things that she never would have even imagined, and her mom was in danger, and her dad was *alive*...

She just wanted it to be simple, to be able to spend time with her friend the way they always had, to laugh and talk and tease.

Him actually coming made her more poignantly aware of how much she had missed him.

"So," Valerie said as she and Sasha started down the hallway toward the cafeteria. "Boys. What are you looking for, exactly? You want a do-for-me boyfriend, or someone who adores you and pays a lot of attention to you, or are you looking for a long-term relationship?"

"I don't know," Sasha said. "I mean, neither of the first two. I want someone to talk to, who makes me laugh, who's... you know. Who's my *person*."

"You want a soulmate," Valerie said, and Sasha looked away, embarrassed.

"I hate to break it to you, but I haven't seen much quality material around school," Valerie said. "I mean, everyone's just too competitive and obsessed with their own magic."

"You and Ethan get along," Sasha said and Valerie nodded, smiling involuntarily again.

"He isn't like them. He doesn't care about all of this so much.

I mean, he knows it's important, but it isn't worth being a jerk over."

"They aren't *all* jerks," Sasha said. "I mean, they are to you, but…"

She stopped and Valerie frowned.

"Your boyfriend doesn't have to *like* me," Valerie said. "I mean, it'd be more fun if he did, but you shouldn't blow someone off because he doesn't like *me*."

Sasha laughed, rubbing her cheeks with her palms for a moment. Valerie wasn't sure if the girl had been crying.

"It's not like anyone has ever expressed any interest," the redhead said. "I don't think I'd turn *anyone* down."

"Would too," Valerie muttered. "You have standards. Don't sacrifice those just because you want a guy."

"Sometimes I'm not sure," Sasha said as they turned into the cafeteria.

"I'm serious," Valerie said. "Guys aren't worth it, okay? I mean, if what you're looking for is someone to give you back rubs and convince you that you're awesome when you're having a bad day, you can get just about any boyfriend you want. But if you want a serious boyfriend… I've seen girls get hooked up with a guy just because he was hot and he winked at them, and they end up wasting years of their lives trying to keep him from being exactly what he liked about himself."

"We're sixteen," Sasha said. "You sound like a sitcom."

Valerie snorted.

"The girls I hung out with started dating in the sixth grade," she said. "And *all* boys were idiots in middle school."

Sasha laughed.

They heard the front doors open and the sound of Lady Harrington's voice as she greeted the visitors, and Valerie stood straight. Hanson rounded the corner into the cafeteria a minute later, and her feet were moving.

She hit him in the chest at speed, and he stumbled back two steps, laughing and wrapping her up tight.

"I forgot how hard you hit," he said.

"I forgot how big you are," she answered, grinning. "Come meet Sasha."

He put an arm around her shoulders and she walked him over to where Sasha was sitting, staring with big eyes.

Hanson's dad was military. He traveled a lot, and he was the kind of guy that everyone stopped talking when he walked in the room because he kind of filled the entire doorway.

Hanson took after him in a lot of ways.

Valerie grinned wider.

"Sasha, this is Hanson. Hanson, this is my roommate and savior Sasha."

"You've been taking care of Val?" Hanson asked, offering his hand to shake hers. "She needs it. Nobody knows it better than I do."

"Um," Sasha said. Hanson grinned, then hugged Valerie again.

"Okay, so apparently there are protocols for these visits, and I'm supposed to be here in time for dinner, which means we've got like thirty minutes for the tour and for me to figure out where to put my stuff."

"Where is it?" Sasha asked. "I'll get it."

"No chance," Hanson said with another easy grin. "It's up in the front hall, and I think it would squish you."

"You brought sportsball stuff, didn't you?" Valerie asked.

"It's a boarding school," he said. "I brought gear for everything."

"You're here for two days," Valerie said. "And I don't *play* anything."

"So?" he asked. "You've also been known to sleep until two on Saturday. I bet I could get a pick-up game of just about anything around here, couldn't I?"

Valerie actually had no idea, so she looked over at Sasha.

"Um," Sasha said.

"Ethan will know," Valerie said. "He said he plays basketball. I bet he plays soccer, too."

"I brought a tennis racket and my baseball mitt," Hanson said.

"Hopelessly optimistic," Valerie said.

What *did* kids do on the weekends? She'd been too busy studying to even try to find out.

"And like six changes of clothes," he said.

They got to the front hall where a set of bags was sitting, and he picked up two of them.

"Where am I headed?" he asked.

"Out," Valerie said. "Did they not tell you anything more than that?"

"I know that I'm assigned to visitor cottage B," he said. "Is that enough?"

"I can show you were that is," Sasha said quickly. "It's a way from the upperclass cottages. I don't know if they've shut down the pool yet."

"There's a *pool* here?" Valerie asked. Sasha glanced at her.

"Three," she said.

Valerie tipped her head back and groaned.

"Why didn't anyone tell me?" she asked as Hanson laughed.

"It was in the campus map," Sasha said. "I told you that you needed to look at it."

"Why?" Valerie asked. "I wasn't planning on getting *lost*."

Hanson snorted again and glanced at Sasha.

"Told you she needs someone looking out for her."

Sasha laughed.

Giggled, actually.

For crying out loud.

They walked across a lawn that crunched underfoot with the beginnings of falling leaves, and Valerie found herself looking around at the property that surrounded Survival School for the first time.

There were some guys, over there, playing Ultimate Frisbee, and a trio of girls sitting on a plaid blanket, talking.

"It's pretty here," Hanson said.

"No kidding," Valerie answered. "I've been cooped up in my room this whole time."

"Well, glad I came to show the place to you," Hanson said. "I really want to catch up, and I've got a birthday present for you in my bag, but there's only about an hour of light left…"

"You can run and play with them," Valerie said. "Just don't get gross for dinner, okay?"

Sasha pointed at the cottages - adorable, white square buildings down in a cove right up against the treeline with, yes, a small pool in the middle of them - and Hanson jogged off to go get his bags put down. Valerie stopped to wait for him.

"He's so *hot*," Sasha said. "You never said he was hot."

Valerie wrinkled her nose.

She still had the image of him in her head as the kid who couldn't sneak up on a frog to save his life, but... okay. If she squinted right she could see it.

"Told you, we're just friends," she said. "He's been my best friend since before I can remember. The idea of him being *sexy* is just..." She shuddered, and Sasha laughed, taking a step sideways.

"And he's so *nice*," Sasha said.

"You know, that's how people are *supposed* to be," Valerie said, though she had to admit that he had always been a relief from the high-amplitude cattiness that was possible with her friends from school. Her friends from her *real* school.

There was a pitting sensation in her stomach, but she pressed through it and moved on.

"I know," Sasha said. "It's just... You know, I had this idea of what school was going to be like, and sitting and studying with friends and talking about *magic* with people, actually having *everyone* around me know what it was so that I was allowed, and..."

"Like one full-time sleepover," Valerie said, and Sasha nodded.

"Yeah. My brothers talk about Light School sometimes, and how rough it can be... Boys don't really talk about it though, do they?"

"Nope."

"I thought the girls would be different," Sasha said. Valerie laughed.

"And they are."

Sasha nodded.

"They're so much worse," she whispered, and Valerie grinned.

Hanson was jogging back up the hill toward them.

"I'm missing two basketball practices to be here," he said. "So I have to put in a good show of getting a workout."

She motioned.

"Be my guest."

She and Sasha followed along behind as Hanson ran over and introduced himself into the game without hesitation.

There was a guy sitting on the sidelines as Hanson arrived, and the two of them both joined to keep the teams even.

Valerie only vaguely understood the rules of Ultimate, but the guys played hard and it was fun to watch.

It felt very much like being back at home, actually.

She was never going home again, she realized. Her mom was out of hiding, and that was all that that place had ever been.

Grief.

It came at her suddenly, and she sat down, trying not to let Sasha see it.

"He's bigger than anyone in the freshman year," Sasha said.

Valerie had actually noticed that - that the magic users tended to be on the petite side, save Shack.

"Shack isn't that much shorter than Hanson," Valerie said. "But Hanson is a freak of nature. I call him that, actually. There are a couple of guys at our school who are taller, but... No, he's one of the biggest guys around, even at a *big* school."

Sasha glanced over at her.

"You don't like being at a small school," she said, and Valerie shrugged.

"I don't think it's the size of the school that disagrees with me," she said honestly. "I would get along just about anywhere that didn't walk in the door assuming I didn't deserve to be there."

"You deserve to be here," Sasha said. "And not only because the Council owes it to your mom. You're one of the best magic users on the campus. That's why Lady Harrington assigned you as Mr. Tannis' research assistant."

"Not exactly the way she put it," Valerie said, considering that day's work with Mr. Tannis.

She'd attempted to cook the man.

And been successful, but for his ability to stop her.

That chilled her, even more out here in the evening sun with Hanson Cox running around and being a goofy idiot the way he always did when he wasn't playing a sport for glory.

She could kill someone with the force of her mind and a rather simple assortment of uninspiring objects.

Kill them dead, like they never saw it coming and never even knew what did it.

And then she saw it.

Her dad.

Her dad had known how to teach her, and she had thought it was because of how closely the way she thought - the way she *learned* - mirrored his. And maybe that was still true. But everyone said how she looked like her mom and how she cast like her mom...

Lady Harrington had needed someone to cast killing spells in order for Mr. Tannis to develop a defense against it.

And they'd brought in the assassin's daughter to do it.

She hugged her knees against her shoulders, angry and ashamed.

It had taken them less than two weeks to teach her how to do it.

That was all it took to turn *Valerie* into a killer.

Hanson looked over and waved, checking his watch and waving his way out of the game.

He was breathing hard as he threw himself onto the ground next to her.

He might have played silly, but he always played hard.

"Who's ready to eat?" he asked.

"I am," Sasha said, and Valerie couldn't help but grin.

"You're supposed to be there for the beginning of dinner?" Valerie asked, and Hanson gave her a more serious nod.

"Yeah. We're supposed to get the rules for being on campus and stuff," he said. "They gave us a little time to get settled in, but... You know."

Valerie nodded.

"Well, we'd better get there while they still have enough food left."

He grinned and stood, pulling her to her feet. Sasha moved like she didn't know whose side to stand on, and Valerie took a step - just being the first one to set off - that left a gap between her and Hanson.

Sasha slid into it easily and they walked back to the main

building.

Valerie took Hanson through the food line and went to the table where she always sat with the Council kids now, raising a hand as Ethan and Shack walked in. Ethan left Shack to come over and greet Hanson.

"Nice to finally meet you," Ethan said after Valerie introduced them. "Heard a lot about you."

"Hey, yeah," Hanson said. "Really neat to meet Val's new friends. All happened really suddenly, actually."

"I was actually a full month later than her," Ethan said. "Was traveling with my family in Europe."

"Cool," Hanson said. "I want to go, someday. Want to see London."

Valerie didn't know that.

"It was mostly continental," Ethan said. "We didn't get up to the UK. Anyway, let me go get some food. Valerie says you play basketball."

"Oh, you don't want to let me get started with that," Hanson said happily. "Sometimes I forget I'm just playing for fun, when it comes to basketball."

Ethan grinned.

"So?"

"So that's him, huh?" Hanson asked as Ethan walked away.

"Him what?" Valerie answered, and he gave her a sideways smile.

"The new guy," he said. "I can always tell. Does he know yet?"

"I don't know what you're talking about," Valerie said.

"Yeah, you do," he teased, then he looked over at Sasha. "So do you play sports?"

"No," Sasha said. "No, not at all. I'm kind of more of a book nerd."

"Don't have to have it one way or the other," Hanson said. "Nothing that says that you can't play sports if you're smart."

She gave him a shy smile and nodded.

"I'm just not very coordinated," she said.

"So?" he asked. "I don't care if you're *good*. The point of playing is to have fun."

"Tell that to every team I've ever been on," Valerie said, and Hanson laughed.

"You're a special brand of don't-care," he said. "I'd be annoyed at you, too."

Valerie shrugged one shoulder at him and continued eating.

"You'd be so good at field hockey, though," he went on, talking to Valerie. "I've never known a girl who hits as hard as you do."

She narrowed her eyes at him and he laughed.

"Just saying."

"Shove a bunch of people around fighting over a little ball that I could buy three of in a can at the store," Valerie said. "Pass."

Hanson leaned over the table toward Sasha.

"So does the new victim know about it yet?" he asked, pointing a thumb at Ethan.

"Victim?" Sasha asked.

"Oh, yeah," Hanson said. "Guys get it *bad* for Val, and she goes along with it for a while and then decides that she's wasting her time with them, and she's the kind you never get over. Can't count the guys that I've seen, still in love with her."

"I don't think Ethan is going to be a *victim*," Sasha said.

"Strong-willed, then," Hanson said. "Gives him a fighting chance. But has he *seen it coming* yet?"

"He hit on me first," Valerie said. "Shut up."

Hanson grinned and returned to his tray. He was going to have to go back for seconds soon.

A minute later, Ethan and Shack came to sit down, and Hanson shook hands with Shack. The two hit it off immediately, talking about sporty things, and Valerie turned her attention to Ethan.

"We're going to have a party for you out at Hanson's cottage tonight," Ethan said.

"No one is going to come," Valerie answered, more of a defiant tone than anything.

"You'd be surprised how many of the guys will turn out for pizza," Ethan said. She considered that.

No, she really *wouldn't* be surprised how many of the guys would turn out for free pizza.

"Fine," she said. "Then we have to do something for your

birthday, when it happens. When is it?"

"December," he said. "Second."

"Do you know that they have pools here?" Valerie asked. He nodded.

"It was in the brochure," he said.

"Stop," she said. "There was a *brochure*?"

"They would have sent it to you, if they'd known where you were," Ethan said.

"No," Valerie said. "They would have decided they were too good for me and saved it for somebody better."

"Nobody is better than you," Hanson said, switching back to his conversation with Shack seamlessly.

He was listening.

Good to know.

"There's a weight-lifting room on the other side of the office," she heard Shack say.

"Cool," Hanson answered. "I'll meet you there in the morning, if you want."

Ethan grinned.

"Kindred spirits," he said.

"Indeed," Valerie answered. "You'll like him, too."

"If he's willing to haul all the way up here to see you, I have no doubt," Ethan answered. Mr. Benson came into the room and held up his hands.

"Visitors?" he called. "I need to see all of the visitors and their hosts for the next ten minutes."

Valerie shoveled another bite of her dinner into her mouth, then wiped her hands off on a napkin and got up to follow Hanson across the room to where Mr. Benson waited. There were six other visitors that weekend, most in groups of two or three. Someone had a younger sibling visiting.

"All right," Mr. Benson said, marking them off on a list. "This is the only time I'm going to interrupt your weekend, so please focus so we can get through this quickly. The only places that visitors are allowed without a student or staff escort are the cottages and the front hallway. Please be direct walking between the buildings and please arrange to have someone with you, the rest of the time. We need you to check in at each meal, and the curfew for all visitors to be back in their cottages is midnight. We ask that you stay there until six AM at the earliest. You are welcome anywhere else on campus with your escort, but we ask that you respect the educations that are progressing even on weekend days and leave closed classroom doors closed. No teenage boys in the girls' dorm rooms and no teenage girls in the boys' dorm rooms. If inappropriate behavior is reported to me or any other member of the staff, we have at our exclusive discretion to cut the visit short and ask the visitor to remain in their cottage until the bus goes back to the city Sunday afternoon, with exceptions made for meals. Is all of that clear?"

"Yes, sir," Hanson said with everyone else. Valerie found it all oppressive and controlling, but she nodded anyway.

She *got* that Hanson could be in danger if he learned about magic - boy did she get it, just now - but *still*.

She sighed.

"All right," Mr. Benson said. "Thank you for visiting us and thank you in advance for your helpful behavior."

He gave them a firm nod and turned to head out. Hanson wrinkled his nose at Valerie as they turned to go back to the table.

"Is it always like that around here?" he asked.

"I had to write you a *letter* to ask if you wanted to come," she said. "Some days, I swear this place is a convent."

He snorted, then grabbed her elbow, pausing her halfway back to the table.

"Sasha," he said. "Is she seeing anyone?"

Valerie blinked at him.

"Wow," she said. "You, too?"

"What do you mean?" he asked.

Boggle.

"Okay," Valerie said. "Um. No. She's not seeing anyone."

She'd forgotten he had a thing for redheads.

"Look, I know this weekend is about getting to see you and…" he started.

"Give me a break," Valerie said. "I missed you, dude, but if you want to talk to her, talk to her. Okay?"

He grinned.

"You're the best."

He went to sit next to Sasha, pulling his tray across the table, and Sasha dipped her head, blushing.

Valerie smiled, watching them, then went to go sit next to Ethan again.

He raised an eyebrow at her and she gave him a what-do-I-know shrug and continued eating.

He grinned.

"Hanson's cottage, eight," he said. "Be there."

"Where are you getting *pizza*?" she asked, and he grinned wider.

"That's my problem, not yours."

Sasha had gone to get changed.

Valerie knew it was because she wanted to look pretty for Hanson, but she had just taken it as a moment to sit with her best friend there on the stairs out front of the school building, watching as the stars began to show overhead and the air finally transitioned from molten to fall-ish.

"It's not a bad place," Hanson said. "If you like this rich-people-and-their-lives-of-leisure thing."

"Yeah," Valerie said skeptically. "You know me. I prefer cement and vacant lots."

He grinned and she put her head on his shoulder, tucking her fingers underneath her shoes.

"It's not the same without you being around," she said.

"Back home, either," he said. "Are you coming back for Christmas?"

"I don't think so," Valerie admitted. "Mom isn't going to be there, I don't think."

She was absolutely certain.

"You could come stay with us," Hanson offered. "You know my mom loves you."

"Yeah," Valerie said, smiling. "How in the world did you talk her into coming out here on your own?"

"Oh, there was no way she was going to let me," he answered.

"And then something huge came up with Dad's work and it was either I was going to have to cancel or I was coming on my own, and I… She let me."

Valerie grinned.

Martha Cox was a loud woman, and when Hanson got home, he just transitioned from this quiet, thoughtful guy to someone who was trying to yell the walls down. They had their conversations from opposite ends of the apartment, and Valerie had been there for more than one fight.

"She really wants to know what your mom is up to," Hanson said. "I was really freaked out, after that guy… I mean… You guys just disappeared."

"I know," Valerie said. "And it turns out he was a *serious* jerk, just manipulating me to try to make things easier for him. He really didn't care about you or any of our friends. He just wanted my mom to do the job he was there to recruit her for, you know?"

"But I *saw* the sidewalk crack," Hanson said. "I saw it."

"I don't have an explanation for that," Valerie said. "He just turned out to be a real jerk."

"But you're here," Hanson said.

"I'm here."

"And Sasha is awesome, and I really like Ethan."

"I'm glad," Valerie said, smiling.

"Is your mom happy?" he asked.

"I haven't talked to her much," Valerie said. "I hope so."

"Where is she?" Hanson asked.

"Truth? I have no idea," Valerie answered. "All I know is that what she's doing is important."

"Are *you* happy?" he asked. "I like the people well enough, and I get that you said that this was a huge opportunity for *you*, but it… This isn't your style. You know?"

"I know," she said. "And I actually came in really behind. I've been working really hard just to try to catch up with the rest of them. But… Yeah. I think I am happy. I don't know when it's going to get easier, but I wouldn't choose to be anywhere else."

"Okay, I'm ready," Sasha said, traipsing down the stairs in a pink blouse and a skirt.

Valerie hadn't been aware the girl owned anything but khakis and stodgy button-ups.

Hanson stood quickly.

"You look pretty," he said, and Sasha skittered sideways.

"Thank you," she said.

Valerie rolled her eyes.

"My birthday party, guys. This is supposed to be about me."

Sasha came over to take Valerie's elbow, peeking around her at Hanson.

"I'll behave," she said.

"No promises," Hanson said.

Valerie elbowed him in the side and he grunted for show, following her and Sasha down the stairs and out toward the cottages.

As they got close, Valerie could hear the sound of music and voices.

"I honestly didn't think anyone would come," Valerie told Sasha, and the redhead shrugged happily.

"Ethan Trent is throwing a party," she said. "It doesn't matter *why*. Everyone will come, just to be around him when he's happy."

Valerie rolled her jaw to the side.

"You're telling me that my birthday party is a political schmoozing event."

"Basically," Sasha said, grinning. "But it's a *party*. I haven't been to one before."

Valerie dropped her chin toward her neck.

"Never?" she asked.

Sasha shook her head quickly.

"No."

"Well, prepare to be disappointed," Valerie said. "It isn't like in the movies."

Hanson snorted, and they changed course to make their way toward his cottage specifically.

"I've never stayed by myself before," he said. "When we travel with the team, I've always got roommates."

The front door of the cottage opened, spilling light and music into the night, and Ethan waved them on.

"Come on, come on," he said. "We have to sing before anyone can eat."

Valerie looked up at Hanson, grinning.

"Looks like you aren't staying by yourself for a while, yet."

She broke loose of Sasha and Hanson, who let her go easily, and she skipped up to Ethan.

"Happy birthday, Valerie Blake," he said, looking her in the eyes.

"It was last week, but thank you," she answered, and he smiled slowly.

"It isn't *real* until it's celebrated," he answered after a moment, then raised his arm.

Valerie went inside.

It was.

Exactly.

Like a movie.

The small cottage was packed out, just barely enough room for people to congregate and talk, with a small zone between the couch and the television eventually emptying out for people to dance. Everyone wished Valerie a happy birthday, holding their red party cups over their heads to keep them from getting bumped, and then they went on with their night.

Furniture was filled, counters were filled, the walls were lined with kids sitting with plates and cups, talking and laughing over the music and each other.

"This is…" Valerie said after about an hour. "Wow. I didn't think this was possible."

"Which part?" Ethan asked cheerfully.

He was fully in his element. Everyone *really* wanted to talk to him, and Valerie could just imagine that they were only tolerating her for the opportunity to talk to him *here* and *now*, but he showed no sign of favoritism or cliquing. He was happy to see everyone like they were a long-lost friend, talking to them like he knew their lives, their folk. Everyone was at ease with him, and Valerie marveled, getting a glimpse of the level of *slick* he was capable of.

225

It wasn't deception.

She didn't see an ounce of deception to him.

It was that he was capable of making people feel *comfortable* and liked and familiar. Exactly the way he'd done it to her.

"You run a pretty good game," Valerie said to him.

"What?" he asked. "Throwing a party?"

"I don't believe anyone actually showed up," she said. "But that's not it. You laid down some *serious* game, the first night we met, and you haven't let up ever since."

He looked directly at her, eyes playful.

"You have a problem with game?" he asked.

"Only if it's a lie," she answered, holding his gaze. He shook his head slowly.

"I've been running the same circles my entire life," he said. "They're *big* circles, but they're all the same. You are a breath of fresh air, Valerie, and I've never met anyone I want to spend time with more than you."

She raised her chin a fraction, then nodded.

"That is an acceptable answer."

He grinned.

"You ought to go spend some time with your friend," he said. "He came all this way to see you. Don't want you to ditch him for my party."

"Oh, I'm not ditching him," Valerie answered. "I'm giving them space."

He raised an eyebrow, lifting up on his toes to find where Hanson was leaning against a wall talking to Sasha.

"Well, well," Ethan said. "Now that's a match I wouldn't have called."

"Yup," Valerie said. "But he's a nice guy and she's a nice girl, and maybe they actually deserve each other."

"Are you saying that I'm not a nice guy?" Ethan asked in mock-hurt.

"And that I'm not a nice girl," Valerie answered with an easy grin. "Own it, wear it."

He grinned.

"As long as you're giving them space, then, you want to give them a little more space?"

"What does that mean?" Valerie asked.

He jerked his chin toward the door, and she frowned, considering.

She hadn't really had her heart set on dancing, and kids continued to wander down from the dorm as they caught wind of the fact that going to Valerie's birthday party wasn't social suicide.

Fear of missing out was beginning to come into play, and the party was threatening to spill out into the common area.

"I don't want Hanson getting banned," Valerie said.

Ethan raised a hand and waved Shack over.

"You're the bouncer," Ethan yelled to his friend. "Anyone starts acting up, place gets too crowded, send people back up to the main building. Keep us under the radar."

Shack nodded, then winked at Valerie.

"Happy birthday," he said, and she smiled, then hugged him.

"Thank you," she said. "For actually meaning that."

He shrugged, then frowned as the front door opened again.

"We're going to have the entire dorm try to pack in here, aren't we?" he asked.

"Yup," Ethan asked. "And you're the one who gets to say who stays and who goes."

Shack grinned, and Ethan took Valerie's arm, weaving her through to the front door and ducking through before it closed again.

"Is he going to make people mad?" Valerie asked. "I don't want anyone coming after Hanson because they got snubbed."

"They know better than to go against Shack," Ethan said. "First because he's capable of planting them face-first into the wall, and second of all because his mom is the second-most powerful person on the Council."

"After your dad?" Valerie asked, and he nodded.

"After my dad."

"Is that a contentious relationship?" Valerie asked, and he shook his head.

"Not always. Usually, it's more like me and Shack. Elvis is going to take over the council, someday, if everything goes to plan, and Shack has two older brothers who actually *want* it, but I actually think everyone would be a lot better off if it was us two leading it, in ten years."

"Only ten?" Valerie asked. He grinned.

"Maybe twenty. My dad has a lot of fight left in him."

The stars were out in force, now. Mostly nights in this part of the country were cloudy, or at least muggy enough that the sky wasn't open, but tonight it was, the Milky Way sprawling across overhead, bright enough that they didn't need a moon to see.

"How much do you tell your dad?" Valerie asked.

"What do you mean?" he asked.

"About stuff," she said. "Do you have a cell phone that you can text him or do you e-mail or anything?"

"Cell phones don't work here," he said. "And I'm not allowed to have internet any more than anyone else is."

"Do you talk to him?" Valerie asked.

He slid his arm down to wrap his hand around hers, walking with an aimlessness that still had intent to it.

"Yes," he said. "I'm supposed to tell him about anyone I see at the school that the Council should recruit."

"But they don't recruit students," she said. "So you're just looking at seniors, right?"

He shrugged, turning his face up to the sky.

"You could drop out of school and not be a student anymore," he said.

"So they recruit students to drop out of school as the way of avoiding the rule?" Valerie asked.

"Look, it's the Council. I just tell my dad the things that he specifically asks about."

"Have you told him about me?" Valerie asked.

He paused for another moment, then looked over at her.

"Yes."

"What have you told him?" Valerie pressed.

"That you're good," he said. "Better than anyone gives you credit for. And that you're working with Mr. Tannis on something, and no one knows what. That you were able to stop the silverthorn the night that the demons attacked, and that a bunch of the girls say that you saved their lives, holding a door against a demon."

Valerie swallowed.

"I don't like you talking to anyone about me," she said.

"I know," he said. "I knew you wouldn't like it, every time I did it. But he's my dad, and it's my job. My whole life, he's had Elvis, and Elvis was going to do all the big things, and then there was me, and he didn't ever know what he was going to do with me. He doesn't have much spare time, and he put it all into my brother. There was a time that he thought that he might not even send me to a magic academy at all."

"You know that's not an excuse," Valerie said. "You spied on me for your dad."

"I did," he said. "And that's not even the half of it."

She stopped walking.

"Tell me everything," she said. "Right now. I trust you, no matter what Sasha or anyone else tells me about you, but if you lie to me right now and I find out about it later, I will never trust you again. Tell me anything you want, I can forgive you, but don't lie to me."

He drew a slow breath and caught her other hand, standing in front of her with calm, serious eyes.

"My father didn't bring me to Europe to expose me to diplomatic contacts over there," he said. "He took me to Europe at the last minute to have an excuse to keep me out of school so that he could figure out who you were and give me a head start, getting close to you. My brother was supposed to, but he blew it because he thinks that you're below us and aren't worth our time. So my dad got a bunch of other information about you and gave it to me, so that you would like me from the beginning."

"Wow," Valerie said. "I've rattled him that bad?"

He laughed.

"Yes."

"Why?"

"Because you're a wildcard. Your mom just goes off-grid and does whatever it is she does, and you're here at school, and... He knows how all of the rest of the kids are, because he's been checking up on them at least once a year since the last war. He's known there

229

would be a second war since the end of the last one, and he says that we're going to be the ones to fight it. So he's been…" Ethan sighed. "He's basically been staffing an army of kids since the last war ended. And he knew that you could be powerful, given who your parents were, but that you would also probably be hard to control, so he needed somebody close to you…"

"And that would be you," Valerie said. He nodded.

"And I jumped, because it gave me something to do that he thought was important. I wanted to prove to him that I could do it."

"So you showed up that first night in the library intending to hit on me," Valerie said, some of the sparkle going out of the evening. "It wasn't serendipity."

"I had your picture from your sophomore year book," he said. "I'm sorry." He paused and Valerie started to say something else, but he cut in again. "No. I'm not. I don't care that it was my dad's idea that I came to find you and get to know you. I *did* find you, and I *did* get to know you, and I wouldn't have done anything different, if I had known from the beginning who you were. That's the truth."

"What if I asked you to stop talking about me to him?" Valerie asked. "Would you do it?"

He considered this, taking a step closer and looking her full in the face.

"I don't know if I can," he said.

"I can't talk to you if I can't trust that you won't pass everything on," Valerie said.

He nodded.

"I get that. And if you can still trust me… What if I just told him the things that I could see, and nothing that you actually *tell* me?"

The cottage was out of sight, from here, and the main building was just a silhouette in the stars behind her. They were alone and he was holding both of her hands.

"You could be the world's best liar," she said.

"I could if I tried," he agreed.

Gemma.

Gemma could have told her if he meant it or not.

Quite abruptly Valerie realized the value of a woman like that standing behind you.

"I don't tell you everything," Valerie said softly after a moment, turning her face down to look at her shoes. "I actually have lots of secrets."

He kissed her forehead.

"Then all I can hope is that someday I'm the person who knows all of them," he said. "But I live with the head of the Council. It's not like I'm going to *begrudge* you secrets."

She looked at him again.

"I swear to you, if you're keeping anything from me, I will find a way to make you regret it."

"Most effective way would be for you to never speak to me again," he said, giving her a half a smile, almost sad. "I spend all day... *knowing* when the next time I'm going to talk to you is."

She nodded.

She did, too.

"I like you," she said. "And I trust you. I may be the stupidest person on the earth, but it's the truth. I want to say that you should have told me before now... that really *is* how I feel... but it's only been about a month since we first met. And we don't really get to sit and talk very much. I don't know when you would have told me, before now."

He nodded.

"I really didn't want to, because I thought you'd dump me on the spot, but I had to tell you. I really like you, too."

"I can't dump you," Valerie said. "We aren't going out."

"Can I fix that?" he asked, a sparkle in his eyes again. He dropped one of her hands, taking a step back and kneeling. "Valerie Blake, will you go out with me?"

She pulled him back up to his feet.

"Yes," she said. "Idiot. You look stupid like that."

He came up onto his feet, but he didn't stop there. It was all one motion, from on one knee to putting his hand into her hair and kissing her.

She was stunned just for a moment, then she kissed him back, letting go of his hand and wrapping her arms around him.

There were techniques to kissing. Tactics and methods that she and her girlfriends had discussed at the lunch table for years.

Ethan Trent knew none of them.

He was still the best kisser she'd ever kissed.

He kissed her slow and deep for a long time, she lost track, and then he put both hands into her hair and rested his forehead against hers.

"Happy birthday, Valerie," he said.

"Thank you," she whispered back.

They stood for a moment, quiet in the dark, then Valerie startled and checked her watch.

It did not light up, and the stars weren't strong enough to see it by. Ethan offered her his watch. It was nearly midnight.

"I need to get back," she said. "The curfew."

"As long as Hanson is in the cottage, they're complying," Ethan said. "It's mostly so that the teachers have a few hours when they can move things around without worrying about the visitors seeing them."

"Still," Valerie said. "I need to get back."

"To the party or the dorm?" Ethan asked, taking her hand and starting off.

"Dorm," she said.

They walked back to the school and quiet through the hallways, stopping at the point where the girls' dorm hallway started.

He wasn't allowed past there; they both knew it.

"Thank you for my party," Valerie said. He kissed her knuckles and looked down the hallway.

"Sleep well," he answered. "I'll see you tomorrow."

"Night," she said, going to her door and opening it. She watched as he turned away, going to find the stairs that would take him up to the boys' dorm rooms, then Valerie stepped into her room and closed the door, leaning with her forehead against it for several moments, just relishing everything.

Everything.

"You need to be careful," a voice said.

Valerie jumped, almost screaming, and spun to find her mother sitting on her bed.

"Mom," she said. "You scared me to death. What are you *doing* here?"

"I came to warn you that you need to be careful of Hanson," she said.

"I what?" Valerie asked, dropping her chin. "You mean Ethan."

"Ethan who?" Susan asked. "I'm talking about your best friend."

"Why would I need to be careful of *Hanson*?" Valerie asked.

"His mom disappeared. When he came here, she should have come with, but she didn't, and I went to go see why, and I ended up going through their apartment. She is a magic user, and he may be, as well."

"What?" Valerie demanded. "No. He doesn't have any clue what's going on here. She had some big thing come up so she couldn't come, and he convinced her to let him come. Case closed. Where have you been?"

"Valerie," Susan said. "The reason she didn't come is because she *attended* Survival School. I just looked it up in Lady Harrington's office. She's changed her name, but she went here."

"You mean your mom's office," Valerie said, sitting down in her chair. Susan tipped her head to the side, surprised, then stood, putting her hands out. With a quick motion, she pulled something from off of her belt and went to stand at the door.

"I'm impressed with this, by the way," she said, marking the outer edge of the door with the thing from her belt.

"Mom, they have me inventing spells to kill people. I have so much I want to talk to you about, and Hanson really isn't it."

"Your father was here," Susan said. "He's the one who told you about Lady Harrington, isn't he?"

"He told me a lot of stuff," Valerie said. "Please come and sit and talk to me. You just dump me off here and disappear and leave me to figure out for myself that magic is actually *real* and I'm *good* at it…"

"I knew you would be," Susan said, taking a step back, then looking at her. "I can't stay. I shouldn't be here at all, but I needed to warn you."

"Warn me what? That Hanson's mom abandoned magic the same way you did?"

"She didn't," Susan said. "She's very good at disguising it, but once I got digging, I found all of it. She's been spying on us your entire life, and she's been using Hanson to do it probably for as long as he's been able to keep the secret. You need to be careful what you tell him."

"What *would* I tell him?" Valerie asked. "I don't *know* anything."

"You know *everything*," Susan said. "You know your dad is alive, you know what I do, you know that I've been here, and you know what Lady Harrington is up to. You might be the only person alive who knows all of those things, except that you told me."

"Mom, I don't want to be an assassin," Valerie said.

"Is that what they told you I am?" Susan asked.

"Mrs. Reynolds danced around the word a lot," Valerie said slowly. "But Dad never said it was wrong."

"Debbie Reynolds is a good woman," Susan said. "Just never got her head in the game."

"That's not an answer, Mom," Valerie said. "Where have you *been?*"

"All over, never the same place two nights in a row. And I need to get going. I know he's your friend, but just be aware that every word you say could reveal a secret that has life-or-death importance to it."

"Mom," Valerie said again, finally getting her mother's attention. "I need to talk to you. I don't understand."

Susan Blake came and knelt in front of her daughter, putting her hands on either side of Valerie's face, such a familiar touch.

"I know," Susan said. "And I'm still… I wish that I had told you everything you needed to know, brought you up in it, but I thought there was a chance we could stay out, and I took it. It would have been so much better if you could have grown up normal."

"Mom, I cast something designed to kill someone. Are you an assassin?"

"I'm tactical," Susan answered, looking over her shoulder and rising slowly, like a cat uncoiling. "They followed me. They knew

I would try to come and they've been waiting. I thought if I got in and out quickly…"

"Mom?" Valerie asked.

"At least the party got most of the students out of the building," Susan said. "So we've got that going for us."

"*Mom,*" Valerie said. Susan glanced back at her, then waved.

"Come on, get your stuff together. We've got a fight coming to us, and we only get home-court advantage if we use it."

"What are you *talking* about?" Valerie asked. "I don't have any stuff. I don't have any *money.* And I don't know what stuff I'd have, if I did have money. And I wouldn't know how to buy it, if I knew what to get."

"I thought I trained you to be more resourceful than that," Susan said. "What about your roommate? I bet Ivory Mills' daughter keeps *everything.*

Valerie went to get Sasha's basket of stuff, holding it out toward her mother with not a little bit of attitude and then going to her desk to unpack it more carefully.

"Who is coming?" she asked.

"Humans," Susan said. "Probably non-propagationists, though they're working with The Pure more and more these days. The Council is driving them together."

"I met Gemma," Valerie said, saying the words out loud a physical relief to her.

"And did you like her?" Susan asked.

"She wished me dead more than once," Valerie said.

"If it helps, she started out on that stuff with me before you were even born," Susan answered. "I think I broke her heart."

Valerie straightened.

"What?"

"Oh, okay, what did she tell you, then?" Susan asked.

"That she's my aunt and she works for the dark side," Valerie said quickly. "What do you mean you broke her heart?"

"We were best friends," Susan said. "I knew her because of Grant and we were really close for a few years. Really, really close. And then she was kind of called up into the big leagues early, while we were still at school, and Grant was staying in touch with her, surreptitiously… Anyway, I decided I wanted no part of playing that game in the long term and I bailed on them. Both of them. But what's funny is that I expect your dad took it better than she did. She started telling me the first year of the war that if I wasn't all-in, fighting the war, that I ought to be dead, so that she didn't have to worry about me. She got really dramatic, seeing everything that was going on up close like that."

"Should I just defend the door?" Valerie asked.

"If you want them to come fight you here in the room," Susan said. "I prefer to fight where my back isn't literally against a wall, if I can help it. But I'm quick. You feel like being quick?"

Valerie shoved the ingredients that felt useful to her into her pockets and went to stand next to her mother.

"Ethan told me that the cast they used to crack open the school showed up on a building in Europe," Valerie said.

"Is that one of the Trent boys?" Susan asked. "I hear nothing but bad things about either of them, but maybe you know better."

"I think he's had a major change of heart recently," Valerie said. Susan reached for the doorknob, as though feeling it out from a distance.

"You have that effect on people," Valerie's mother said. "You ready to move?"

"What does it mean, that the same cast was used in Europe as here?" Valerie asked.

"It means the European belief that they're immune to our war and can play both sides against the middle has already blown up, and they just don't know it yet," Susan answered. "Are you ready?"

"As I'm going to be," Valerie answered.

Susan nodded, pulling the door open and shouting words down the hallway. If there was anyone around to hear them, they didn't give a sign. Valerie wondered if the *entire* dorm hadn't emptied itself out into Hanson's cottage.

Susan was moving quickly, facing the end of the hallway that met with the rest of the building, but walking backwards.

"Where's the potions room?" Susan asked.

"You've never been here?" Valerie answered.

"Nope," Susan said. "Not through the doors, anyway."

"It's upstairs," Valerie said.

"Stairs are that way?" Susan asked, indicating the way she was facing. Valerie nodded.

Still nothing.

Apart from her mother acting like the world had ears, the hallway felt just like any other night after most everyone had gone to sleep.

"They're testing the defenses on the school," Susan said. "Can you copy a cast?"

"Maybe," Valerie said. "It kind of depends."

Susan got two red marking sticks out of her back pocket and handed one to Valerie, then turned and went to the last dorm room on the hall, putting a complex mark on it in a thick paint-like grease.

As though she'd been studying those shapes from Kindergarten, Valerie nodded.

"I can do that."

"You get that side, I'll do this side," Susan asked. "They'll have a heck of a time getting these girls *out* in the morning, but it will keep The Pure from using them as hostages while they're chasing us down."

"Why do they care so much?" Valerie asked. "This is the second time they've come here."

"The new leader of The Pure," Susan said, looking over her shoulder as she did the second door. "He and I have history, and he's pretty sure that between the two of us - meaning you and me - that one of us would be the key to his loss. So he wants to kill us both, just to be sure he gets the right one."

"Why would *I* matter?" Valerie asked.

Susan stopped, turning to face her, body unanimated for the first time since Valerie had opened her dorm room door.

"No one told you?" Susan asked. "No. I guess they wouldn't have. How would they have known? Most of them don't believe, anyway. The curse. You're a part of it, as far as any of us can figure out."

"What?" Valerie asked. "I thought that was just on council kids."

"You do know about it," Susan said cheerfully, turning to mark the next door. "Well, neither of us were *on* the council, but your dad and I both had close ties to it. And I was in the room when the curse was launched. Len hated me."

"I have *dark* magic?" Valerie asked.

"Don't be cute," Susan answered. "You're a mage. You have control of all three."

Valerie didn't see how that could be considered anything resembling cute. She marked the next door on her side of the hallway.

"I don't understand," Valerie said.

"Lady Harrington is an old traditionalist," Susan answered. They were moving quickly, still, though it felt less like someone was coming to kill them and more like Valerie's grandmother was going to catch them graffitiing the walls.

"That doesn't help," Valerie said. "Will you people talk sense, just for like a *minute*?"

"Mage," Susan said easily. "A person who possesses the skill to control all three branches of magic."

"How do you *know*?" Valerie asked.

"I've been testing you since you were five," Susan said. "And you prefer the light, without a doubt, but you have deep strengths in all of them."

"Does light magic kill people?" Valerie asked. Susan glanced back at her.

"You do see how there's a natural conflict between light and dark," her mother said. "Almost everything in dark magic has a light magic equivalent."

They got to the end of the hallway and Susan pointed left and then right.

"This way," Valerie said.

"Running is better," Susan answered. They are going to be right on top of us."

"Usually I can hear the front doors open," Valerie said.

"Easy to overcome that," Susan told her. Valerie was jogging, heading for the stairs up to Mr. Tannis' room.

She'd never much liked running, and running up stairs when she would have preferred to have been in bed…

She didn't mind when her mother stopped to mark the wall with a different design.

"Lady Harrington is going to be so mad when she finds that," Valerie said.

"She's mad all the time," Susan answered. "Not like I ever change anything."

They reached the top of the stairs. Mr. Tannis' room was the next one over.

Valerie tried the knob, but nothing happened.

"Here," Susan said, jamming a wicked-looking black key into the lock and twisting it. Something in the door popped and hissed, and Susan shouldered the door open.

"Go to work," she said.

"What?" Valerie asked.

"You said that you made a cast to kill someone with," Susan said. "I need to order up a dozen."

"*What?*" Valerie asked.

Susan glanced at her.

"You have a room full of weapons and an unknown number of people coming with the intent of killing you. I assume I don't have to remind you about our conversations on how this works."

"Mom, I don't *want* to kill people," Valerie said.

"Oh, honey, I know," Susan answered. "And you aren't warded any better than a baby seal. I'm leaving you in here and I'm going to fight them on my own. I just need your arsenal."

Valerie went over to the boxes, collecting things.

She was reserved.

She could partially make them, and then refuse to complete them or turn them over. She was just making progress with the time that she had, in case she decided to actually make them.

As she sat at a desk, Susan was a blur of motion, going around the classroom and peering into this box and that, taking a little of this and the entire container of that and tossing them onto desks.

Their apartment had always been spotless and organized to within an inch of its life. Valerie had never seen this side of her mother before.

There were footsteps outside and Susan went back to the door, marking it in blue.

Valerie had a hard time focusing as she heard the voices out there.

"They're human?" she asked quietly, and Susan nodded.

"Possible they have a demon with them, but not likely. Mostly the demons don't care about you or me."

"It was demons who came for me last time," Valerie said, and Susan nodded, watching the door.

"Hired. They may not care, but they'll take money or favors. And at the end of the day, they enjoy that sort of thing. Terrorizing teenagers? Sure. Hunting down Susan Blake? A lot less mercenaries for hire."

The door thumped, and Susan went back to one of the tables, tossing things together and speaking over it in a low voice that kept Valerie from catching any of the specific sounds. For her part, Valerie was getting close, but watching her mother she realized she didn't *have* to be anywhere near that precise, as long as she did it *right*.

It was a profound realization, that right and precise were… different for her.

And she went cold.

Her hands worked mechanically over the ingredients, always moving, often before the previous ingredient had finished settling on the table. It was something she could do by *touch*, even as she'd been doing it by instinct. She didn't have to look carefully at the barra barra. She just needed to split it and twist it with the red thelp. Power built, she was good.

She went on.

The door thumped again, and the ceiling shifted overhead by enough that dust drifted down at them.

Susan shifted her table to avoid it. Valerie, mercifully, didn't have to because of the specific alignment of the dust.

"Keep moving," Susan said at one point as the door thumped again, cracking. "Whatever you do, keep moving."

"What do I do?" Valerie asked, putting aside one of the full casts that she'd used on Mr. Tannis. It wouldn't work in this room, if she understood it right. Susan had to use it before the people outside got in.

"I trust you," Susan said, looking up for a moment. "I trust you more than anyone alive to have my back. I know I kept all of this from you, but you've always had such good instincts. Just go with them."

Valerie frowned, then Susan gave her a tight-lipped smile and came over to take the casts Valerie had finished.

"Keep two," her mother said.

"They won't work in here," Valerie said, and Susan nodded.

"You have to use them before anyone makes it through the door," Susan said. "But I'll drive them back. Okay? You only have to use them as a last resort."

Valerie looked at her mother and nodded.

"I've missed you," Valerie said, and Susan gave her a tighter smile.

"Not as much as I've missed you," she said, then shook her head. "Bygones. We can't have it back because that's not the world we live in. Finish these. I may be back for them."

Valerie nodded quickly and Susan went to stand in front of the door, putting both hands out toward it to form a diamond with her thumbs and forefingers. She shouted her cast, now, a language Valerie didn't recognize at all, and the doorframe glowed red, first dully and then so brightly and with so much heat that Valerie had to look away.

There was an explosion and bits of wood went flying past Valerie, and her mother was gone.

There were shouts in the hallway and other noises - impact, hissing, thuds and clinks and groans - that indicated that the fight had successfully gone outside. Valerie looked over her shoulder at the door, then walked around the desk so that she could face it while she continued to work.

Keep moving.

Just keep making *stuff*. Some of it was bound to be right.

Maybe some of it would be a bomb. Literally. Maybe there were worse things in the world, right now.

Valerie went back to the bins, watching as cement dust floated into the room. Her hands worked mechanically and unemotionally, commandeering a new desk and setting off on a new cast that she couldn't identify any more than she could identify any of the ingredients.

It didn't matter.

She knew what she was doing and she did it, eventually soaking a papyrus rag in a purplish fluid and going to get a lighter out of one of the front bins. She walked to the back of the room, standing with her back to the door as she listened to her mother fight out there, completely outnumbered.

Assassins weren't intended to fight even hand-to-hand. They were supposed to simply kill and vanish.

Her mother wasn't an assassin.

She was special forces.

Valerie smiled at the thought, then lit the papyrus and tossed it out into the hallway.

What had she just done?

Not a clue.

But that was how you used it, so she went on, scavenging through boxes and bins that were beginning to fall on the floor with the intensity of the battle outside.

It was late enough that all of the teachers would be in their personal cottages, asleep. Valerie doubted that the magic going on out in the hall was well-enough warded that Lady Harrington didn't know about it, but Valerie didn't actually know where the woman slept, and she wasn't sure that she was hoping Lady Harrington showed up. As fearsome as everyone made her out to be, the fight out there... it was lethal. Valerie could feel it, even as she stood in Mr. Tannis' well-warded classroom.

Maybe the teachers would put together a rally of some kind to save Susan Blake. Maybe Mrs. Gold and Franky Frank - the boy's dorm supervisor - would come storming in and get themselves killed.

There was no way of knowing.

Valerie kept working.

She mixed and cut and threw and painted and ate. She actually ate one of her own casts.

That was how strange the world had gotten.

And then there was a thud, one that her mind simply recognized was her mother's body, and Valerie looked up from the table where she was working to find two men in view of the door.

It was smoky and dim out in the hallway, and it was possible they were teachers.

Possible.

Valerie picked up the two casts from the table, the ones she'd built for Mr. Tannis, and she walked slowly toward the door, watching as the men approached something just outside of her field of vision. They were afraid of it.

And then one of them turned his head and looked Valerie in the eye.

He grinned.

"Hello, little girl," he said.

The other straightened.

"Is that her?" he asked.

The first man nodded, coming to lean against the doorframe.

"Can't you tell, just looking at her?"

The second man spoke, opening his hand at her as though he expected something to happen.

Valerie *felt* it happen.

The warding stretched around her like a spider's web, tensing with the effort it took to hold back the cast, breaking under the force. It hit her, but there was little enough of it left that she simple had to breathe a simple spell of healing and protection that put up a little invisible bubble around her and kept the rest of the cast from hitting her at all.

She held up the two killing casts in her palms as the men changed posture, preparing to come into the room.

Nothing to do but let them come in and physically beat her to death, or.

Or.

She launched them both simultaneously.

She hadn't known it was possible, but it suddenly was.

It was *her* magic, and she controlled it, sending it at two chests, two rib cages, knowing where it would hit.

Knowing what it could do.

The second man, the one who had cast at her, was the first one to feel the hit. He grabbed at his chest and stumbled back, trying to rip at his shirt. The second man just slumped sideways against the doorframe, eyes wide at Valerie. His feet slid across the floor until they hit the other side of the doorframe, and there they stayed.

"Shouldn't…" he said, then there was a gargle and a groan as he tipped over backwards into the hallway.

The other man was spinning in a circle, ripping at his shirt like he was trying to put out a fire, and then he, too, gurgled and fell to the floor.

She'd done it.

She'd *killed* two men.

The men who had killed her mother.

It all hit her at once, and Valerie staggered into a desk, trying to find the surface with her fingers so that she wouldn't fall onto the floor.

"Don't give yourself too much credit," Susan said, coming around the corner. "Though it was a great assist. You didn't kill them, daughter."

Valerie ran into her mother's arms and hugged her hard.

"I thought…" she whispered, and her mother nodded.

"I know you did," she said. "Healing warding makes us exceedingly hard to kill unless you really know your stuff. Are you okay?"

Susan held Valerie out at arms' length and looked her up and down.

"I'm fine," Valerie said. "Are you okay?"

"I'm harder to kill than you can imagine," Susan said, looking around the room. "Henry is going to be impossible, after this. All right. One of my secrets to survival is to never stay in the same place for too long. And I've been here *way* too long. I need to go."

"What about me?" Valerie asked. "I have to come with you."

Susan gave her another hug, then held her by her elbows.

"You have to *stay*. You are safe here, as safe as anyone can make you, and you're learning how to take care of yourself. Look at what you just did. That jamming vapor was… one of the best I've ever seen. I know it's hard, but it will get easier as you figure it out."

"But they just tried to *kill* us," Valerie said.

"They're going to keep trying," Susan answered. "But you better believe if they leave themselves open like that, sending this kind of people out here to get you, I'm going to take advantage. That's why I have to go *right now*. People are out of position, and that's when I get my opportunities. I mean it about Hanson, though. Be careful."

"I think he's dating my roommate, as of tonight," Valerie answered. "*You* be careful of Hanson."

Susan stretched her mouth to the side, then shook her head.

"I can't convince you," she said. "All I can do is warn you. Why isn't his mom here? Think hard about that."

"I *told* you," Valerie started, but Susan shook her head.

There were voices out in the hallway again.

"I have to go now," her mother whispered. "I hate to leave you with the cleanup, but clearly no one will blame *you* for this."

Valerie gave her mother a dark look, and Susan smiled brightly.

"So proud of you," she whispered, then kissed Valerie's forehead and went out the door.

There was perhaps a fifteen second gap, and then Lady Harrington's voice.

"Who's in there?" she called.

"It's me," Valerie called back. "Valerie Blake. And it isn't my fault."

Aftermath

Back in the big conference room.

And every teacher in the school was pressed in there, with Valerie sitting at the table and Lady Harrington sitting at the other end.

"I will remind the faculty that I plan on dismissing all of you before we get to the sensitive portion of this interview, but that I know all of you have questions and it wouldn't be right to hold the entire interview in private."

Valerie wasn't sure she wanted to answer *any* questions, just now, not to mention *all of them*, but she sat still, doing her best not to fidget.

She *wanted* to go to bed and lay and think on what her mother had said and everything else that had happened that night.

But, no.

The teachers had questions.

"What happened?" Mr. Jamison started. Valerie shook her head.

"I don't know what I'm supposed to say," she answered.

"We'll save that for the private interview," Lady Harrington said. "I'm opening the floor to questions about the magic exchange and nothing else."

"How many casts happened in my room?" Mr. Tannis asked.

"Um," Valerie said. "A few? I… I don't know what counts as *in* and what was in the hallway. Where it started or where it finished?"

"Mr. Tannis, you can probe at the specifics on your own time, if you don't mind," Lady Harrington said.

"Are you okay?" Mrs. Reynolds asked. Valerie nodded.

"They tried to hit me, but the warding in the room protected me, and I cast something that healed it and blocked it."

"What was that?" someone else asked. Valerie tried to

remember the words that she'd used, but they fumbled on her lips, no longer mechanical and easy.

"That worked?" another teacher asked.

"You've never worked with a natural before," Lady Harrington murmured.

"Who did the casts on the doors in the girls' dormitory hallway?" another teacher asked.

"I did some of them," Valerie said.

"You?" several people asked.

"Yes," Valerie said slowly. "Me."

Was she insulted?

She was too tired and too overwhelmed to be insulted.

"Do we need to do anything to repair the damage specifically caused by your casts?" someone asked.

"I don't know," Valerie said.

"I will detail all casts that she knew of and recommend a course of action for all of the classrooms facing the hallway," Mr. Tannis said. For a moment, Valerie genuinely liked him.

"Who were they?" another teacher asked. "How did they get in?"

"She is very much unlikely to know that," Lady Harrington said.

"Are you controlling your magic?" Mr. Jamison asked. Valerie shrugged.

"Some more, some less. Practicing with Mr. Tannis has been helping."

That was actually true, in point of fact.

"Did you use dark magic?" another of Valerie's teachers asked.

"I don't know," Valerie said. "Mr. Tannis can help me figure that out."

If the man was going to volunteer, she wasn't going to turn him down.

Lady Harrington held up a hand.

"It is very late and we have guests on campus. We are very lucky that Mr. Trent had organized for all of the students to be out of the building, but we need to be able to get the girls into their rooms as they return, and we need to conceal the damage for our visitors by morning. Everyone here who is *not* going to be staying for the private interview has plenty of things to occupy themselves with before they retire to bed. Thank you."

Valerie watched as the teachers filed out, Mrs. Reynolds and Mr. Tannis both getting indications that they were dismissed, leaving just Valerie, Mr. Jamison, and Mr. Benson there with Lady Harrington.

"All right, Valerie," Lady Harrington said. "Mr. Benson will be inspecting every inch of ground that you covered tonight, and if I find that you left anything out, I will expel you."

"If you expel me, I will die," Valerie answered. It wasn't intended to be defiant - she *hoped* it didn't come out defiant - but it wasn't a plea, either.

"I will expel you from the school, but you will be permitted to reside on campus through the end of the spring semester. You have no guardians to release you into their care, so we will continue to be your custodians. But I will not have you in the dorm, nor in classes if I cannot trust you to tell me the truth after something like this happens."

Valerie pause for a long time, considering this.

"I don't know what I'm supposed to say and what I'm not," she finally said. "There are so many secrets, and I don't know who to trust."

She looked at Mr. Jamison, and he gave her a sympathetic smile.

"Look at me," Lady Harrington said. "This is about your best interests, child. I care about them more than anyone in the building, and I take the charge of your care very seriously. If I cannot protect you, then I will not continue to put you in harm's way. I will lock you away in a protected building and wait for your mother to claim you."

"She was here tonight," Valerie finally said.

Lady Harrington crossed her arms.

"You say that like it's supposed to surprise me," the woman said. "There are eight dead men and women in my classroom hallway upstairs, and you were the only one left standing there. Did you expect me to think that *you* killed them?"

"No," Valerie sulked.

"Why was she here?" Lady Harrington asked.

"To warn me to be careful around Hanson," Valerie said. "But that makes no sense. He's been my best friend forever, and this is the first time she's *ever* been concerned about him."

"Who *is* your friend?" Lady Harrington asked.

"I grew up with him," Valerie answered. "He's no one."

"He's here by himself," Mr. Benson said. "Not all families consider it strange for a teenage young man to travel on his own, but most of the time an older relative would have come with."

"Who is his mother?" Lady Harrington asked.

"Her name is Martha," Valerie said. "Martha Cox. And his dad is Victor. I don't know his dad very well."

"Victor Cox," Lady Harrington said, then shook her head and looked at Mr. Benson. "Does that ring any bells for you?"

"No," he said.

"It was weird for her to not be here," Valerie admitted. "But he's my *best* friend. You don't understand. I trust him more than anyone. And he doesn't even know magic exists."

"I'll look into it," Mr. Benson said.

"What happened after your mother got here?" Lady Harrington asked, turning her attention back to Valerie.

"She told me to be careful with Hanson, which is just stupid, and then she said someone had come for her, and we marked the doors. She marked something in the stairwell, too, and then she broke us into Mr. Tannis' room. I don't know what she cast, and I don't even know if I'll *remember* what I cast. We were fighting for our lives."

"I believe that," Lady Harrington said. "But you will still assist Mr. Tannis in repairing what you damaged, and you will, in particular, be responsible for keeping your guest off of the second floor of the building on Saturday. We will have reconstruction finished by Sunday, but I think you have two hours' of work to do with Mr. Tannis in the meantime."

"It's going to be the middle of the night before it's done," Valerie said. "And it wasn't my fault."

"I don't care if it was your fault or not," Lady Harrington said. "You made the mess. There is no one more capable or *safer* cleaning it up than you."

"Are the men still up there?" Valerie asked quietly, trying not to show her shudder at the memory.

"I've had them taken care of," Mr. Benson said. "It's just the physical damage, at this point."

Valerie nodded, looking at the table for a moment.

"I didn't choose any of this," she said. "I just want to go home and be normal."

"You were never destined for normalcy, my dear," Lady Harrington said with what might have been genuine compassion. "Please get yourself cleaned up and into some working clothes and meet Mr. Tannis upstairs."

Valerie nodded, standing.

"I'm sorry," she said after a pause. "I'm glad no one else got hurt."

"You and your mother locked all of the girls who were still here into their rooms, including Mrs. Gold. It's a good thing that Franky was hard enough asleep that he didn't hear it, or else he *might* have ended up dead."

Valerie nodded, then frowned.

"How does he manage the boys, if he sleeps that hard?" she asked, and Lady Harrington gave her a cool, humored smile.

"An elaborate system of alarms that he changes almost every day," she said. "Go on, now. You aren't the only one who's missing sleep." She paused, then pursed her lips. "Oh, and the next time you see her, you ask my daughter what the *hell* she was thinking, locking me out of my own school."

Valerie looked at her fingers there on the table, not moving, *unable* to move. Finally she raised her head and Lady Harrington raised her eyebrows and nodded.

So there.

They both knew that they knew.

Valerie shook her head.

"I don't know when that's going to be," she said, and Lady Harrington nodded.

"I know."

Valerie pressed her lips, then nodded and left.

She didn't want to go back up to the room, but her feet got her there, anyway. Mr. Jamison was there, helping Mr. Tannis get the debris there swept up - there didn't appear to be any magic involved - and Mr. Jamison straightened as Valerie arrived.

"Are you okay?" he asked.

"I'm tired," Valerie said. "And I just want to go to bed, but I have to help clean up everything here, instead."

"Was your mother okay?" Mr. Jamison asked, his voice lower. Valerie nodded.

"They hit her hard, there at the end, but it didn't seem to bother her at all. I don't really know what happened, but she ran out like nothing had happened."

"The structural damage out here will be easy enough to deal with," Mr. Tannis said from across the hall, cutting in. "I'd prefer you start in my classroom with picking things up and putting them away."

"*That* has to be done tonight?" Valerie asked. "Can't you just close the door so that no one sees?"

"You, as much as anyone, should recognize the risk we run if we allow those things to mingle unattended," Mr. Tannis said. "The room will be as you found it before any of us go back to bed."

Valerie frowned, then sighed and did as she was told.

The room was a disaster.

Even more than she'd remembered.

There were half-completed casts on every table, and only half of the wall containers were still attached, at a rough count. She wasn't just going to have to go through everything on the floor; every box and bag and crate, she was going to have to go through it to make sure that it *only* had in it a single ingredient, and that all of them were packaged safely.

She worked for two and a half hours, easy, methodically going through every box one by one, cleaning up messes and asking Mr. Tannis what to do with spoiled ingredients - there was *dust* everywhere, and just mixing them all into a dustpan was unacceptable, even to Valerie.

As she was getting through to the front of the room and

thinking about how to unwind the casts on the desks - no one had even *begun* to teach her *that* skillset - someone cleared their throat, and she turned to find Mr. Benson standing in the doorway.

"I need to show you a picture," he said, and Valerie nodded, straightening.

Her back hurt.

"Okay."

"I went through the yearbooks from the four years I attended here, and I found a picture. This is Martha Combs and Vick McIntire."

Valerie's stomach clenched, knotted itself, as she walked across the room to look at the picture.

Mr. Cox's build was impossible to mistake, even at seventeen years old. He was the spitting image of Hanson, though Hanson Cox had his mother's smile and her wavy hair. She put her hand over her mouth.

"They were here," she whispered.

He nodded.

"I don't know what he knows, what motivation his parents might have had to do whatever it was they've done, or even what your mother knows, but I remember that girl. She was an underclassman when I was an upperclassman, and she had big dreams."

"Did my mother know?" Valerie asked, and Mr. Benson shrugged.

"There's no reason to suspect that they would have crossed paths between then and now. It's possible that they were strangers to each other before your mother decided to run away with you. I don't know."

"He's been spying on me," Valerie said. "Just like Ethan."

"Don't jump to conclusions," Mr. Benson said. "You... You aren't the first person who comes to mind when you think about people it would be *worth* spying on, if you'll forgive me saying it."

Valerie sighed, putting her hands over her eyes.

She was *so* tired.

"Go to bed," Mr. Benson said. "Lady Harrington thinks that the best therapy for shocking situations is dealing with the aftermath in a mechanical, pragmatic fashion, but I personally think that a good night's sleep will do wonders."

Valerie let her arms drop.

"It's all a disaster," she said. "Nothing is true."

"Everything is true," Mr. Benson said, tipping his head to look at her. "It's people telling you things that might not be true. But what *is*, has *always* been true."

She frowned, and he gave her a half a smile.

"Go on. You'll feel better in the morning. I can almost promise it."

She nodded, going to the sink and washing her hands, then walking past Mr. Benson as he picked up a conversation with Mr. Tannis. The potions teacher had been in and out enough to ask questions on every single one of the half-casts, and about every one of them that Valerie had constructed and used. He was apparently putting together the entire fight out in the hallway the way a crime-scene investigator would have, and he was very excited.

It just made Valerie more tired.

She went downstairs, finding girls asleep on the floors under towels. Mrs. Gold's door was in splinters, and she and Lady Harrington were standing in front of one of the dorm doors, speaking quietly.

"You can't open them?" Valerie asked, feeling wretched.

"It's a strong ward," Lady Harrington said. "I expect it will vaporize with the sunrise, but I can't be sure."

"Then if I just let everyone in…?" Valerie asked.

"Be my guest to try," Mrs. Gold said.

Valerie walked up to the nearest door and put her hands on it, feeling the energy there. It was one that she had drawn.

She remembered words that her mother had said, and she spoke them again, not even knowing what they meant, but the magic clicked, and she turned the knob, opening the door.

"Make sure everyone pees before they go to bed," Valerie said, starting for the next door. "That would suck."

"Miss Blake, I'm going to have to insist that you tell me how you did that," Lady Harrington said.

"And I'm going to have to insist that you let me go to bed,"

Valerie answered, speaking to the next door and opening it. "I don't have the... I don't want to deal with you tonight, and I'm making bad decisions."

She was upset.

Earth-shaken upset.

Hanson wasn't her best friend.

He was a spy, and he always had been.

Who was he even reporting to?

Why would they care how she wore her hair to school in the fourth grade?

She went all the way up and down the hallway, opening the doors, then she went to her own room and closed it, even as Lady Harrington and Mrs. Gold were trying to say something to her.

She didn't care.

None of it made sense, and everything that had *ever* made sense was a lie.

She had a bed.

It felt good under a sore back.

Ethan Trent had kissed her, and she'd liked it.

It felt like a lifetime ago.

Too much.

It was all too much.

She lay down in her clothes and went to sleep.

She woke stiff, sore, and very confused.

She knew that she'd been upset when she went to sleep, but it was all a mush of things and she didn't remember why.

And then she saw Sasha sitting on the side of her bed, watching Valerie, and she remembered.

Valerie groaned.

"What time is it?" she asked.

"Almost ten," Sasha said. "Hanson and Shack went to the weight room first thing this morning, and they're hanging out in the cafeteria now, waiting for you."

Valerie rubbed her face.

Hanson was the *last* person she wanted to see, right now.

254

"How much do you know?" she asked Sasha.

"I know that the doors stayed shut until almost eight, and everyone is freaking out because they heard that you did it. Was it a prank?"

"Is that seriously all they've told you?" Valerie asked, sitting up. "Evil jerks. That's why there are so many secrets. The good guys shouldn't *keep* all of these secrets, Sasha."

"So you tell me," Sasha said. "And let's go from there. What happened last night?"

Valerie threw herself back down onto the bed.

"Ethan kissed me," she said.

"He *what?*" Sasha asked. "Oh, my gosh, that's… I'm so excited for you. I mean, I am, really, but… what has that got to do with you locking everyone in their rooms?"

"Nothing," Valerie said. "It's just the only part I feel like talking about."

"Okay," Sasha said, with a tone that said she was willing to drop it.

"No," Valerie said. "It's that the rest of it *sucks.*"

"Okay," Sasha said again, settling onto her bed once more.

"My…" Valerie paused. "How safe are we, in here? Can anyone listen in to what we're saying?"

"Electronic devices are pretty easy to mask over, if you know what you're doing," Sasha said. "And magic doesn't really work like that. You can't bug somebody's room and listen in."

"So… short answer, no, they can't?" Valerie asked.

"Short answer, no they can't," Sasha affirmed.

"All right," Valerie said, checking to make sure there weren't any shadows under the door to give away someone standing there. "So, my mom came last night. She wanted to warn me about something… and that's a secret I have to keep until I find out a few more things, but she came to warn me about something, and some people who were hunting her or me or both of us… I'm not entirely sure, anyway… they showed up. So we locked the doors so that anyone who was here in the girls' dorm would be safe, because the people coming only *really* cared about the two of us. And then we went up to Mr. Tannis' room and… My mom killed all of them. I was right there, and… I saw them, after. It was… It was awful."

"Oh, my gosh," Sasha said. "Are you okay?"

"No," Valerie said. "I don't even want to think about it, because if I *don't* think about it, then maybe it didn't happen. I mean, I'm glad we lived and not them, and I even… Sasha, I tried to cast on them, and I think it *worked*. It wasn't *enough*, but I think I actually cast something at a pair of men that might have killed them, if they weren't ready for it."

"Wow," Sasha said. "I would have died."

"No, Sasha," Valerie said. "Don't…"

"I'm serious," Sasha cut in. "You wouldn't have cast at someone unless they were actually coming to *kill* you, and I would have stood there and *died*. I would be dead. You aren't. You defended yourself, and I'm amazed at that."

Valerie paused.

Got up and went to sit down next to Sasha, wrapping her arms around the girl.

"Thank you," Valerie whispered. "That was exactly what I needed to hear."

"I'm so sorry it happened," Sasha said. "But I'm glad you're alive."

Valerie nodded.

"I'm going to go take a shower," she said. She was still covered in spell debris; she could feel it on her skin.

"Will you go see Hanson first?" Sasha asked. "He's feeling really bad that he hasn't given you your birthday present yet. We spent your entire party together, and then when he went to look for you, you were gone…"

Valerie clamped her jaw and nodded.

"No, you didn't do anything wrong," Valerie said. "I'll… I'll go find him first. I really need to talk to him."

"Okay," Sasha said. "We both really did feel bad."

Valerie nodded, numb, changing her clothes and going out into the hallway.

It was the same as it had always been. Mrs. Gold had a door, there was no graffiti anywhere, girls came and went from their rooms, talking to each other and heading for leisure time or the bathroom or a late breakfast…

They went silent when they saw her, but that wasn't actually new.

Valerie turned her face away from it and headed for the cafeteria.

Hanson was sitting with Ethan and Shack, and both his face and Ethan's lit up when they saw her.

"Heard about your prank," Ethan called. "Epic."

Valerie shook her head, motioning to Hanson.

"Can we talk?" she asked.

"Yeah, sure," he said. "I'm really sorry I abandoned you all night last night…"

"Outside," Valerie said. "Please?"

He frowned, but gave a casual farewell wave to Ethan and Shack, then followed her down the hallway, past the offices, and out onto the front steps.

"I left your birthday present in my cottage," he said as he sat. "I didn't forget. I just… I really liked talking to Sasha, and then when we turned around, we couldn't find anyone, and Shack said that you'd left…"

"How long have you known?" Valerie asked, staring out at the tree line.

"That I like Sasha? I mean, maybe since kind of the first time I saw her…"

"About magic?" Valerie asked.

He fell silent.

It was an admission, and they both knew it.

"What do you know?" he asked. She snorted.

"How dare you?" she asked. "Going to cover up the secrets you think I haven't figured out?"

He sighed, resting his forehead on his palms.

"I told my mom that nothing gets past you," he said finally. "That you'd figure it out."

"How long have you been spying on me?" Valerie asked.

"Since were little," he said, looking over at her. "I didn't know that that's what it was, at the time. I just thought my mom was really interested in you and your mom, because she asked me a lot of questions. But she got straight with me around middle school, I guess."

"So you've known about magic since then," Valerie said.

"More or less," he said quietly. "I don't know how to *do* magic. I mean, my mom never taught me anything like that. But I knew she used it around the house, and that it was important to her, and that... I knew that it was involved with you and your mom, but she was never really specific how." He paused for a long time, though Valerie sensed there was more. "Not until the day you left."

There was a kneejerk reaction to apologize, but Valerie mastered it.

"And what were you going to do this weekend?" she asked. "Come up here and spy on me some more?"

"Yes," he said. "It doesn't mean that I don't miss you. Everything I've ever told you, everything I've ever been to you, it's *true*. You're my best friend, and there's a giant hole at school without you there. But, yeah... I'm supposed to go home and answer all of my mom's questions tomorrow."

"Who does she report to?" Valerie asked.

"I don't know," Hanson said.

"Not good enough," Valerie told him, and he put the side of his face down on his knees.

"I don't know what to tell you," he said. "I don't *know*."

"Then I don't know if you're with the good guys or the bad guys," Valerie said.

"I'm not a bad guy," Hanson protested. "You *know* that."

"No," Valerie said. "I don't. I don't know you, I don't know your mom, I don't know *my* mom... I don't know *anyone*. I'm completely alone and orphaned, and I think the only person I trust right now is Sasha Mills."

"I like her a lot," Hanson said, and Valerie shook her head.

"I want you to go," she said. "You aren't going to lay *eyes* on her or *me* again until the war is *over*. Do you understand? You don't get to spy on us. I'm going to tell Sasha everything, and I'll leave it up to her if she wants to wait for you. I don't think *I* ever want to see you again."

There was a very long pause, and she looked over at him, just wanting to know what he would say. Finally he shook his head.

"I don't believe you," he said. "I mean... You've been my best friend since we were six. And I've been yours. I love you and you love me. I get that you're angry and that... I deserve it. I know I do. But I don't believe that this is the end of us."

She felt the stinging behind her eyes that told her if she spoke just that moment, she was going to cry.

Swallowing hard, she looked out again.

More than anything, she wanted to put her head on his shoulder, tell him about the night before, how *angry* she was at her mom, how much she didn't *want* to be good at magic... Tell him that her dad was alive and that there were all of these *things* happening... How hard her classes were and how bad the kids were to her...

Tell him everything.

The way she always had.

"I need you to go," she finally said as she mastered all of it.

"It's not us," he said, standing. "It's our parents' fight. Whatever it is that's going on, she never told me, and I don't think your mom ever told you. But it's their fight. And when it's over... I hope we can be friends again."

"I'm not coming home again," Valerie said. "There's no home there anymore."

"You'll find me. Or I'll find you," he said, taking a step down and looking back up at her. "This isn't the end of us."

She frowned.

"I don't know you," she said, then turned before the tears escaped.

She looked up at the school as she heard his footsteps go down the stairs and then fall silent in the grass.

She couldn't go home. It was entirely true. There was no home left for her there.

Her mother... No one had any idea where her mother was, least of all Valerie, and her father was even less of an option.

No.

Much as it was impossible for her to have said it out loud, this place was her home now, and this was where she belonged.

She pulled the doors open and went in.
She had work to do.

Epilogue

Susan Blake sat on a worn couch at the back of a coffee shop, knees up, notebook spread across them as she wrote nonsense in it. It was a longstanding affectation, one that tended to keep people from talking to her, and left her with a misdirect should she find anyone significant watching her.

Leave the notebook, they tended to be willing to pounce on it and give her an extra moment to disappear.

Given how long she'd been doing it, it actually freed her mind to think through magic from a more chaotic perspective; this was where her biggest eureka moments had come from, there at the end of the war, and the habit hadn't left her.

"We need to talk about our daughter," a man's voice said.

"I made you fifteen minutes ago," Susan answered. "The minute you hit the door."

"Is that all?" he asked. "I thought you'd have felt the soulmerge. You not paying attention to that anymore?"

Susan smiled.

"You quit using it three blocks ago when you figured out where I was going to be," she said. "And you've been standing outside for the last hour trying to figure out if you actually wanted to see me."

She heard Grant snort softly as he sat down by her feet on the couch.

"Risky, coming back here," he said.

"Thought it was appropriate, once I knew you were looking for me," she said. "Besides, I wiped out their attack squad two nights ago. They'll still be reorganizing."

"Hadn't heard," Grant said, and Susan closed her notebook, tucking it under the couch.

"No, they wouldn't advertise that they got bested by a single operator and a teenage girl."

There was a pause, and Susan smiled again.

He hadn't anticipated she would go see Valerie.

She hadn't even known she was going to do it, herself, until that day when she'd finally had the good sense to check up on Martha Cox.

Victor had been the giveaway. The man couldn't hide in a pitch-dark room. He was too big and too notable in every way.

Martha, on the other hand, was only mediocre in any way that mattered to Susan. Most of the spies were. Helped them to blend in.

And it had worked on Susan.

"You took her away from me," Grant said.

"You were dangerous to everyone, including yourself," Susan answered, crossing her legs now so that she could actually see Grant.

He'd aged well.

He'd always had a solid nature to him, not heavy, but a fighter's build.

He'd always been a fighter.

She loved that about him.

"Haven't gotten any better," he admitted. "You still had no right."

"It was that moment," Susan said. "That moment or never. You would have done the same thing, if you were me and you'd had the opportunity."

"She's amazing," Grant said.

"I'm jealous that you've gotten to train her," Susan said. "It shows, by the way."

"Can't believe you brought a fight to her," Grant said, though he didn't sound angry. That. Susan smiled. That was jealousy.

"You wish you'd been there to see it," she said, and he covered a smile with his hand and nodded.

"I do."

"She did you proud," Susan said. She licked her lips and watched him. "Are we really going to do this?"

"Do what?" he asked.

That wasn't ignorance. He just wanted to hear her say it first.

"Sneak around on the wrong side of the line," she said. "Pretend like the last fifteen years didn't happen."

"I never left," he said. "And as far as I can see, there's no way we can end this once and for all without the two of us working together the way we did the last time we ended it."

"They're going to keep going after her," Susan said.

"And you're the one who stole her away so we couldn't train her."

"If I'd have stayed, every single person we'd ever known would have been trying to buy influence. She's my daughter and nobody else's. You won't make

me apologize for that."

"I know," Grant said, surprising Susan. *"You haven't heard about the Council brats."*

Susan could sense what that meant without him even having to explain it. She sighed.

"I wish she'd known you," she said finally. *"I genuinely do. There just wasn't any way."*

"You saved her," Grant said abruptly. *"I may never forgive you for stealing her, but I'll always know you saved her, too."*

Susan nodded and he looked at his hands.

"You clocked them?"

"Two minutes before you," Susan said. *"Probably don't even know who you are yet."*

"Kill them?" Grant asked.

"I've got my decoy set," she said. *"It's time for you to be a real player again."*

"If I come out, Gemma dies," Grant said. *She gave him a sideways smile and stood.*

"You think I don't have a plan for that?"

The End

More Fiction by Chloe Garner

Science Fiction

Monte and the crew of his ship The Kingfisher keep ending up in the middle of some of the galaxy's biggest problems.

Following Cassie, an analyst and former jumper at the Air Force's portal base in Kansas we chase foreign terrestrial (you know, space alien) Jessie to other planets. This is about as sci-fi as it gets, with a side helping of military politics.

Sarah Todd is the law in Lawrence, a mostly abandoned mining town at the end of the rail line. But when a new deposit of absenta is found trouble starts pouring into town. Mostly in the form of Jimmy Lawson, head of the Lawson clan and the former enforcement in town.

ABOUT THE AUTHOR

I'm Chloe and I am the conduit between my dreaming self and the paper (well, keyboard, since we live in the future). I write paranormal, sci-fi, fantasy, and whatever else goes bump in the night, I also write mystery/thriller as Mindy Saturn. When I'm not writing I steeplechase miniature horses and participate in ice cream eating contests. Not really, but I do tend to make things up for a living.

I have a newsletter that goes out about twice a month with promotions on my books and other authors' books, cover reveals, book releases, and freebies from me. It's a great way to discover a lot of new writers and find your next favorite series. Check out my website, for more info.

www.blenderfiction.wordpress.com